# EARTH HAD WON
# THE LONG MARTIAN WAR

Ray Stanton set his jaw as he stared at the molded lead seal on the door of the Martian museum. The seal was not really lead; nothing on Mars was exactly like its Earthly counterparts. And perhaps the institution was not a museum, either, as much as it was a—what would you call it? Maybe a cenotaph? Or a time capsule? Or a biographical sketch . . .

Or a suicide note.

He deciphered its inscription, his tongue stumbling over the unfamiliar sibilants of the Martian language:

"To the . . . strangers from the third planet . . . who have won their . . . bitter . . . triumph . . . we of Mars charge you . . . not to wantonly destroy . . . that which you will find . . . within this door . . . our codified learning . . . may serve you . . . better than we ourselves . . . might have done."

# OUR BEST

### THE BEST OF
## FREDERIK POHL AND
## C.M. KORNBLUTH

BAEN BOOKS

OUR BEST: THE BEST OF FREDERIK POHL AND
C.M. KORNBLUTH

Copyright © 1987 by Frederik Pohl and C.M. Kornbluth

A Baen Books Original

Baen Publishing Enterprises
260 Fifth Avenue
New York, N.Y. 10001

First printing, February 1987

ISBN: 0-671-65620-1

Cover art by Isidre Mones

Printed in the United States of America

Distributed by
SIMON & SCHUSTER
1230 Avenue of the Americas
New York, N.Y. 10020

# Contents

# Introduction

**Because** Cyril Kornbluth isn't with us any more, the task of writing an introduction to this collection of our shorter fiction falls on me alone. I'm sorry about that. We collaborated on a great deal of fiction, but never on anything like an introduction; it would have been fun to see how it came out.

We collaborated so much that, for a while, the joint works overpowered the things we were writing on our own. (One critic, on being introduced to me, said, "But I always thought your last name was 'and C. M. Kornbluth'.") Over the years, when lecturing or just chatting with fans and other writers, I've been asked many questions of how, and especially why, and they all began to sound familiar. But just the other day I was asked a new one.

It was at an academic symposium at a university, the subject being science fiction. One of the scholars raised a point that, he said, had been troubling him for some time. "Collaboration," he said. "You don't find much of that in mainstream literature, or even in the old pulps. But in science fiction there has always been a significant amount of it—Pournelle and Niven today, plus Silverberg and Garrett, Pratt and de Camp, all the way back to the brothers Earl and Otto, writing as 'Eando', Binder. And there was Cyril Kornbluth and yourself. How come?"

I surprised myself when he asked. I came up with an answer. I'm not sure it's the only one, because writers do things out of their own personal needs and habits and we're all different, but I think it may be statistically true. It has to do with one of the basic attributes of science fiction, namely that sf is more or less a literature of ideas.

(I say "more or less" because there's an awful lot of science fiction that no one would say that about. *Star Wars* is science fiction, all right, and it's certainly a lot of fun—but if there is an idea in it anywhere I haven't detected it.)

You can see the difference if you look at almost any of the masterpieces of "mainstream" literature. One can't imagine *Huckleberry Finn* or *The Remembrance of Things Past* being team-written; the things that make them great are very personal and largely autobiographical. Twain and Proust recorded what was. Science fiction tells us what has never been— but might be. The methodology for writing science fiction is simple. (I said "simple." I didn't say "easy.") You think of an idea. You consider what its implications are. You imagine the details and consequences. You conceive of what sorts of characters might exist in this setting and situation; then you embody all this in a story. None of this need be practiced in solitude. In the development and elaborations of the basic idea, it is not difficult, and sometimes it is better, to have a partner to bounce them off, and to receive new notions from.

There is a second answer; it's sociological, and it

has to do with the herding instinct of the people who write (and even who read) science fiction. Science-fiction people of any class or degree tend to want to associate with other science-fiction people. They form clubs. They hold conventions. They keep in touch. This is another quality you won't usually find among the people involved in westerns, mysteries or the works of James Michener. (There is a little of it among poets, maybe.) Because of this, every week of the year there are from one to a dozen "cons" in some motel, hotel or campus facility, somewhere in the United States (and almost as many in other parts of the world, from Australia and Japan to Yugoslavia and Sweden). And the clubs, societies and associations are past numbering.

When I first began to read (and to try to write) science fiction, the herding instinct was easy to understand. We were a tiny and beleaguered band. Nobody but us took science fiction seriously. All the authority figures, from teachers to parents, thought it was at best silly and, at worst, certain to rot our minds. To find another person who read the stuff, in school or on the block, was a direct gift from God. To be able to join a club was heaven. Those of us who lived in out-of-the-way places like Kansas or New Mexico had no hope of flesh-and-blood contact, but found solidarity in writing to the letter columns of the magazines or to each other. Those of us in or near cities found actual assemblages to attend.

One of these, in New York City, was called The Futurians; and it was there that I met Cyril Kornbluth for the first time.

The Futurians survived less than ten years and hardly ever had more than twenty or thirty mem-

bers. It scarcely even existed in any formal sense—
was not incorporated or registered, rarely had business
meetings, maintained nothing much in the way of a
treasury. All it was, really, was a permanent rotat-
ing bull session, where a bunch of us could get
together to talk—and collaborate.

We were all fans anxious to become pros; the membership included Donald A. Wollheim, James Blish,
Richard Wilson, Walter Kubilius, Judith Merril,
Hannes Bok, Damon Knight, Isaac Asimov and Robert W. Lowndes and, as you see, a good many
Futurians made it. One of the ways we got started
was by collaborating, which is to say by leaning on
each other to do what we didn't have the confidence
(and probably not the skill, either) to do by ourselves
just yet. X had a half-baked idea; Y had a part of a
notion; we put them together and got—well, not a
masterpiece, but fairly often a story that actually got
into print somewhere.

Cyril Kornbluth showed up around 1938, a pudgy,
bright young fellow from the far north of New York
City. He was about fourteen years old, and already
sardonic, witty and inventive. I was three years older.
I was already almost a pro—that is, I had sold a
poem to *Amazing Stories*—but not *quite* a pro, because they hadn't yet paid me for it, although it was
published in 1937. We began collaborating early on,
and our first story was published in 1940. (As it
happens, by me. Most of our—and of my own—early
stories were published in the two science-fiction magazines I had miraculously been given to edit at the
age of nineteen.)

There was already a war in Europe by the time we
got serious about writing. The war itself got serious
for us when the United States came in. By 1942

Cyril was off doing war-work in another state. In 1943 we both went into uniform. When the war was over Cyril settled in Chicago, first to go to school, then to work as a rewrite man, later bureau chief, for a small news-wire service called Trans-Radio Press. Meanwhile I had settled down in New York as an advertising copywriter. We kept in touch, but we didn't collaborate.

Actually, Cyril didn't do much writing of any kind for about a five-year period in there; the Army, the University of Chicago and the wire service successively kept him pretty busy. I didn't do much more, being involved as a literary agent (first part-time, then all the way), and it didn't seem fair to compete with my own clients. But then we both began writing again and, when Cyril came back East around 1951, it seemed natural to start to collaborate once more. The first thing we wrote was a novel called *The Space Merchants*, nee *Gravy Planet*. It surprised us by doing quite well, and so, over the next few years, we wrote six more together.

We also kept doing our own solo work—by the latter part of the 1950s, quite a lot of it—and so I don't know how many other novels we might have written together. Surely some; it was just too good a thing to give up forever. But that option was foreclosed. One snowy March morning Cyril shoveled out his driveway and ran to catch a train. He had strained his heart carrying a heavy machine-gun around the Ardennes Forest in the Battle of the Bulge, and the condition had been getting worse. That was the final straw. He collapsed on the platform of the Long Island Rail Road, and died there.

Working with Cyril Kornbluth was one of the great

professional (as well as personal) experiences of my life. That, and my time as an editor, taught me most of what I know about the skills of the profession. I'm grateful for what I had of it. I only wish there could have been more.

—Frederik Pohl

# The Stories of the Sixties

**When** Cyril Kornbluth died he left a number of incomplete or abandoned stories, sometimes only a scrap of two or three pages. Cyril was not the orderly sort of writer who prepared outlines before beginning to commit a work to paper (neither am I), so there was seldom any indication of where any given fragment was meant to go.

However, that was not a wholly unprecedented situation. The way we routinely collaborated was similar. We wrote, most of the time, in four-page stints, turn and about, and it was rare that either of us would give the other any indication of what was to come next after our own four pages were done. We didn't really have to. We relied very heavily on what might almost be called a sort of telepathy—or, less fancifully, on the fact that our minds tended to go in pretty much the same directions anyway. We would look on what the other person had put on paper, we would consider what options the events, characters and situations already established offered, we would choose the ones that looked most promising, and we would write them down.

13

So, one by one, with many of those fragments Cyril left behind, I sat myself down at the typewriter, pretended Cyril was sitting on my front porch two stories below, thought about what we might have wanted to do, and did it. In such fashion were (mostly) written these first six stories, most of them published within a decade of Cyril's death.

There were exceptions. "The Engineer" was actually completed while Cyril was still alive. It was a chapter that got squeezed out of our novel, *Gladiator-at-Law;* it didn't fit there, but it made a pretty nearly complete short story in itself (with the addition of an ending best, or anyway most charitably, called a "homage" to Graham Greene's *Brighton Rock*.) "Critical Mass" wasn't from a single fragment; it was from three separate false starts Cyril had made on different stories, which happily fitted together pretty well after I discarded some aberrant elements. "Nightmare with Zeppelins" began, actually, as the opening of a novel of Cyril's own; the rest of the novel he had researched in great detail, but was never written. "A Gentle Dying," too, was meant to be the first chapter of a novel, this one actually intended to be a collaboration between us. It was in fact the first collaboration of any sort we did, and was misplaced until after his death. (We never really tried to write the rest of the novel; when we began it we were both teen-agers and a long way from able to cope with that sort of project.) "The World of Myrion Flowers" existed only as a character sketch. "The Quaker Cannon" was an opening and no more.

It is a source of curiosity to me that—although I know that, for example, the fragment Cyril left for "The Quaker Cannon" was only about 3,000 words and the finished story is four times as long, which means that 9,000 or so of those words I wrote—I can't easily tell which parts of the story were Cyril's and which were mine.

But I can't always tell that with the novels, either; and that is just one of the reasons why collaborating with Cyril was so satisfactory to us both.

# Critical Mass

The neutron was a plump young man named Walter Chase, though what he thought he was was a brandnew Engineering graduate, sitting mummified and content with the other 3,876 in Eastern's class of '98, waiting for his sheepskin.

The university glee club sang the ancient scholastic song *Gaudeamus Igitur* with mournful respect and creamy phrasing, for they and most of the graduates, faculty members, parents, relatives and friends present in the field house thought it was a hymn instead of the rowdy drinking song it was. It was a warm June day, conducive to reverence. Of Eastern's 3,877 graduating men and women only three had majored in classical languages. What those three would do for a living from July on was problematical. But in June they had at least the pleasure of an internal chuckle over the many bowed heads.

Walter Chase's was bowed with the rest. He was of the Civil Engineering breed, and he had learned more about concrete in the four years just ended than you would think possible. Something called The Cement Research and Development Institute, whose

vague but inspirational commercials were regularly
on the TV screens, had located Walter as a promising
high-school graduate. He was then considering the
glamorous and expensive field of nuclear physics. A
plausible C.R.D.I. field man had signed him up and
set him straight. It took twelve years to make a
top-of-the-line nuclear physicist. Now, wasn't that a
hell of a long time to wait for the good things of life?
Now, here was something he ought to consider: four
years. In four years he could walk right into a job
with automatic pay raises, protected seniority, stock
participation *and* Blue Everything, paid by the company. Concrete was the big industry of tomorrow.
The C.R.D.I. was deeply concerned over the lack of
interest in concrete engineering, and it was prepared
to do something about it: Full four-year scholarship,
tuition, living costs and pocket money. Well?

Walter signed. He was a level-headed eighteen-
year-old. He had been living with a pinch-penny
aunt and uncle, his parents dead; the chance of the
aunt and uncle financing twelve years of nuclear
studies for him he estimated to lie midway between
the incredible and the impossible.

Two solid hours dwindled past in addresses by the
Chancellor, the Governor of the State and a couple
of other politicos receiving honorary degrees. Walter
Chase allowed the words to slip past him as though
they were dreams, although many of them concerned
his own specialty: shelters. You knew what politician
talk was. He and the 3,876 others were coldly realistic
enough to know that C.S.B. was a long way from
being enacted into law, much less concrete-and-steel
Civilian Shelters in fact. Otherwise why would the
Institute have to keep begging for students to give
scholarships to? He drowsed. Then, as if with an
absent-minded start, the program ended.

Everybody flocked away onto the campus.

In the hubbub was all the talk of the time: "Nice weather, but, Kee-*rist!* those speeches!" "Who d'ya like in the All-Star?" "Nothing wrong with C.S.B. if it's *handled* right, but you take and throw a couple thousand warheads over the Pole and—" "My feet hurt." Chase heard without listening. He was in a hurry.

There was no one he wanted to meet, no special friend or family. The aunt and uncle were not present at his graduation. When it had become clear from their letters that they expected him to pay back what they had spent to care for him as soon as he began earning money, he telephoned them. Collect. He suggested that they sue him for the money, or, alternatively, take a flying jump for themselves. It effectively closed out a relationship he loathed.

Chase saw, approaching him across the crowded campus, another relationship it was time to close out. The relationship's name was Douglasina MacArthur Baggett, a brand-new graduate in journalism. She was pretty and she had in tow two older persons who Chase perceived to be her parents. "Walter," she bubbled, "I don't believe you were even *looking* for me! Meet Daddy and Mom."

Walter Chase allowed his hand to be shaken. Baggett *père* was something in Health, Education and Welfare that had awakened Walter's interest at one time; but as Douglasina had let it slip that Daddy had been passed over for promotion three years running, Walter's interest had run out. The old fool now began babbling about how young fellows like Walter would, through the Civilian Shelters Bill, really give the country the top-dog Summit bargaining position that would pull old Zhdetchnikov's cork for him. The mother simpered: "So *you're* the young man! We've heard so much about you in Douglasina's letters. I tell you, why don't you come and spend the All-Star weekend with us in Chevy Chase?"

Walter asked blankly: "Why?"

"Why?" said Mrs. Baggett in a faint voice, after a perceptible pause. Walter smiled warmly.

"After all," he said, shrugging, "boy-girl college friendships. . . . She's a fine girl, Mrs. Baggett. Delighted to have met you, Mr. Baggett. Doug, maybe we'll run into each other again, eh?" He clapped her on the shoulder and slipped away.

Once screened from the sight of their faces, he sighed. In some ways he would miss her, he thought. Well. On to the future!

In the dormitory he snapped the locks on his luggage, already packed, carried them down to be stowed in the luggage compartment of the airport bus and then circulated gently through the halls. He had in four years at Eastern made eleven Good Contacts and thirty-six Possibles, and he had an hour or two before his plane to joke with, shake the hand of, or congratulate the nine of those on the list who shared his dorm. He fooled the fools and flattered the flatterable, but in his wake a few of his classmates grimly said: "That young son of a bitch is going to go far, unless he runs out of faces to step on."

Having attended to his nine he charitably spread some of his remaining time among the couple dozen Outside Chances he ran into. To a sincere, but confused, servo-mech specialist he said, man-to-man, "Well, Frankie, what's the big decision? Made up your mind about the job yet?"

The servo-mech man clutched him and told him his tale of woe. "God no, Walt. I don't know *which* way to turn. Missile R and D's offering me a commission right away, captain inside of two years. But who wants to be a soldier all his life? And there's nothing in private industry for inertial guidance, you know. Damn it, Walt, if only they let you resign from the service after a couple of years!" Chase said something more or less comforting and moved on. He was careful not to chuckle until he was out of sight.

Poor Frankie! Got himself educated in what amounted to a military speciality—who else could afford servomechanisms?—and discovered he hated the Army.

Still, Chase meditated while nodding, smiling and handshaking, thirty years as an Engineering Officer might not be so bad. As it was one of the alternatives open to himself—that was what C.S.B. was all about—he allowed his mind to drift over the prospects. It wasn't like the bad old days of fighting. A flat and rigid policy of atomic retaliation had been U.S. military doctrine for fifty-nine years, and backing it up was a large, well-trained U.S. military establishment of career men. And the regulations said *career*. The only way out short of thirty-year retirement was with a can tied to your tail and a taint to your name. He dismissed that thirty-year dead end with light contempt, as he had before.

The air-raid warning sirens began to howl their undulating hysteria.

Chase sighed and glanced at his watch. Not too bad. He should still be able to make his plane. Everyone around him was saying things like, "Ah, damn it!" or "Oh, dear," or "*Jeez!*" But they were all dutifully following the arrows and the "S" signs that dotted the campus.

Chase trailed along. He was kind of annoyed, but nothing could really spoil his day. The first shelter he came to was full up. The freshman raid warden

stood at the door—Chase had been a raid warden
himself three years before—chanting: "Basement filled
to capacity, folks. Please proceed to Chemistry building. Don't block the exit, folks. Basement here
filled—"

Because of the extra crowd caused by the graduation the Chemistry building basement was filled,
too, but Chase got into the Administration building
and sat down to wait. Like everybody else. Women
fussed about their dresses—they always had, in every air raid drill he had taken part in, say, four a
week for fifty-two weeks of each year for the nearly
twenty years since he had been old enough to toddle
alongside his late mother and father. Men grumbled
about missing appointments. *They* always had. But
for the most part the battery-fed air-raid lights gleamed
equally on them all, the warden fussed with the air
conditioner and the younger folk smooched in the
corners.

It wasn't a bad shelter, Walter Chase thought. The
Law School basement was a mess—too high a pH in
the mortar mix, and the aggregate showing hygro-
scopic tendencies because of some clown not watching his rock crusher, so the walls were cracked and
damp. Chemistry's had been poured in a freeze.
Well, naturally it began to sinter and flake. This was
better; trust the Chancellor to make sure his own
nest was downy! Of course, in a *raid* none of them
would be worth a hoot; but there weren't to be any
real raids. Ever.

A jet plane's ripping path sounded overhead.

Evidently this was going to be a full-dress affair, at
least regional in scope. They didn't throw simulated
manned-bomber attacks for a purely local do. Walter
frowned. It had suddenly occurred to him that with
the air-transport flight lanes screwed up by military

fighters on simulated missions everything within a thousand miles might be rerouted into stack patterns. What the devil would that do to his plane's departure time?

Then he smiled forebearingly. He was, in a way, pleased to be annoyed. It meant he was entering into the adult world of appointments and passages. They said that when a raid drill began to be a damn interruption instead of a welcome break from classes and a chance to smooch, then, brother, you were growing up. He guessed he was growing up.

"Goddamn foolishness," growled the man who sat next to Chase on the bench, as though it were a personal attack. More jets shredded sound overhead and he glared at Chase. Walter inventoried his English shoes, seal ring and pale cigar and at once engaged him in conversation. The man was some graduate's father; they had got separated in the raid drill, and Pop was sore as a tramped bunion. The whole drill thing was damned childishness, didn't Walter see that? And *vindictive* damned childishness when they chose to throw one on graduation day of a major university. If only Crockhouse had been elected in '96 instead of Braden, with his packed ballots in Indiana and Puerto Rico!

Here Walter Chase's interest cooled, because Pop sounded like a politician, revealed himself to be a Nationalist and thus was out of power. But there was no escaping the bench. What Pop objected bitterly to was the multiple levels of expense. Here the drill was knocking men out of production, but the damn Middle-Road Congress said they had to be paid anyhow. And if the Defense Department was making it a full-scale simulated raid, did Walter know what that meant? That meant that there went thirty or forty *Nineveh Able*s at a hundred and fifty thousand dollars apiece, and was that enough? No. Then they sent up four or five *Tyre*s at ninety thousand apiece to knock down the *Nineveh*s. Did that make sense? He paused to glare at Walter Chase.

Walter said, "Well, that's the Cold War for you. Say, who d'you like in the All-Star—" He didn't get to finish the sentence.

"L.A." snapped Pop, without losing a beat. "Get the damn monkey-business over with, that's what I say. I'm a sneak-puncher and I'm proud of it. If we'd put our man in the White House instead of that psalm-singing Braden there wouldn't *be* any Moscow or Peking or Calcutta by now and we wouldn't be sitting here on our butts!"

Somebody clawed through from the bench in front; with horror, Chase recognized old man Baggett. But Douglasina's Daddy did not recognize him. Flushed with rage and politics he had eyes only for the sneak-punch advocate. "You're right it's monkey-business, fat-mouth!" he snarled. "No thanks to you and your Crockhouse we aren't dead in this cellar instead of safe and secure! President Braden is a hundred per-cent pledged to the C.S.B., God bless it, and—"

The rest of his sentence and Sneak-Punch's angry reply were drowned out by a further flight of jets overhead, and then the *wham-wham-wham* of interceptor missiles blowing simulated attackers out of the sky.

Somehow, heaven knew how, Walter Chase managed to sneak away, inching through the packed rows of benches. As soon as the All Clear siren toots began he was up and out, ignoring the freshman warden's puppy-like yaps that they should remain in their seats until the front benches had been emptied—

Routine. It was all strictly routine.

Out on the campus, Chase headed for the airport in earnest, and was delighted to find that his flight was still on time. How lucky he was, he thought, with more pride than gratitude. "What are you, sir?" asked the robot baggage-checker, and he said, "Washington," with pleasure. He was on his way. He was headed for Washington, where Dr. Hines of The Cement Research and Development Institute would assign him to his job, doubtless the first rung of a dizzying climb to wealth and fame. He was a young man on his way. Or so he thought. He did not know that he was only a neutron ambling toward events.

## II

Arturo Denzer, in the same sense, was a nucleus. He knew no more about it than Walter Chase.

Denzer woke to the rays of a rising sun and the snarl of his wake-up clock. He took a vitamin capsule, an aspirin tablet, a thyroid injection; a mildly euphoric jolt of racemic amphetamine sulphate; caffeine via three cups of black coffee with sucaryl; and nicotine via a chain of nonfiltering filter-tip cigarettes. He then left his apartment for the offices of *Nature's Way Magazine*, which he edited.

June's blossom was in the air, and so was the tingle of the All-Star Game Number One. The elevator operator said to him respectfully, "Who d'ya like in the All-Star game, Mr. Denzer?" Denzer turned the operator's conversation circuit off with a handwave. He didn't feel like talking to a robot, at least until the aspirin began to work.

Absent-mindedly he waved a cab to him and climbed in. Only after it took off did he notice, to his dismay, that he had picked a Black-and-White fleet hack. They were salty and picturesque—and couldn't be turned off. The damned thing would probably call him "Mac."

"Who ya like inna All-Star, Mac?" the cab asked genially, and Denzer winched. Trapped, he drummed his fingers on the armrest and stared at the Jefferson Memorial in its sea of amusement rides and hot-dog stands. "Who ya like inna All-Star, Mac?" it asked again, genially and relentlessly. It would go on asking until he answered.

"Yanks," Denzer grunted. Next time he'd watch what he was doing and get a sleek, black Rippington Livery with a respectful BBC accent.

"Them bums?" groaned the cab derisively. "Watcha think Craffany's up to?"

Craffany was the Yankee manager. Denzer knew that he had benched three of his star players over the last weekend—indeed, it was impossible to avoid knowing it. Denzer struck out wildly: "Saving them for the All-Star, I guess."

The cab grunted and said: "Maybe. My guess, Fliederwick's in a slump so Craffany benched him and pulled Hockins and Waller so it'd look like he was saving 'em for the All-Star. Ya notice Fliederwick was 0 for 11 in the first game with Navy?"

Denzer gritted his teeth and slumped down in the seat. After a moment the cab grunted and said: "Maybe. My guess is Fliederwick's in a slump so Craffany benched him and pulled. . . ." It went through it twice more before Denzer and his hang-over could stand no more.

"I hate baseball," he said distinctly.

The cab said at once, "Well, it's a free country. Say, ya see Braden's speech on the C.S.B. last night?"

"I did."

"He really gave it to them, right? You got to watch

those traitors. Course, like Crockhouse says, where we going to get the money?"

"Print it, I imagine," snarled Denzer.

"Figgers don't lie. We already got a gross national debt of $87,912.02 per person, you know that? Tack on the cost of the Civilian Shelters and whaddya got?"

Denzer's headache was becoming cataclysmic. He rubbed his temples feverishly.

"Figgers don't lie. We already got a gross national debt . . ."

Desperate situations require desperate measures. "I hate p-politics too," he said, stuttering a little. Normally he didn't like smutty talk.

The cab broke off and growled: "Watch ya language, Mac. This is a respectable fleet."

The cab corkscrewed down to a landing in North Arlington-Alex and said, "Here y'are, Mac." Denzer paid it and stepped from the windy terrace of the Press House onto a crowded westbound corridor. He hoped in a way that the cab wouldn't report him to a gossip columnist. In another way he didn't care.

Around him buzzed the noise of the All-Star and the C.S.B. ". . .Craffany . . . $87,912.02, and at *least* $6,175.50 for Shelters . . . Foxy Framish and Little Joe Fliederwick . . . well, this *is* next year . . . nah, you sneak-punch 'em a couple thousand missiles over the Pole and . . . needs a year in the minors."

"Hello, Denzer," someone said. It was Maggie Frome, his assistant.

"Hello, Maggie," he said, and added automatically: "Who do you like in the All-Star game?"

In a low, ferocious voice she muttered: "You can take the All-Star game, tie it up in a b-b-b-brassiere

and dump it in a Civilian Shelter. I am sick of the
subject. *Both* subjects."

He flushed at her language and protested: "Really,
Maggie!"

"Sorry," she grunted, sounding as though she didn't
mean it. He contrasted her surly intransigence with
his own reasoned remarks to the cab and tolerantly
shook his head. Of course, he could have been taken
the wrong way . . . He began to worry.

They stepped off together at the *Nature's Way*
offices. Sales & Promotion was paralyzed. Instead of
rows of talkers at rows of desks, phoning prospects
out of city directories and high-pressuring them into
subscriptions, the department was curdled into little
knots of people cheerfully squabbling about the C.S.B.
and the All-Stars. Denzer sighed and led the girl on
into Transmission. The gang should have been tun-
ing up the works, ready to shoot the next issue into
seven million home terminals. Instead, the gang was
talking All-Stars and C.S.B. It was the same in Typography, the same in Layout, the same in Editorial.

The door closed behind them, isolating their twin
office from the babble. Blessed silence. "Maggie," he
said, "I have a headache. Will you please work on the
final paste-ups and cutting for me? There isn't anything that should give you any trouble."

"Okay, Denzer," said she, and retreated to her
half of the office with the magazine dummy. Denzer
felt a momentary pang of conscience. The issue was
way overset and cutting it was a stinker of a job to
pass on to Maggie Frome. Still, that was what you
had assistants for, wasn't it?

He studied her, covertly, as she bent over the
dummy. She was a nice-looking girl, even if she was
a hangover from the administration of President Dan-

ton and his Century of the Common Woman. Maggie's
mother had been something of an intergrationist leader
in Sandusky, Ohio, and had flocked to Washington as
one mote in Danton's crackpot horde, bringing her
subteenage daughter Maggie. No doubt there had
been a father, but Maggie never mentioned him.
The mother had died in a car crash that looked like
suicide after Danton lost all fifty-four states in his bid
for reelection, but by then Maggie was a pert teen-
ager who moved in with cousins in Arlington-Alex
and she stayed on. Must just like Washington, Denzer
thought. Not because of Female Integration, though.
Danton's Century of the Common Woman had lasted
just four years.

He winced a little as he remembered her coarse-
ness of speech. She was round and brown-haired.
You couldn't have everything.

Denzer leaned back and shut his eyes. The hubbub outside the office was just barely audible for a
moment—some red-hot argument over the Gottshalk
Committee's Shelter Report or Fliederwick's R.B.I.
had swelled briefly to the shrieking stage—and then
died away again. Heretically he wondered what the
point was in getting excited over baseball or the
building or nonbuilding of air-raid shelters capable of
housing every American all the time. One was as
remote from reality as the other.

"Sorry, Denzer."

He sat up, banging his knee on his desk.

"Lousy staff work, I'm afraid. Here's the Aztec
Cocawine piece and no lab verification on the test
results." She was waving red-crayoned galleys in his
face.

He looked at the scrawling red question-mark over
the neat columns of type with distaste. *Nature's Way*
promised its seven million subscribers that it would

not sell them anything that would kill them; or, at
least, that if it did kill them nobody would be able to
hang it on the product directly. At substantial expense, they maintained a facility to prove this point.
It was called The Nature's Way National Impartial
Research Foundation. "So call the lab," he said.

"No good, Denzer. Front-office memo last month.
Lab verifications must be *in* writing *with* notary's
seal *on* hand before the issue goes to bed."

"Cripes," he protested, "that means somebody's
got to go clear over to Lobby House." He did not
meet her eye. Going over to Lobby House was a
worthwhile break in the day's routine; the free snack-
bar and free bar-bar the lobbies maintained was up
to the best expense-account standards, and everyone
enjoyed talking to the kooks in the lab. They were so
odd.

"I'll go if you want, Denzer," she said, startling
him into looking at her.

"But the issue—"

"Did most of it last night, Denzer. The Aztec story
is all that's left."

"We'll both go," he said, rising. She had earned it;
he needed a bromo and a shot of B-1 vitagunk in the
Lobby House snack-bar; and since there would be
two of them in the cab he had a ruse for cutting out
the cab's talk about All-Stars and the C.S.B.

The ruse was this: As soon as the cab took off he
flung his arms around her and bore her back against
the arm rest.

The cab chuckled and winked at them with its
rear-view lens, as it was programmed to do. They
discussed proofreading, the vacation sked and the
choice of lead commercials for the next issue of *Nature's Way* in soft whispers into each other's ears all

the way to Lobby House, while the cab winked and chuckled at them every fifteen seconds.

The kooks on the 93rd floor were under the care of a sort of half-breed race of semi-kooks. These were science majors who had minored in journalism . . . or in marrying rich . . . and thus wandering into press agentry for scientific concerns. As liaison men between *Nature's Way* and the test-tube manipulators the semi-kooks occupied an uncertain middle ground. It sometimes made them belligerent. Denzer and the girl were let in to see the Director of Bennington's Division, a Dr. Bennington, and Denzer said: "We came for the Aztec Cocawine certification."

Dr. Bennington boomed: "Damn right! Coming right up! Say, who's gonna take it in the Game?" He thumped a button on his desk and in a moment a tall, stooped youth with a proudly beaked nose swept in and threw a document on his desk. "Thanks, Valendora. Lessee here, um, yeah. Says it's harmless to the nerves, ya-ta-ta, ya-ta-ta, all signed and stamped. Anything else today, Arturo? Gland extract, fake a heroin prescription, shot of Scotch?"

The beaked youth said loftily: "Our findings are set forth precisely, Dr. Bennington. The fluid contains an alkaloid which appreciably eroded the myelin sheaths of the automatic nerve trunks."

Denzer blanched, but the semi-kook administrator agreed carelessly, "Right, that's what I said. It's that word 'appreciably.' Anything less than 'markedly,' we write it down as negative." He slipped it in an envelope that was already marked *Confidential Findings, Aztec Wine of Coca Corporation, Sponsor*, and sailed it across to Denzer. "Well, what about C.S.B., boy? They gonna get us dug in before it's too late?" He made them promise to stop in at the snack-bar or bar-bar before leaving the building, then offered them a drink out of his private stock. They refused, of course. That was just his way of saying good-bye. It was the only way he knew to end a conversation.

With the certification in his pocket and the issue locked up, Denzer began to feel as though he might live, especially if he made it to the B-1 vitagunk dispenser in the snack-bar. He took Maggie Frome by the arm and was astonished to feel her shaking.

"Sorry, Denzer. I'm not crying, really. If somebody's going to sell crazy-making dope to the public, why *shouldn't* it be you and me? We're no better than anybody else, d-d-damn it!"

He said uncomfortably, "Maybe a drink's not such a bad idea. What do you say?"

"I'd love it," she sobbed. But then the sirens began to wail and they said, "Damn it," and "Oh, dear"—respectively, she did and he did—and they took their bearings by the signs and made for the shelters. Under Lobby House was nothing like enough space, so the air-raid shelter was the interior parts of the 10th through 85th floors, away from the flying glass of the curtain walls but not too near the elevator shafts. It was not a bad shelter, actually. It was proof against any bomb that the world had ever known, up to, say, early 1943.

There was plenty of room but not enough benches. Maggie and Denzer found a place on the floor where they could put their backs against a wall, and he allowed her to lean against his shoulder. She wasn't such a bad kid, he thought sympathetically, especially as the perfume in her hair was pleasant in his nostrils. There wasn't anything really *wrong* with Female Integration. Maggie wasn't a *nut*. Take baseball. Why, that was the Integrationists' major conquest, when women demanded and got equal representation on every major-league team in spite of the fact that they could not throw or run on competitive terms with men. They said that if all the teams had the same number of women it wouldn't matter. And it hadn't. And Integrationists were still crowing over the victory; and yet Maggie had refused to fall into the All-Star hysteria.

A roar like an outboard motor in the crown of your hat shook the building; A. A. "carpet" cannon laying a sheet of sudden death for missiles across the sky above them. Denzer relaxed. His headache was almost gone. He inclined his head to rest his cheek against Maggie's hair. Even with a hangover, it had been pleasant in the cab with his arms around her. He had been kind of looking forward to the return trip. If Denzer were indeed a nucleus, as in a way he was, he was beginning to feel a certain tugging of binding energy toward certain other nuclear particles.

As soon as the noise stopped, he thought he would speak to her.

The noise stopped. The voices of the men beside them bellowed into the sudden quiet: "—damned foolish idea of Therapeutic War was exploded ten years ago! And that's what we'd be if your idiot Crockhouse was in—exploded!"

And the man next to him: "At least Crockhouse wouldn't have us sitting in these fool imitation shelters! He'd *do* something."

"Whadya think *Braden* wants, for God's sake? Not these things. He's right on the record for C.S.B."

And then Maggie Frome, breathing fire, her head no longer resting on Denzer's shoulder: "What the hell is so great about C.S.B.? Shelters, no shelters, can't you get it through your head that if this keeps up we're *dead?* Dear God above, deliver me from fools, baseball players and p-p-politicians!"

Denzer tried to look as though he'd never met her; he was white-faced. Round, yes, sweet-smelling, yes, warm—but how could he ever get used to her dirty *talk?*

# III

If Denzer was a nucleus and Walter Chase a neutron, what can we call the President of the United States? He played a part. Without him nothing could happen. Perhaps what he did was to shape the life of the neutron before fission happened; in that sense one could call him a "moderator." This was an apt term for President Braden.

On this bright June morning in Washington—not Arlington-Alex or the bedroom municipalities in Maryland but the little old Federal District itself—the President of the United States held what was still called a "press" conference. He was late. The cathode-tube "newspapermen" grumbled a little as Secret Service men frisked them, but it was habit. They were used to being frisked, ever since that fanatic Alaskan nationalist publisher emptied a .32 at then-President Hutzmeyer. And they were used to now-President Braden being late.

They rose when President Braden came in. As usual, he protested in his pleasant adopted border-South accent: "Please, ladies, please, gentlemen, don't bother—" So they sat down and smiled, and waited while Braden arranged some papers on his desk. He always did that. He never referred to them during the session, because he didn't have to, but every week there was the minute or two of silence in the room while the President, his rimless glasses gleaming studiously, pursed his lips over the documents in their red, blue and cream-colored folders.

He looked up and beamed.

Unobtrusive camera-eyes mounted flush with the walls of the conference room began to record. The elephantine Giuseppe von Bortoski, N.B.C. Washington bureau chief, incomparably senior correspondent, was privileged to lead off. He did: "Good morning, Mr. President. Do you have a statement for us today?"

"Nothing prepared, Joseph. It's been a quiet week, hasn't it?"

Von Bortoski said solemnly, "Not for Craffany," and everybody roared. Von Bortoski waited out his laugh and said: "But seriously, Mr. President, is there any comment on the radar picket situation?"

The President paused, then looked faintly surprised. "I didn't know there was a 'situation,' Joseph. Our radar picket vessels off the Atlantic and Pacific coasts have been pulled in approximately two hundred miles. They all have the new microradar; they don't have to be so far out. This gives us a gratifying economy, since the closer we can pull them in the fewer ships we need to stick out there on picket duty. Is that what you wanted to know, Joseph?"

"No, Mr. President. I was referring to Representative Simpson's telecast yesterday. He alleged that the new radars haven't been adequately field-tested. Said the move was premature and, well, dangerous."

The President paused, then looked faintly angry. "I seem to recall that Illinois Simpson. A Democrat." Everybody nodded. "I am surprised that you are taking up our time, Joseph, with the wild charges that emanate with monotonous regularity from the Party of Treason." Everyone looked at the stout N.B.C. man with annoyance. The President turned toward a young lady correspondent, paused, and said, "Miss Bannerman, do you have a question?"

She did. What about the Civilian Shelters Bill?

The President paused, grinned and said, "I'm for it." He got a small laugh.

"I mean, Mr. President, what is its status now? As the leader of your Party, is it going to go through?"

The President paused longer than usual. Everyone in the room knew what he was waiting for, though it was a convention of the Press Conference to pretend he was answering off the cuff. At last the other end of the transprompter circuit got its signals cleared and the President said levelly: "As the leader of my Party, Miss Bannerman, I can say this thing is being hammered out. Slower than some of us would wish, true. But it will be done. It is the platform of my Party; on that platform I was elected, and I have not the reputation of going back on my pledges." He inclined his head to an approving stir among the correspondents.

Von Bortoski made a mental calculation. He decided that the press conference had supplied enough matter for his upcoming newscast and to hell with the rest of them. "Thank you, Mr. President," he said. The other reporters swore under their breaths once more at the tyranny of the senior-correspondent rule, the President rose smiling and the armed guards stepped away from the doors.

C.S.B., C.S.B., the President mediated. Someday he would have to ask a question himself and find out just what this C.S.B. was all about. No doubt the R & I desk that fed him answers or speeches via the transprompter could tell him. He promised himself he would get around to it first thing, say, Monday. Or wait, wasn't Monday the first All-Star game?

A swift conveyor belt whisked him from the Annex to the Old White House and an escalator to the Oval Room. His personal secretary ventured to say: "You made good time, Governor. There's thirty-five minutes clear before the first appointment. How about a nap?"

President Braden snapped: "I see General Standish has been talking to you again, Murray. Tell that quack when I want doctoring I'll ask for it, and get me a drink."

The President, who liked to think he was a hard-riding, hard-drinking southern gentleman, although he had been a New Jersey accountant until he was thirty, sipped a glass of mineral water lightly tinted with whiskey, decided he was refreshed and buzzed for the first appointment to start ahead of time.

The first appointment was with Senator Horton of Indiana. While he was coming in, the transprompter whispered into the President's ear: "Call him David, not Dave. No wife. Ex-professor, for God's sake. Watch him."

The President rose, smiling, and gripped Horton's hand with warmth and the pressure of an old campaigner. "It's a great pleasure, David. How's Indiana shaping up for next year? Lose all your best seniors?"

Senator Horton had a shock of gray hair, a mournful face and a surprisingly springy, lean body for a fifty-year-old ex-professor. He said abruptly: "I don't follow the school's football schedule. Mr. President, I want something."

"Unto the half of my kingdom," Braden said gaily, attempting to throw him off balance.

Horton gave him a meager smile. "I want you to bear down on the Civilian Shelters Bill. You are, after all, committed to it. It helped elect you. But twenty-two months have gone by and the bill is still in the Public Works Committee. I am on that committee, Mr. President, and it is my impression that I am the only member interested in seeing it enacted into law."

The President said gravely, "That's a mighty serious charge, David. One I cannot act on without the fullest—"

"Excuse me for interrupting, Mr. President, but your time is valuable and there are some things you needn't bother explaining to me." Deeply affronted, the President stared at him. "Believe me when I say that I've come to you as a last resort. I get only bland evasions from Harkness. The Interior Department—"

Harkness was the committee chairman and he had been Braden's personal campaign manager in the election run. The President rose and said, "Excuse *me*, Senator, but I don't permit people to speak about Jim Harkness like that in my presence."

Senator Horton distractedly ran his hands through his shock of hair. "I didn't mean to offend you. God knows I don't mean to offend anyone. Not even the Secretary of Interior, though if he thinks— No, I won't say that. All I want is to get the C.S.B. on the floor and get the construction work under way. Mr. President, how long can all this go on?"

The President remained standing, looked at his watch and said coolly, "All what, David?"

"We are in the fifty-ninth year of the Political War, Mr. President. Somehow, by a succession of last-minute, hairs-breadth accidents, we have escaped nuclear bombing. It can't go on forever! If the missiles came over the Pole today they'd annihilate this nation, and I don't give one juicy damn that China and Russia would be annihilated in the next forty minutes—"

He was trembling. The President's earphone whispered tinnily: "Hospitalized one year; nervous breakdown. The guard-ports have him covered with sleep guns, sir." That was a relief; but what about this Horton? He was Doane's personal choice, chairman of the National Committee; had Doane put a raving maniac in the Senate? The President remembered, from those young, county-committeeman days when he remembered things clearly, that something like that had happened before. It had been during the Party of Treason's first years—a lunatic from the Northwest got elected to Congress and was mighty embarrassing until he committed suicide. The President, then a schoolboy, had chuckled with the rest of the nation over Congressman Zioncheck; but now he was not chuckling. It was *his* Administration and in the *Senate*. And a member of, God help him, *his* party.

The President did not look toward the guard-ports and the riflemen behind them. He said quietly, "David, I want you to calm down. No pledges have been forgotten and no pledges are going to be violated. I'll speak to Jim Harkness about the Shelter Bill today. That's a promise."

"Thank you," Horton said gratefully, and tried to smile. "I'll hold you to that, sir. Good day."

The President buzzed, not for his next appointment but to talk to his secretary. "Murray, get me Senator Harkness on the phone." And to his chest microphone: "Trans-prompter desk? Get out of circuit. I'll buzz you." He heard the faint carrier tone in his ear die and the guard-ports' click. For the first time since he stepped out of his shower that morning, the President was able to say a word that no one but himself could hear. He said it. It had only one syllable, but it improved his mood very much.

Harkness's voice was resonant and comforting. The President, sometimes nagged by a secret feeling that he was not very bright, knew damned well that he was brighter than Harkness.

He said: "Jim, I've got to wondering about this C.S.B. that you've got in Public Works. The day's young yet and I've had two questions about it. I know we campaigned on it—what is it, exactly?"

Harkness said comfortingly: "It's under control, Brad. That fellow Horton is trying to unbottle it, but we can keep him quiet. He doesn't know the ropes."

"Know that, Jim. I just had him in here, wailing and mad. What's it all about?"

"Why," said Senator Harkness, with something less of assurance in his voice, "it's about building shelters, Brad. Against nuclear attack." He pronounced it "nookyoular," in the approved White House fashion.

"Not quite my point, Jim. I mean—" the President searched for what it was he did mean—"I mean, I can find out the facts and so on, but what's got people so stirred up? Put it this way, Jim: What's your philosophy about the Civilian Shelters Bill?"

"Philosophy?" Harkness sounded vaguely scared. "Well, I would not know about philosophy, Brad. It's an issue, C.S.B. is, and we're very fortunate to have got it away from the Nationalists. C.S.B.'s very popular." The President sighed inaudibly and relaxed; Senator Harkness was clearly about to launch into one of his famous explanations of things that never needed to be explained. "You see, Brad, an issue is lifeblood to a party. Look over the field today. What's to argue about? Damn little. Everybody knows the Party of Treason is the Party of Treason. Everybody knows the Commies are crazy hoodlums, can't trust 'em. Everybody knows atomic retaliation is the only sound military policy. There, at one sweep, you knock domestic, foreign and military policy off the board and haven't anything left to play with except C.S.B." He paused for breath, but before the President could try to get him back on the track of the question he was rushing on: "It's a godsend, Brad! The Nationalists guessed wrong. They turned C.S.B. down in the name of economy. My opinion, they listened too much to the Defense Department people; naturally the generals didn't want to admit they can't intercept whatever the Commies throw at us, and naturally they want the money for interception instead of shelters. Well, that's all right, too, but the people say the last word. We Middle-Roaders guessed right. We slapped C.S.B. in our platform, and we won. What else is there to say about it? Now, we're not going to turn loose of an issue like that. Fools if we did. The strategy's to milk it along, get it on the floor just before we adjourn for campaign trips and if a Nationalist filibuster kills it, so much the better. That saves it for us for next year! You know, you never get credit in this game for what you've done. Only for what you're going to do. And, *hell*, Brad," he crowed, suddenly exultant as a child who has found a dime in the street, "this thing is good for years! There has to be a big conference committee with the House on financing C.S.B., we haven't even set up liaison with Military Affairs. We've got four more years easy. How's that sound, Brad, eh? Ride right in to reelection with a *tested* issue, that you *know* works, and no worry about opinion-sampling or testing trial balloons?"

"Thanks, Jim," said the President, "I knew I could get a straight answer out of you." It was the only way to stop him. Otherwise he might go clear on to the C.S.B. and its effect on the Integrationists, the C.S.B. and Labor, the C.S.B. and Colorado water diversion or the C.S.B. as viewed in the light of Craffany's benching of Little Joe Fliederwick.

And yet, pondered the President, he still didn't know even the question, much less the answer. *Why* was C.S.B. a good issue? The missiles hadn't hit in the past fifty-nine years, why should a voting population march to the booths and elect its leaders because of their Shelter philosophy now?

Braden changed the subject. "What do you think of Horton, Jim?"

He could always count on Harkness being frank, at least. "Don't like him. A boat-rocker. You want my advice, Brad? You haven't asked for it, but it's get rid of him. Get the National Committee to put a little money in his district before the primaries."

"I see," said the President, thanked his former campaign manager and hung up.

He took a moment before buzzing Murray for the next appointment to sip his lightly tinted soda water and close his eyes. Well, he'd wasted most of the thirty-five minutes he'd gained, and not even a nap to show for it. Maybe General Standish was right.

Once when Braden was younger, before he was governor of New Jersey, before he was state senator, when he still lived in the old Rumford house on the beach and commuted to Jersey City every day—once he had been a member of the National Guard, what he considered his obligation as a resigned West Pointer. And they had killed two of their obligatory four-hours-a-month one month watching a documentary film on nuclear attack. The arrows marched over the Pole and the picture dissolved to a flight of missiles. The warheads exploded high in the air.

Then the film went to stock shots, beautifully selected and paced: the experimental houses searing and burning on Yucca Flats, the etched shadows of killed men on the walls of Hiroshima, a forest fire, a desert, empty, and the wind lifting sand-devils. The narration had told how such-and-such kind of construction would be burned within so many miles of Ground Zero. It remarked that forest fires would blaze on every mountain and mentioned matter-of-factly that they wouldn't go out until the winter snow or spring rains, and of course then the ground would be bare and the topsoil would creep as mud down to the oceans. It estimated that then, the year was no later than 1960, a full-scale attack would cost the world 90 percent of its capacity to support life for at least a couple of centuries. Braden had never forgotten that movie.

He had never forgotten it, but he admitted that sometimes he had allowed it to slip out of his mind for a while. This latest while seemed to have lasted quite a few years. Only C.S.B. had brought it back in his recollection.

Because that was the question, the President thought, sipping his tinted soda water. What was the use of C.S.B.? What was the use of any kind of shelters, be they deep as damn-all, if all you had to come out of them to was a burned-out Sahara?

## IV

Now that the simulated raid was over everybody was resuming their interrupted errands at once. Denzer was crammed in any-which-way with Maggie Frome wedged under an arm and that kook from the

Institute—Venezuela?—gabbling in his ear about computer studies and myelin sheaths.

The elevator jollied them all along. "Don't forget tomorrow, folks. Be a lot of grandmothers buried tomorrow, eh?" It could not wink, but it giggled and, well, nudged them. Or at least it shook them. It was overloaded with the crowds from the shelter floors, and its compensators flagged, dropping it an inch below the sill of the lobby door, then lifting it. "Sorry, folks," it apologized. "Good night, all!"

Denzer grabbed Maggie's arm. The laboratory man called after him, but he only nodded and tugged the girl away through the crowds, which were mumbling to each other: "Foxy Framish . . . slip 'em a couple thousand nookyoular . . . caught off first . . . *oh, hell.*" The "oh, hells" became general as they reached the main lobby outside of the elevator bays.

Civilian Air Wardens formed chains across the exits. Like fish weirs they chuted the exiting civilians into lines and passed each line through a checkpoint.

"Denzer," groaned Maggie, "I'm cooked. I *never* wear my dosimeter badge with this old green dress."

The wardens were checking every person for his compulsory air-raid equipment. Denzer swore handily, then brightened. They did have their press cards; this *was* official business. Aztec Wine of Coca was a powerful name in industry, and didn't they have a right to take care of its affairs even if they overlooked a few formalities that nobody really took very seriously anyway? He said confidently: "Bet I get us out of it, Maggie. Watch this." And he led her forcefully to the nearest warden. "You, there. Important morale business; here's my card. I'm Denzer of *Nature's Way*. This's my assistant, Frome. I—"

Briskly the warden nodded. "Yes, *sir*, Mr. Denzer. Just come this way." He led them through the purse-seine of wardens, out of the building, into—why, Denzer saw, outraged, into a *police cab*.

"You fixed us fine, Denzer," gloomed Maggie at his side as they got in. He didn't have the spirit to listen to her.

The roundup had bagged nearly fifty hardened criminals, like Denzer and Maggie, caught flagrantly naked of dosimeters and next-of-kin tags. They were a surly lot. Even the C.S.B. adherents among them belligerently protested their treatment; the sneak-punchers were incandescent about the whole thing. Office girls, executives, errand boys, even one hang-dog A.R.P. guard himself; they were a motley assortment. The research man, Valendora, was among them, and so was the girl from the Institute's reception room. Valendora saw Denzer and slipped through the crowd toward him, holding a manila envelope as though it contained diphtheria vaccine and he was the first man to arrive at the scene of an epidemic. "Mr. Denzer," he said darkly, "I ask you to assist me. Eleven months of my time and twenty-two computer hours! And this is the only copy. *Statist. Analysis Trans.* expects this by tomorrow at the latest, and—"

Denzer hardly heard. *Statist. Analysis Trans.* was not the only periodical expecting something from one of the fish in this net. With an inner ear Denzer was listening to what his Front Office would say. He was, he saw clearly, about to miss a deadline. Seven million paid-up subscribers would be complaining to the Front Office when their copies were late, and Denzer knew all too well who Front Office would complain to about *that*. He whimpered faintly and reached for an amphetamine tablet, but an A.R.P. cop caught his arm. "Watch it, Mac," said the cop, not unkindly. "No getting rid of evidence there. You got to turn all that stuff in."

Denzer had never been arrested before. He was in a semi-daze while they were waiting to be booked. Ahead of him in line a minor squabble arose— Valendora seemed to be clashing with a plump young fellow in a collegiate crew-cut—but Denzer was paying little attention as he numbly emptied his pockets and put all his possessions on the desk to be locked away for him.

It was not until Maggie Frome repeated his name for the fifth time that he realized she was talking to him. She indicated a lanky, homely woman talking into an autonoter, seemingly on terms of amiable mutual contempt with the police.

"Denzer," Maggie hissed urgently, "that girl over there. The reporter. Name's Sue-Mary Gribb, and I know her. Used to work with her on the *Herald*."

"That's nice. Say, Maggie," he moaned, "what the devil are we going to do about the Aztec Wine of Coca piece? The Front Office'll have our heads."

"What I'm trying to tell you, Denzer! Give her the lab report. She'll take it in for us!"

The sun rose in pink glory for Arturo Denzer.

Half blinded by the radiance of sudden, unexpected hope, he staggered back to the desk. Valendora and the plump youth were still at it, but he pushed past them, picked up the Nature's Way National Impartial Research Foundation envelope and clawed his way back to Maggie. "Pencil!" he snapped. She produced one and Denzer scribbled a note to Joe, in Production:

> Joe, we're in a jam. Fix this up for us somehow. Run it pp 34–35, push it through soonest, I've already got all okays so just jam it

in. God bless you. If Front Office asks where I
am I'm dead.

He thought of adding, "Will explain later," but he
wasn't so very sure he could. He thought of kissing
Sue-Mary Gribb; but she was another Female Inte-
grationist, wearing slacks, carrying a corncob pipe;
he only shook her hand briskly and watched her
leave.

It was not until she was out the door that he
realized why she had been there in the first place.

She was a reporter, gathering names. It was customary to run a list of A.R.P. violators in the
newspapers. It was inevitable that someone who
worked for *Nature's Way* would see his and Maggie's
names on that list; and it was beyond hope that that
someone would fail to show it to the Front Office.

With the help of Sue-Mary Gribb he might have
made his deadline, but his troubles were not over.
Front Office was solid C.S.B.

"Maggie," he said faintly, "when you left the *Herald*,
did you part friends? I mean, do you think they
might give us a job?"

The next thing was that they had to wait for their
hearing and, in the way of police courts, that took
some time. Meanwhile they were all jammed together,
noisy and fretful.

The bull-pen roared: "Quiet down, you mokes!
You think this is a debating society?" Denzer sighed
and changed position slightly so as not to disturb
Maggie Frome, again placidly dozing on his shoulder. (This could become a habit, he thought.)

Well, that was something else the Century of the
Common Woman had accomplished. They had integrated the lockups, for better or for worse. Not that

Maggie, asleep, was deriving the benefit she might from the integrated, but still very loud, yammering of the inmates of the bullpen.

They weren't all A.R.P. violators. A sizeable knot in one corner were clearly common drunks, bellowing about the All-Star Game when they were not singing raucously. They were the chief targets of the bullpen's repeated thunderings for quiet, as its volumetric ears registered an excessive noise level. They must wear out those tapes in a week, Denzer thought.

A diffident finger touched his arm. "Mr. Denzer?" It was the research fellow from the Institute.

Softly, to refrain from disturbing Maggie, he said: "Hello, Venezuela. Make yourself comfortable."

"Valendora, Mr. Denzer."

"Sorry," said Denzer absently, inhaling Maggie's hair.

"I ask you, Mr. Denzer," Valendora said, choosing his words with as much care as though he were taping a question for his computers, "is it proper that I should be arrested for being twenty-six feet away from where I would not be arrested?"

Denzer stared at him. "Come again?" Maggie stirred restlessly on his shoulder.

"I was two floors below the Foundation, Mr. Denzer, no more," said the research man. "We are not required to wear dosimeters in the Institute itself. Two floors is twenty-six feet."

Denzer sighed. This was not a time when he had patience for nuts. The girl on his shoulder stirred and he said, "Good morning, Maggie." Valendora swept on:

"Naturally, Mr. Denzer, it did not occur to me to go back for my dosimeter. My probable error was more than twenty-four hours minus, though zero plus, and it might have been the real attack. I was carrying a most important document and I could not endanger it."

Maggie looked at him with faint curiosity and then twisted around to look at Denzer's face. "The deadline, Denzer?" she muttered. He crossed his fingers and shrugged.

"Mr. Denzer," cried Valendora, "you are a man of influence. *Statist. Analysis Trans.* is waiting for this study—and besides," he added wonderingly, "I suppose if the attack is to come tomorrow someone should do something about it. Can you not secure justice for me in this matter?"

Rocked by the sudden vision of himself as a man of influence, Denzer hardly heard the rest of what the research man was saying. Maggie Frome pushed herself away from him and stared thoughtfully at Valendora.

"We're all in the same boat, friend," she said kindly.

Valendora scowled at the floor.

"But what's this about an attack?"

With bitter sarcasm Valendora said, "Nothing at all, Miss Frome. Merely what I have spent eleven months of my time on. *And* twenty-two computer hours."

"I'm impressed, friend. You said something about an attack?"

Valendora said, "You would not understand single-event prediction, Miss Frome. It is a statistical assessment of probabilities. Oh, nothing in itself that has not previously been studied, true; but it is in the establishing of quantitative values for subjective data that I have, I do know, made a contribution." He shrugged moodily. "And by tomorrow? The event, you see. If I have not published before the event it is only a mathematical statement. The test of a theory is the prediction that can be made from it; I have made my prediction. During the All-Star Game, you see—"

"There you are!" cried a new voice.

It was the plump youth who had been quarreling with Valendora at the booking desk. He was still angry. "Baseball," he snapped, "that's all I hear. Can't I make anyone understand that I am a special investigator on Senator Horton's *personal* staff? The senator is waiting to interview me right now! And this man has stolen my thesis!" He put a hand out and briskly pumped Denzer's. "Walter Chase, sir. M.A., C.E., and all the rest of that nonsense," he twinkled, for he had made a quick estimate of Denzer's well-cut clothes and hangdog look and pigeonholed him at once as *second-string executive, subject to flattery*.

"Denzer. *Nature's Way*," he mumbled, trying to let go of the hand, but Chase hung on.

"I'm in cement, Mr. Denzer," he said. "Did a bit of research—my dissertation, actually—just received another degree—and Senator Horton is most taken by it. Most taken, Mr. Denzer. Unfortunately I've just the one copy, as it happens and it's, well, rather important that it not be lost. It concerns cement, as it affects our shelter program—and, after all, what *is* a shelter but cement? Eh? Probably should've been classified at the start, but—" He shrugged with the faint amused distaste of the man of science for the bureaucrat. "Anyway, I must have it; the senator must see it with his own eyes before he'll give me the j—before making final arrangements. And this man has stolen it."

"Stolen!" screamed Valendora. "Man! It is your fault, man! I was only—"

"Be careful!" commanded Chase furiously. "Don't blame *me!* I was merely—"

Denzer felt a tug on his arm. Maggie Frome winked and led him away, near the group of singing drunks. They sat down again. "Quieter here!" she shouted in his ear. "Put your shoulder back, Denzer! I want to go back to sleep!"

"All right!" he yelled, and helped her settle her head against him; but in a moment she raised it again.

"Denzer!" she asked over the singing of the group, "did you hear what your friend from the Institute was saying? Something about an attack? I had the funny idea he meant missile attack—a real one, I mean."

"No," he shouted back, 'it was only baseball! All-Star Game, you know."

And he hardly heard the raucous bellowing of the drunks for the next half hour, inhaling the fragrance of her hair.

They were released at last, Denzer making bail; the bail corresponded to the amount of their fines for A.R.P. violation, and small print at the bottom of their summons pointed out that they could forfeit it if they chose, thus paying their fines, simply by failing to appear at the magistrate's trial. They got out just in time to get the bulldog edition of *Nature's Way* from a sidewalk scriber.

They looked at once on the spread, pages 34 and 35, expecting anything, even blank pages.

Tragically, the pages were not blank at all.

Pages 34 and 35 had nothing to do with Aztec Wine of Coca. It was a straight news story, headlined:

U.S. MISSILE VULNERABILITY TOTAL IN
ALL-STAR GAME, SAYS GOVERNMENT
STATISTICS EXPERT

From there it got worse. Maggie screamed faintly over Denzer's shoulder as she read parts of it aloud: " 'The obsessive preoccupation of the American public with baseball stems from a bread-and-circuses analogy with ancient Rome. Now, as then, it may lead to our destruction.' Denzer! Does this maniac want us to get lynched?"

"Read on," moaned Denzer, already several laps ahead of her. Neatly boxed on the second page was a digested, sexed-up version of something Denzer recognized faintly as the study of cement in the shelter program Chase had mentioned. What the *Nature's Way* semantic-digester had made of it was:

### SHELTERS DEATH TRAPS

Study of the approved construction codes of all American shelter projects indicates that they will not withstand even large chemical explosives.

"I think," sobbed Arturo Denzer, "that I'll cut my throat."

"Not here, Mac," snapped the news-scribing machine. "Move on, will you? *Hey!* Late! Whaddya read?"

Shaking, the couple moved on. "Denzer," Maggie gasped, "where do you think Joe got this stuff?"

"Why, from us, Maggie," Denzer tried to swallow, but his throat was dry. "Didn't you hear Chase before? That was the mix-up at the desk; we must have got his papers, and I suppose what's his-name's, Venezuela's, and bundled them off to Joe. Nice job of rush typography, though," he added absently, staring into space. "Say, Maggie. What Venezuela was talking about. You think there's any truth to it?"

"To what, Denzer?"

"What it says here. Optimum time for the Other Side to strike—during the All-Star Game, it says. You think—?"

Maggie shook her head. "I don't think, Denzer," she said, and they walked on for a moment.

They heard their names called, turned, and were overtaken rapidly by Valendora and the cement engineer. "You!" cried Chase. "You have my thesis!"

"And you have my study!" cried Valendora.

"Not I but humanity," said Denzer sadly, holding out the damp faxed edition of *Nature's Way*.

Valendora, after one white-faced oath in Spanish, took it calmly. He glanced up at the sky for a second, then shrugged. "Someone will not like this. I should estimate," he said thoughtfully, "that within five minutes we will all be back in the *calabozo*."

But he was wrong.

It was actually less than three.

# V

It was the third inning, and Craffany had just benched Little Joe Fliederwick. In spite of the sudden ban on air travel the stadium was full. Every television screen in the country followed Little Joe's trudging walk to the dugout.

In the White House, President Braden, shoes off, sipping a can of beer, ignored the insistent buzzing in his ear as long as he could. He wanted to watch the game. "—and the crowd is *roaring*," roared the announcer, "just a-*boiling*, folks! What's Craffany up to? What will he do next? Man, don't we have one going here *today*? Folks, was that the all-important turning point in today's all-im—in today's record-breaking All-Star Game, folks? Well, we'll see. In sixty seconds we'll return to the field, but meanwhile—"

The President allowed his attention to slip away from the commercial and took another pull at his beer. Baseball, now. That was something he could get his teeth into. He'd been a fan since the age of five. All his life. Even during the Century of the Common Woman, when that madman Danton had listened to the Female Lobby and put girls on every second base in the nation. But it had never been this good. This Fliederwick, now, he was *good*.

Diverted, he glanced at the screen. The camera was on Little Joe again, standing at the steps to the dugout, looking up. So were his teammates; and the announcer was saying: "Looks like some more of those air-to-air missile-busters, folks. A huge flight of them. *Way* up. Well, it's good to know our country's defense is being looked after and, say, speaking of defense, what do you suppose Craffany's going to do now that—"

The buzzing returned. The President sighed and spoke to his invisible microphones. "What? Oh. Well, damn it . . . all right."

With a resentful heart he put down the beer can and snapped off the television set. He debated putting his shoes back on. He decided against it, and pulled his chair close to the desk to hide his socks.

The door opened and Senator Horton came in.

"Mr. President," cried Horton, "I want to thank you. There's no doubt your prompt action has saved your country, sir. I imagine you've been filled in on the, ah, incident."

Well, he had been, the President thought, but by Senator Harkness, and maybe the time had come when Jim Harkness' view of world affairs needed a little broadening. "Suppose you tell me about it," he said.

Horton looked faintly perplexed, but said promptly: "It was basically an accident. Two men, working independently, came up with reports, strictly unofficial, but important. One was a graduate student's thesis on shelter construction; happens the boy was looking for a job, the Cement Research and Development Institute recommended him to me, he was on his way to see me when the thing happened. That's how I became involved in it. The other fellow's a lab worker, at least as far as earning a living's concerned, but he's a mathematician something-or-other and was working out a problem with his lab's computers. The problem: If the Reds are going to sneak-punch us, when will they do it? The answer: today. While we're all off base, with the All-Star Game. In the old days they'd maybe pick a presidential election to put one over, just like Hitler used to pick the long weekends. Now all they need is a couple of hours when everybody's looking the other way, you see. All-Star Game's a natural."

The President said mildly, "I can see that without using a computer, Senator."

"Certainly, sir. But this boy proved it. Like to meet him, by the way? I've got the lot of them, right outside."

In for a penny, in for a pound, thought the President, motioning them in. There were three men and a girl, rather young, rather excited. Senator Horton rattled off introductions. The President gathered the other two had been involved in the security leak that had occurred on the reports.

"But I've talked to them," cried Senator Horton, "and I can't believe there's a grain of malice in all of them. And what they say, Mr. President, requires immediate action."

"I was under the impression I'd taken immediate action," said the President. "You asked me to ground all civilian air traffic so the missile-watchers could have a clear field; I did. You asked me to put all our defense aircraft airborne; I did. You asked for a Condition Red defense posture and you got it, all but the official announcement."

"Yes, Mr. President. The immediate danger may have been averted, yes. But what about the future?"

"I see," said the President, and paused for a second. Oddly, there was no voice from the prompter in his ear to suggest his next words. He frowned.

"I see," he said again, louder. The tiny voice in his ear said at last:

"Well, sir, uh—" It cleared its throat. "Sir, there seems to be some confusion here. Perhaps you could ask the Senator to continue to brief you."

"Well—" said the President.

"David," whispered the prompter.

"—David, let's get our thinking organized. Why don't you continue to fill me in?"

"Gladly, sir! As you know, I'm Shelters all the way. Always have been. But what this young man here says has shaken me to the core. Mr. Venezuela says—" Valendora grinned sullenly at the rug—"that at this very moment we would be in atoms if it hadn't been for his timely publication of the statistical breakdown of our vulnerability. He's even a little sore about it, Mr. President."

"Sore?"

The senator grinned. "We spoiled his prediction," he explained. "Of course, we saved our own lives . . . The Other Side has computers too; they must have assessed our national preoccupation with baseball. Beyond doubt they intended to strike. Only the commotion his article caused—not only in our own country but, through their embassies, on the Other Side—plus of course your immediate reaction when I telephoned you asking for a Red Alert, kept the missiles from coming down today, sir. I'm certain of it. And this other young fellow, Mr. Chase—" Walter Chase bowed his head modestly—"brought out a lot of data in his term paper, or whatever it was. Seemed like nonsense, sir, so we checked it. Everything he said is not only fact but old stuff; it's been published hundreds of times. Not a word of new material in it." Chase glared. "That's why we've never built deep shelters. They simply won't stand up against massive attack—and cannot be made to stand up. It's too late for shelters. In building them we're falling into the oldest strategic trap of human warfare: We're fighting yesterday's war today."

President Braden experienced a sinking feeling when the earprompter said only, and doubtfully, "Ask him to go on, sir."

"Go on, si—Go on, David."

"Why," said the senator, astonished, "that's all there is, Mr. President. The rest is up to you."

President Braden remembered vaguely, as a youth, stories about the administration of President—who was it? Truman, or somebody around then. They said Truman had a sign on his desk that read: *The buck stops here*.

His own desk, the President noticed for the first time, was mirror-smooth. It held no such sign. Apart from the framed picture of his late wife there was nothing.

Yet the principle still held, remorselessly, no matter how long he had been able to postpone its application. He was the last man in the chain. There was no one to whom the President could pass the buck.

If it was time for the nation to pick itself up, turn itself around and head off in a new direction, he was the only one who could order it to march.

He thought about the alternatives. Say these fellows were right. Say the shelters couldn't keep the nation going in the event of all-out attack. Say the present alert, so incredibly costly in money and men, could not be maintained around the clock for any length of time, which it surely could not. Say the sneak-punchers were right . . .

But no, thought the President somberly, that avenue had been explored and the end was disaster. You could never get *all* the opposing missile bases, not while some were under the sea and some were touring the highways of the Siberian tundra on trucks and some were orbital and some were airborne. And it only took a handful of survivors to kill you.

So what was left?

Here and now, everybody was waiting for him to speak—even the little voice in his ear.

The President pushed his chair back and put his feet up on the desk. "You know," he said, wiggling his toes in their Argyle socks, "I once went to school too. True," he said, not apologizing, "it was West Point. That's a good school too, you know. I remember writing a term paper in one of the sociology courses . . . or was it history? No matter. I still recall what I said in that paper. I said wasn't it astonishing that things always got worse before they got better. Take monarchy, I said. It built up and up, grew more complex, more useless, more removed from government, in any real sense, until we come to things like England's Wars of the Roses and France's Sun King and the Czar and the Mikado—until most of the business of the government was in the person of

the king, instead of the other way around. Then—
bang! No more monarchy."

"Mr. President," whispered the voice in his ear,
"you have an appointment with the Mongolian
Legate."

"Oh, shut up, you," said the President amiably,
shocking his prompter and confusing his guests.
"Sorry, not you," he apologized. "My, uh, secretary.
Tells me that the Chinese representatives want to
talk about our 'unprecedented and unpeace-loving
acts'—more likely, to see what they can find out."
He picked the plug out of his ear and dropped it in a
desk drawer. "They'll wait. Now, take slavery," he
went on. "It too became more institutionalized—and
ritualized—until the horse was riding the man; until
the South here was existing on slaves, it was even
existing *for* slaves. The biggest single item of wealth
in the thirteen Confederate states was slaves. The
biggest single line of business, other than agricul-
ture, was slavery, dealing and breeding. Things get
big and formal, you see, just before they pop and
blow away. Well, I wrote all this up. I turned it in,
real proud, expecting, I don't know, maybe an honorary
LL.D. At least a compliment, certainly . . . It came
back and the instructor had scrawled one word across
the top of it: *Toynbee*. So I read up on Toynbee's
books. After, of course, I got over being oppressed
at the instructor's injustice to me. He was right.
Toynbee described the whole thing long before I
did.

"But, you know, I didn't know that at the time. I
thought it up myself, as if Toynbee had never lived,"
said the President with some pride. He beamed at
them.

Senator Horton was standing with open mouth.
He glanced quickly at the others in the room, but

they had nothing but puzzlement to return to him
He said, "Mr. President, I don't understand. You
mean—"

"Mean? I mean what's happened to us," said the
President testily. "We've had our obsessive period.
Now we move on to something else. And, Senator,
Congress is going to have to help move; and, I'm
warning you, you're going to help me move *it*."

When they left the White House it was late afternoon. The lilacs that bordered the wall were in full,
fragrant bloom. Denzer inhaled deeply and squeezed
the hand of Maggie Frome.

Passing the sentry box at the end of the drive,
they heard a voice from a portable radio inside. It
was screaming:

"It's going . . . it's *going* . . . it's GONE, folks!
Craffany has pulled one out of the fire again! And
that wraps it up for him, as Hockins sends one *way*
out over centerfield and into the stands . . ." The
guard looked out, rosily beaming, and waved them
on. He would have waved them on if they had worn
beards and carried ticking bombs; he was a Craffany
rooter from way back, and now in an ecstasy of
delight.

"Craffany did it, then," said Walter Chase sagely.
"I *thought* when he benched Hockins and moved
Little Joe Fliederwick to—"

"Oh, shut up, Chase," said Denzer. "Maggie, I'm
buying drinks. You want to come along, Venezuela?"

"I think not, Mr. Denzer," said the research man.
"I'm late now. *Statist*. *Analysis Trans*. is expecting
me."

"Chase?" Politeness forced that one out of him.
But Chase shook his head.

"I just remembered an old friend here in town,"

said Chase. He had had time for some quick thinking. If the nation was going over to a non-shelter
philosophy—if cave-dwelling was at an end and a
dynamic new program was going to start—maybe a
cement degree wasn't going to be the passport to
security and fame he had imagined. Walter Chase had
always had a keen eye for the handwriting on the
wall. "A young lady friend," he winked. "Name of
Douglasina Baggett. Perhaps you've heard of her father; he's quite an important man in H.E. and W."

The neutron, properly placed, had struck the nucleus; and the spreading chain was propagating rapidly through their world. What was it going to be
from now on? They did not know; does a fissioned
atom know what elements it will change into? It
*must* change; and so it changes. "I guess we did
something, eh?" said Denzer. "But . . . I don't know.
If it hadn't been us, I expect it would have been
someone else. Something had to give." For it doesn't
matter which nucleus fissions first. Once the mass is
critical the chain reaction begins; it is as simple as
that.

"Let's get that drink, Denzer," said Maggie Frome.

They flagged a cab, and all the way out to Arlington-
Alex it chuckled at them as they kissed. The cab
spared them its canned thoughts, and that was as
they wished it. But that was not why they were in
each other's arms.

# The World of Myrion Flowers

The world of Myrion Flowers, which was the world of the American Negro, was something like an idealized England and something like the real Renaissance. As it is in some versions of England, all the members of the upper class were at least friends of friends. Any Harlem businessman knew automatically who was the new top dog in the music department of Howard University a week after an upheaval of the faculty. And as it was in the Florence of Cellini, there was room for versatile men. An American Negro could be a doctor-builder-educator-realist-politician. Myrion Flowers was. Boston-born to a lawyer-realtist-politician father and a glamorous show-biz mother, he worked hard, drew the lucky number and was permitted to enter the schools which led to an M.D. and a license to practice in the State of New York. Power vacuums occurred around him during the years that followed, and willy-nilly he filled them. A construction firm going to waste, needing a little capital and a little common sense—what could he do? He did it, and accepted its stock. The school board coming to him as a sound man to represent

"Ah, your people"? He was a sound man. He served the board well. A trifling examination to pass for a real-estate license—trifling to him who had memorized a dozen textbooks in pathology, histology, anatomy and materia medica—why not? And if they would deem it such a favor if he spoke for the Fusion candidate, why should he not speak, and if they should later invite him to submit names to fill one dozen minor patronage jobs, why should he not give him the names of the needy persons he knew?

Flowers was a cold, controlled man. He never married. In lieu of children he had protégés. These began as Negro kids from orphanages or hopelessly destitute families; he backed them through college and postgraduate schools as long as they worked to the limit of what he considered their abilities; at the first sign of a let-down he axed them. The mortality rate over the years was only about one nongraduate in four—Myrion Flowers was a better predictor of success than any college admissions committee. His successes numbered forty-two when one of them came to him with a brand-new Ph.D. in clinical psychology and made a request.

The protégé's name was Ensal Brubacker. He took his place after dinner in the parlor of Dr. Flower's Brooklyn brownstone house along with many other suppliants. There was the old woman who wanted an extension of her mortgage and would get it; there was the overstocked appliance dealer who wanted to be bailed out and would not be; there was the mother whose boy had a habit and the husband whose wife was acting stranger and stranger every day; there was the landlord hounded by the building department; there was the cop who wanted a transfer; there was the candidate for the bar who wanted a powerful name as a reference; there was a store-front archbishop who wanted only to find out whether Dr. Flowers was right with God.

Brubacker was admitted to the doctor's study at 9:30. It was only the sixth time he had seen the man who had picked him from an orphanage and laid out some twenty thousand dollars for him since. He found him more withered, colder and quicker than ever.

The doctor did not congratulate him. He said, "You've got your degree, Brubacker. If you've come to me for advice, I'd suggest that you avoid the academic life, especially in the Negro schools. I know what you should do. You may get nowhere, but I would like to see you try one of the Four-A advertising and public relations firms, with a view to becoming a motivational research man. It's time one Negro was working in the higher levels of Madison Avenue, I believe."

Brubacker listened respectfully, and when it was time for him to reply he said: "Dr. Flowers, I'm very grateful of course for everything you've done. I sincerely wish I could—Dr. Flowers, I want to do research. I sent you my dissertation, but that's only the beginning—"

Myrion Flowers turned to the right filing card in his mind and said icily, "The Correlation of Toposcopic Displays, Beta-Wave Amplitudes and Perception of Musical Chord Progressions in 1,107 Unselected Adolescents. Very well. You now have your sandwich board with 'P,' 'H' and 'D' painted on it, fore and aft. I expect that you will now proceed to the job for which you have been trained."

"Yes, sir. I'd like to show you a—"

"I do not," said Dr. Flowers, "want you to be a beloved Old George Washington Carver humbly bending over his reports and test tubes. Academic research is of no immediate importance."

"No, sir. I—"

"The power centers of America," said Dr. Flowers, "are government, where our friend Mr. Wilkins is ably operating, and the executive levels of the large corporations, where I am attempting to achieve what is necessary. I want you to be an executive in a large corporation, Brubacker. You have been trained for that purpose. It is now perhaps barely possible for you to obtain a foothold. It is inconceivable to me that you will not make the effort, neither for me or for your people."

Brubacker looked at him in misery, and at last put his face into his hands. His shoulders shook.

Dr. Flowers said scornfully: "I take it you are declining to make that effort. Good-bye, Brubacker. I do not want to see you again."

The young man stumbled from the room, carrying a large pigskin valise which he had not been permitted to open.

As he had expected to overwhelm his benefactor with what he had accomplished he had made no plans for this situation. He could think only of returning to the university he had just left where, perhaps, before his little money ran out, he might obtain a grant. There was not really much hope of that. He had filed no proposals and sought no advice.

It did not help his mood when the overnight coach to Chicago was filling up in Grand Central. He was among the first and took a window seat. Thereafter the empty place beside him was spotted gladly by luggage-burdened matrons, Ivy-League-clad youngsters, harrumphing paper-box salesmen—gladly spotted—and then uncomfortably skimmed past when they discovered that to occupy it they would have to sit next to the gorilla-rapist-illiterate-tapdancermugger-menace who happened to be Dr. Ensal Brubacker.

But he was spared loneliness at the very last. The fellow who did drop delightedly into the seat beside him as the train began to move was One of His Own Kind. That is, he was unwashed, unlettered, a quarter drunk on liquor that had never known a tax stamp, and agonizingly high-spirited. He spoke such pure Harlem jive that Brubacker could not understand one word in twenty.

But politeness and a terror of appearing superior forced Brubacker to accept, at 125th Street, a choking swallow from the flat half-pint bottle his seatmate carried. And both of these things, plus an unsupportable sense of something lost, caused him to accept his seatmate's later offer of more paralyzing pleasures. In ten months Brubacker was dead, in Lexington, Kentucky, of pneumonia incurred while kicking the heroin habit, leaving behind him a badly puzzled staff doctor. "They'll say everything in withdrawal," he confided to his wife, "but I wonder how this one ever heard the word 'cryptesthesia.' "

It was about a month after that that Myrion Flowers received the package containing Brubacker's effects. There had been no one else to send them to.

He was shaken, that controlled man. He had seen many folk-gods of his people go the same route, but they were fighters, entertainers or revivalists; he had not expected it of a young, brilliant university graduate. For that reason he did not immediately throw the junk away, but mused over it for some minutes. His next visitor found him with a silvery-coppery sort of helmet in his hands.

Flowers's next visitor was a former Corporation Counsel to the City of New York. By attending Dr. Powell's church and having Dr. Flowers take care of his health he kept a well-placed foot in both the principal political camps of the city. He no longer much needed political support, but Flowers had pulled him through one coronary and he was too old to change doctors. "What have you got there, Myrion?" he asked.

Flowers looked up and said precisely, "If I can believe the notes of the man who made it, it is a receiver and amplifier for beta-wave oscillations."

The Corporation Counsel groaned, "God preserve me from the medical mind. What's that in English?" But he was surprised to see the expression of wondering awe that came onto Flowers's withered face.

"It reads thoughts," Flowers whispered.

The Corporation Counsel at once clutched his chest, but found no pain. He complained testily, "You're joking."

"I don't think I am, Wilmot. The man who constructed this devise had all the appropriate dignities— summa cum laude, Dean's List, interviewed by mail by nearly thirty prospective employers. Before they found out the color of his skin, of course. No," he said reflectively, "I don't think I'm joking, but there's one way to find out."

He lifted the helmet toward his head. The Corporation counsel cried out, "Damn you, Myrion, don't do that!"

Flowers paused. "Are you afraid I'll read your mind and learn your secrets?"

"At my time of life? When you're my doctor? No, Myrion, but you ought to know I have a bad heart. I don't want you electrocuted in front of my eyes. Besides, what the devil does a Negro want with a machine that will tell him what people are thinking? Isn't guessing bad enough for you?"

Myrion Flowers chose to ignore the latter part of

what his patient had said. "I don't expect it to electrocute me, and I don't expect this will affect your heart, Wilmot. In any event, I don't propose to be wondering about this thing for any length of time, I don't want to try it when I'm alone and there's no one else here." He plopped the steel bowl on his head. It fit badly and was very heavy. An extension cord hung from it, and without pausing Flowers plugged it into a wall socket by his chair.

The helmet whined faintly and Flowers leaped to his feet. He screamed.

The Corporation Counsel moved rapidly enough to make himself gasp. He snatched the helmet from Flowers's head, caught him by the shoulders and lowered him into his chair again. "You all right?" he growled.

Flowers shuddered epileptically and then controlled himself. "Thank you, Wilmot. I hope you haven't damaged Dr. Brubacker's device." And then suddenly, "It hit me all at once. It *hurt!*"

He breathed sharply and sat up.

From one of his desk drawers he took a physicians' sample bottle of pills and swallowed one without water. "Everyone was screaming at once," he said. He started to replace the pills, then saw the Corporation Counsel holding his chest and mutely offered him one.

Then he seemed startled.

He looked into his visitor's eyes. "I can still hear you."

"What?"

"It's a false angina, I think. But take the pill. But—" he passed a hand over his eyes—"you thought I was electrocuted, and you wondered how to straighten out my last bill. It's a fair bill, Wilmot. I didn't overcharge you." Flowers opened his eyes very wide and said, "The newsboy on the corner cheated me out of my change. He—" He swallowed and said, "The cops in the squad car just turning off Fulton Street don't like my having white patients. One of them is thinking about running in a girl that came here." He sobbed, "It didn't stop, Wilmot."

"For Christ's sake, Myrion, lie down."

"*It didn't stop.* It's not like a radio. You can't turn it off. Now I can hear—everybody! Every mind for miles around *is pouring into my head* WHAT IT THINKS ABOUT ME—ABOUT ME—ABOUT US!"

Ensal Brubacker, who had been a clinical psychologist and not a radio engineer, had not intended his helmet to endure the strain of continuous operation nor had he thought to provide circuit-breakers. It had been meant to operate for a few moments at most, enough to reroute a few neurons, open a blocked path or two. One of its parts overheated. Another took too much load as a result, and in a moment the thing was afire. It blew the fuses and the room was in darkness. The elderly ex-Corporation Counsel managed to get the fire out, and then picked up the phone. Shouting to be heard over the screaming of Myrion Flowers, he summoned a Kings County ambulance. They knew Flowers's name. The ambulance was there in nine minutes.

Flowers died some weeks later in the hospital—not Kings County, but he did not know the difference. He had been under massive sedation for almost a month until it became a physiological necessity to taper him off; and as soon as he was alert enough to do so he contrived to hang himself in his room.

His funeral was a state occasion. The crowds were enormous and there was much weeping. The Corporation Counsel was one of those permitted to cast a clod of earth upon the bronze casket, but he did not weep.

No one had ever figured out what the destroyed instrument was supposed to have been, and Wilmot did not tell. There are inventions and inventions, he thought, and reading minds is a job for white men. If even for white men. In the world of Myrion Flowers many seeds might sturdily grow, but some ripe fruits would mature into poison.

No doubt the machine might have broken any mind, listening in on every thought that concerned one. It was maddening and dizzying, and the man who wore the helmet would be harmed in any world; but only in the world of Myrion Flowers would he be hated to death.

# The Engineer

It was very simple. Some combination of low temperature and high pressure had forced something from the seepage at the ocean bottom into combination with something in the water around them.

And the impregnable armor around Subatlantic Oil's drilling chamber had discovered a weakness.

On the television screen it looked more serious than it was—so Muhlenhoff told himself, staring at it grimly. You get down more than a mile, and you're bound to have little technical problems. That's why deep-sea oil wells were still there.

Still, it did look kind of serious. The water driving in the pitted faults had the pressure of eighteen hundred meters behind it, and where it struck it did not splash—it battered and destroyed. As Muhlenhoff watched, a bulkhead collapsed in an explosion of spray; the remote camera caught a tiny driblet of the scattering brine, and the picture in the screen fluttered and shrank, and came back with a wavering sidewise pulse.

Muhlenhoff flicked off the screen and marched

into the room where the Engineering Board was waiting in attitudes of flabby panic.

As he swept his hand through his snow-white crew cut and called the board to order, a dispatch was handed to him—a preliminary report from a quickly-dispatched company trouble-shooter team. He read it to the board, stone-faced.

A veteran heat-transfer man, the first to recover, growled:

"Some vibration thing—and seepage from the oil pool. Sloppy drilling!" He sneered. "Big deal! So a couple hundred meters of shaft have to be plugged and pumped. So six or eight compartments go pop. Since when did we start to believe the cack Research and Development hands out? Armor's armor. Sure it pops—when something makes it pop. If Atlantic oil was easy to get at, it wouldn't be here waiting for us now. Put a gang on the job. Find out what happened, make sure it doesn't happen again. Big deal!"

Muhlenhoff smiled his attractive smile. "Breck," he said, "thank God you've got guts. Perhaps we were in a bit of a panic. Gentlemen, I hope we'll all take heart from Mr. Breck's level-headed—what did you say, Breck?"

Breck didn't look up. He was pawing through the dispatch Muhlenhoff had dropped to the table. "*Nine*-inch plate," he read aloud, white-faced. "And time of installation, not quite seven weeks ago. If this goes on in a straight line—" he grabbed for a pocket slide-rule—"we have, uh—" he swallowed—"less time than the probable error," he finished.

"Breck!" Muhlenhoff yelled. "Where are you going?"

The veteran heat-transfer man said grimly as he sped through the door: "To find a submarine."

The rest of the Engineering Board was suddenly

pulling chairs toward the trouble-shooting team's dispatch. Muhlenhoff slammed a fist on the table.

"Stop it," he said evenly. "The next man who leaves the meeting will have his contract canceled. Is that clear, gentlemen? Good. We will now proceed to get organized."

He had them; they were listening. He said forcefully: "I want a task force consisting of a petrochemist, a vibrations man, a hydrostatics man and a structural engineer. Co-opt mathematicians and computermen as needed. I will have all machines capable of handling Fourier series and up cleared for your use. The work of the task force will be divided into two phases. For Phase One, members will keep their staffs as small as possible. The objective of Phase One is to find the cause of the leaks and predict whether similar leaks are likely elsewhere in the project. On receiving a first approximation from the force I will proceed to set up Phase Two, to deal with countermeasures."

He paused. "Gentlemen," he said, "we must not lose our nerves. We must not panic. Possibly the most serious technical crisis in Atlantic's history lies before us. Your most important job is to maintain—at all times—a cheerful, courageous attitude. We cannot, repeat cannot, afford to have the sub-technical staff of the project panicked for lack of a good example from us." He drilled each of them in turn with a long glare. "And," he finished, "if I hear of anyone suddenly discovering emergency business ashore, the man who does it better get fitted for a sludgemonkey's suit, because that's what he'll be tomorrow. Clear?"

Each of the executives assumed some version of a cheerful, courageous attitude. They looked ghastly, even to themselves.

Muhlenhoff stalked into his private office, the nerve-center of the whole bulkheaded works.

In Muhlenhoff's private office, you would never know you were 1,800 meters below the surface of the sea. It looked like any oilman's brass-hat office any-where, complete to the beautiful blonde outside the door (but white-faced and trembling), the potted palm (though the ends of its fronds vibrated gently), and the typical section chief bursting in the typical flap. "Sir," he whined, frenzied, "Section Six has pinholed! The corrosion—"

"Handle it!" barked Muhlenhoff, and slammed the door. Section Six be damned! What did it matter if a few of the old bulkheads pinholed and filled? The central chambers were safe, until they could lick whatever it was that was corroding. The point was, you had to stay with it and get out the oil; because if you didn't prove your lease, PetroMex would. Mexi-can oil wanted those reserves mighty badly.

Muhlenhoff knew how to handle an emergency. Back away from it. Get a fresh slant. Above all, *don't panic*.

He slapped a button that guaranteed no interrup-tion and irritably, seeking distraction, picked up his latest copy of the *New New Review*—for he was, among other things, an intellectual as time allowed.

Under the magazine was the latest of several confi-dential communications from the home office. Muhlen-hoff growled and tossed the magazine aside. He re-read what Priestley had had to say:

"I know you understand the importance of beating our Spic friends to the Atlantic deep reserves, so I won't give you a hard time about it. I'll just pass it on the way Lundstrom gave it to me: 'Tell Muhlenhoff he'll come back on the Board or on a board, and no alibis or excuses.' Get it? Well—"

Hell. Muhlenhoff threw the sheet down and tried to think about the damned corrosion-leakage situation.

But he didn't try for long. There was, he realized, no point at all in him thinking about the problem. For one thing, he no longer had the equipment.

Muhlenhoff realized, wonderingly, that he hadn't opened a table of integrals for ten years; he doubted that he could find his way around the pages well enough to run down a tricky form. He had come up pretty fast through the huge technical staff of Atlantic. First he had been a geologist in the procurement section, one of those boots-and-leather-jacket guys who spent his days in rough, tough blasting and drilling and his nights in rarefied scientific air, correlating and integrating the findings of the day. Next he had been a Chief Geologist, chairborne director of youngsters, now and then tackling a muddled report with Theory of Least Squares and Gibbs Phase Rule that magically separated dross from limpid fact . . . or, he admitted wryly, at least turning the muddled reports over to mathematicians who specialized in those disciplines.

Next he had been a Raw Materials Committee member who knew that drilling and figuring weren't the almighty things he had supposed them when he was a kid, who began to see the Big Picture of off-shore leases and depreciation allowances; of power and fusible rocks and steel for the machines, butane for the drills, plastics for the pipelines, metals for the circuits, the computers, the doors, windows, walls, tools, utilities. A committeeman who began to see that a friendly beer poured for the right resources-commission man was really more important than Least Squares or Phase Rule, because a resources commissioner who didn't get along with you might get along,

for instance, with somebody from Coastwide, and
allot to Coastwide the next available block of leases—
thus working grievous harm to Atlantic and the bil-
lions it served. A committeeman who began to see
that the Big Picture meant government and science
leaning chummily against each other, government
setting science new and challenging tasks like the
billion-barrel procurement program, science backing
government with all its tremendous prestige. You
consume my waste hydrocarbons, Muhlenhoff thought
comfortably, and I'll consume yours.

Thus mined, smelted and milled, Muhlenhoff was
tempered for higher things. For the first, the technical directorate of an entire Atlantic Sub-Sea Petroleum Corporation district, and all wells, fields,
pipelines, stills, storage fields, transport, fabrication
and maintenance appertaining thereto. Honors piled
upon honors. And then—

He glanced around him at the comfortable office.
The top. Nothing to be added but voting stock and
Board membership—and those within his grasp, if
only he weathered this last crisis. And then the
rarefied height he occupied alone.

And, by God, he thought. I do a damn good job of
it! Pleasurably he reviewed his conduct at the meeting; he had already forgotten his panic. Those shaking fools would have brought the roof down on us, he
thought savagely. A few gallons of water in an unimportant shaft, and they're set to message the home
office, run for the surface, abandon the whole project. The Big Picture! They didn't see it, and they
never would. He might, he admitted, not be able to
chase an integral form through a table, but by God
he could give the orders to those who would. The
thing was organized now; the project was rolling; the
task force had its job mapped out; and somehow,

although he would not do a jot of the brain-wearing, eyestraining, actual work, it would be *his* job, because he had initiated it. He thought of the flat, dark square miles of calcareous ooze outside, under which lay the biggest proved untapped petroleum reserve in the world. Sector Forty-one, it was called on the hydrographic charts.

Perhaps, some day, the charts would say: *Muhlenhoff Basin.*

Well, why not?

The emergency intercom was flickering its red call light pusillanimously. Muhlenhoff calmly lifted the handset off its cradle and ignored the tinny bleat. When you gave an order, you had to leave the men alone to carry it out.

He relaxed in his chair and picked up a book from the desk. He was, among other things, a student of Old American History, as time permitted.

Fifteen minutes now, he promised himself, with the heroic past. And then back to work refreshed!

Muhlenhoff plunged into the book. He had schooled himself to concentration; he hardly noticed when the pleading noise from the intercom finally gave up trying to attract his attention. The book was a study of that Mexican War in which the United States had been so astonishingly deprived of Texas, Oklahoma and points west under the infamous Peace of Galveston. The story was well told; Muhlenhoff was lost in its story from the first page.

Good thumbnail sketch of Presidente Lopez, artistically contrasted with the United States' Whitmore. More-in-sorrow-than-in-anger off-the-cuff psychoanalysis of the crackpot Texan, Byerly, derisively known to Mexicans as "El Cacafuego." Byerly's raid at the head of his screwball irredentists, their prompt annihilation by the Mexican Third Armored Regiment, Byerly's impeccably legal trial and execution at Tehuantepec. Stiff diplomatic note from the United States. Bland answer: Please mind your business, Señores, and we will mind ours. Stiffer diplomatic note. We said *please*, Señores, and can we not let it go at that? *Very* stiff diplomatic note; and Latin temper flares at last: Mexico severs relations.

Bad to worse. Worse to worst.

Massacre of Mexican nationals at San Antonio. Bland refusal of the United States federal government to interfere in "local police problem" of punishing the guilty. Mexican Third Armored raids San Antone, arrests the murderers (feted for weeks, their faces in the papers, their proud boasts of butchery retold everywhere), and hangs them before recrossing the border.

United States declares war. United States loses war—outmaneuvered, outgeneraled, out-logisticated, outgunned, outmanned.

And outfought.

Said the author:

"The colossal blow this cold military fact delivered to the United States collective ego is inconceivable to us today. Only a study of contemporary comment can make it real to the historian: The choked hysteria of the newspapers, the raging tides of suicides, Whitmore's impeachment and trial, the forced resignations of the entire General Staff—all these serve only to sketch in the national mood.

"Clearly something had happened to the military power which, within less than five decades previous, had annihilated the war machines of the Cominform and the Third Reich.

"We have the words of the contemporary military analyst, Osgood Ferguson, to explain it:

"The rise of the so-called 'political general' means a decline in the efficiency of the army. Other things being equal, an undistracted professional beats an officer who is half soldier and half politician. A general who makes it his sole job to win a war will infallibly defeat an opponent who, by choice of constraint, must offend no voters of enemy ancestry, destroy no cultural or religious shrines highly regarded by the press, show leniency when leniency is fashionable at home, display condign firmness when voters demand it (though it cause his zone of communications to blaze up into a fury of guerrilla clashes), choose his invasion routes to please a state department apprehensive of potential future ententes.

"It is unfortunate that most of Ferguson's documentation was lost when his home was burned during the unsettled years after the war. But we know that what Mexico's Presidente Lopez said to his staff was: 'My generals, win me this war.' And this entire volume does not have enough space to record what the United States generals were told by the White House, the Congress as a whole, the Committees on Military affairs, the Special Committees on Conduct of the War, the State Department, the Director of the Budget, the War Manpower Commission, the Republican National Committee, the Democratic National Committee, the Steel lobby, the Oil lobby, the Labor lobby, the political journals, the daily newspapers, the broadcasters, the ministry, the Granges, the Chambers of Commerce. However, we do know—unhappily—that the United States generals obeyed their orders. This sorry fact was inscribed indelibly on the record at the Peace of Galveston."

\*     \*     \*

Muhlenhoff yawned and closed the book. An amusing theory, he thought, but thin. Political generals? Nonsense.

He was glad to see that his subordinates had given up their attempt to pass responsibility for the immediate problem to his shoulders; the intercom had been silent for many minutes now. It only showed, he thought comfortably, that they had absorbed his leading better than they knew.

He glanced regretfully at the door that had sheltered him, for this precious refreshing interlude, from the shocks of the project outside. Well, the interlude was over; now to see about this leakage thing. Muhlenhoff made a note, in his tidy card-catalog mind, to have Maintenance on the carpet. The door was bulging out of true. Incredible sloppiness! And some damned fool had shut the locks in the ventilating system. The air was becoming stuffy.

Aggressive and confident, the political engineer pressed the release that opened the door to the greatest shock of all.

# A Gentle Dying

Elphen DeBeckett lay dying. It was time. He had lived in the world for one hundred and nine years, though he had seen little enough of it except for the children. The children, thank God, still came. He thought they were with him now: "Coppie," he whispered in a shriveled voice, "how nice to see you." The nurse did not look around, although she was the only person in the room besides himself, and knew that he was not addressing her.

The nurse was preparing the injections the doctor had ordered her to have ready. This little capsule for shock, this to rally his strength, these half-dozen others to shield him from his pain. Most of them would be used. DeBeckett was dying in a pain that once would have been unbearable and even now caused him to thresh about sometimes and moan.

DeBeckett's room was a great twelve-foot chamber with hanging drapes and murals that reflected scenes from his books. The man himself was tiny, gnomelike. He became even less material while death (prosey biology, the chemistry of colloids) drew inappropriately near his head. He had lived his life remote from everything a normal man surrounds himself with. He now seemed hardly alive enough to die.

DeBeckett lay in a vast, pillared bed, all the vaster for the small burden he put on it, and the white linen was whiter for his merry brown face. "Darling Veddie, please don't cry," he whispered restlessly, and the nurse took up a hypodermic syringe. He was not in unusual pain, though, and she put it back and sat down beside him.

The world had been gentle with the gentle old man. It had made him a present of this bed and this linen, this great house with its attendant horde of machines to feed and warm and comfort him, and the land on which stood the tiny, quaint houses he loved better. It had given him a park in the mountains, well stocked with lambs, deer and birds of blazing, spectacular color, a fenced park where no one ever went but DeBeckett and the beloved children, where earth-moving machines had scooped out a Very Own Pond ("My Very Own Pond/Which I sing for you in this song/Is eight Hippopotamuses Wide/And twenty Elephants long.") He had not seen it for years, but he knew it was there. The world had given him, most of all, money, more money than he could ever want. He had tried to give it back (gently, hopefully, in a way pathetically), but there was always more. Even now the world showered him with gifts and doctors, though neither could prevail against the stomping pitchfire arsonist in the old man's colon. The disease, a form of gastroenteritis, could have been cured; medicine had come that far long since. But not in a body that clung so lightly to life.

He opened his eyes and said strongly, "Nurse, are the children there?"

The nurse was a woman of nearly sixty. That was why she had been chosen. The new medicine was utterly beyond her in theory, but she could follow directions; and she loved Elphen DeBeckett. Her love was the love of a child, for a thumbed edition of *Coppie Brambles* had brightened her infancy. She said, "Of course they are, Mr. DeBeckett."

He smiled. The old man loved children very much. They had been his whole life. The hardest part of his dying was that nothing of his own flesh would be left, no son, no grandchild, no one. He had never married. He would have given almost anything to have a child of his blood with him now—almost anything, except the lurid, grunting price nature exacts, for DeBeckett had never known a woman. His only children were the phantoms of his books . . . and those who came to visit him. He said faintly, "Let the little sweetlings in."

The nurse slipped out and the door closed silently behind her. Six children and three adults waited patiently outside, DeBeckett's doctor among them. Quickly she gave him the dimensions of the old man's illness, pulse and temperature, and the readings of the tiny gleaming dials by his pillow as well, though she did not know what they measured. It did not matter. She knew what the doctor was going to say before he said it: "He can't last another hour. It is astonishing that he lasted this long," he added, "but we will have lost something when he goes."

"He wants you to come in. Especially you—" She glanced around, embarrassed. "Especially you children." She had almost said "little sweetlings" herself, but did not quite dare. Only Elphen DeBeckett could talk like that, even to children. Especially to children. Especially to these children, poised, calm, beautiful, strong and gay. Only the prettiest, sweetest children visited Elphen DeBeckett, half a dozen or a score every day, a year-in, year-out pilgrimage. He would not have noticed if they had been ugly and dull, of course. To DeBeckett all children were sweet, beautiful and bright.

They entered and ranged themselves around the bed, and DeBeckett looked up. The eyes regarded them and a dying voice said, "Please read to me," with such resolute sweetness that it frightened. "From my book," it added, though they knew well enough what he meant.

The children looked at each other. They ranged from four to eleven, Will, Mike, blonde Celine, brown-eyed Karen, fat Freddy and busy Pat. "You," said Pat, who was seven.

"No," said five-year-old Freddy. "Will."

"Celine," said Will. "Here."

The girl named Celine took the book from him and began obediently. " 'Coppie thought to herself—' "

"No," said Pat. "Open."

The girl opened the book, embarrassed, glancing at the dying old man. He was smiling at her without amusement, only love. She began to read:

> Coppie thought to herself that the geese might be hungry, for she herself ate Lotsandlots. Mumsie often said so, though Coppie had never found out what that mysterious food might be. She could not find any, so took some bread from Brigid Marie Ann-Erica Evangeline, the Cook Whose Name Was So Long That She Couldn't Remember It All Herself. As she walked along Dusty Path to Coppie Brambles's Very Own Pond—

Celine hesitated, looking at the old man with sharp worry, for he had moaned faintly, like a flower moaning. "No, love," he said. "Go on." The swelling soft bubble before his heart had turned on him, but he knew he still had time.

The little girl read:

—As she walked along Dusty Path to Coppie Brambles's Very Own Pond, she thought and thought, and what she thought finally came right out of her mouth. It was a Real Gay Think, to be Thought While Charitably Feeding Geese:
They don't make noise like little girls and boys,
And all day long they're aswimming.
They never fret and sputter 'cause they haven't any butter,
They go where the water's wetly brimming.
But say—
Anyway—
I
Like
Geese!

There was more, but the child paused and, after a moment, closed the book. DeBeckett was no longer listening. He was whispering to himself.

On the wall before him was painted a copy of one of the illustrations from the first edition of his book, a delightful picture of Coppie Brambles herself, feeding the geese, admirably showing her shyness and her trace of fear, contrasted with the loutish comedy of the geese. The old man's eyes were fixed on the picture as he whispered. They guessed he was talking to Coppie, the child of eight dressed in the fashions of eighty years ago. They could hardly hear him, but in the silence that fell on the room his voice grew stronger.

He was saying, without joy but without regret.

"No more meadows, no more of the laughter of little children. But I do love them." He opened his eyes and sat up, waving the nurse away. "No, my dear," he said cheerfully, "it does not matter if I sit up now, you know. Excuse me for my rudeness. Excuse an old and tired man who, for a moment, wished to live on. I have something to say to you all."

The nurse, catching a sign from the doctor, took up another hypodermic and made it ready. "Please, Mr. DeBeckett," she said. Good humored, he permitted her to spray the surface of his wrist with a fine mist of droplets that touched the skin and penetrated it. "I suppose that is to give me strength," he said. "Well, I am grateful for it. I know I must leave you, but there is something I would like to know. I have wondered . . . For years I have wondered, but I have not been able to understand the answers when I was told them. I think I have only this one more chance."

He felt stronger from the fluid that now coursed through his veins, and accepted without fear the price he would have to pay for it. "As you know," he said, "or, I should say, as you children no doubt do not know, some years ago I endowed a research institution, the Coppie Brambles Foundation. I did it for the love of you, you and all of you. Last night I was reading the letter I wrote my attorneys—No. Let us see if you can understand the letter itself; I have it here. Will, can you read?"

Will was nine, freckled darkly on pale skin, red haired and gangling. "Yes, Mr. DeBeckett."

"Even hard words," smiled the dying man.

"Yes, sir."

DeBeckett gestured at the table beside him, and the boy obediently took up a stiff sheet of paper.

"Please," said DeBeckett, and the boy began to read in a highpitched, rapid whine.

" 'Children have been all my life and I have not regretted an instant of the years I devoted to their happiness. If I can tell them a little of the wonderful world in which we are, if I can open to them the miracles of life and living, then my joy is unbounded. This I have tried, rather selfishly, to do. I cannot say it was for them! It was for me. For nothing could have given me more pleasure.' "

The boy paused.

DeBeckett said gravely, "I'm afraid this is a Very Big Think, lovelings. Please try to understand. This is the letter I wrote to my attorneys when I instructed them to set up the Foundation. Go on, Will."

" 'But my way of working has been unscientific, I know. I am told that children are not less than we adults, but more. I am told that the grown-up maimers and cheats in the world are only children soiled, that the hagglers of commerce are the infant dreamers whose dreams were denied. I am told that youth is wilder, freer, better than age, which I believe with all my heart, not needing the stories of twenty-year-old mathematicians and infant Mozarts to lay a proof.

" 'In the course of my work I have been given great material rewards. I wish that this money be spent for those I love. I have worked with the heart, but perhaps my money can help someone to work with the mind, in this great new science of psychology which I do not understand, in all of the other sciences which I understand even less. I must hire other eyes.

" 'I direct, then, that all of my assets other than my books and my homes be converted into cash, and that this money be used to further the study of the child, with the aim of releasing him from the corrupt adult cloak that smothers him, of freeing him for wisdom, tenderness and love.' "

"That," said DeBeckett sadly, "was forty years ago."

He started at a sound. Overhead a rocket was clapping through the sky, and DeBeckett looked wildly around. "It's all right, Mr. DeBeckett," comforted little Pat. "It's only a plane."

He allowed her to soothe him. "Ah, loveling," he said. "And can you answer my question?"

"What it says in the 'Cyclopedia, Mr. DeBeckett?"

"Why—Yes, if you know it, my dear."

Surprisingly the child said, as if by rote: "The Institute was founded in 1976 and at once attracted most of the great workers in pediatric analysis, who were able to show Wiltshanes's Effect in the relationship between glandular and mental development. Within less than ten years a new projective analysis of the growth process permitted a reorientation of basic pedagogy from a null-positive locus. The effects were immediate. The first generation of—"

She stopped, startled. The old man was up on his elbow, his eyes blazing at her in wonder and fright. "I'm—" She looked around at the other children for help and at once wailed, "I'm *sorry*, Mr. DeBeckett!" and began to cry.

The old man fell back, staring at her with a sort of unbelieving panic. The little girl wept abundantly. Slowly DeBeckett's expression relaxed and he managed a sketchy smile.

He said, "There, sweetest. You startled me. But it was charming of you to memorize all that!"

"I learned it for you," she sobbed.

"I didn't understand. Don't cry." Obediently the

little girl dried her eyes as DeBeckett stretched out a hand to her.

But the hand dropped back on the quilt. Age, surprise and the drug had allied to overmaster the dwindling resources of Elphen DeBeckett. He wandered to the plantoms on the wall. "I never understood what they did with my money," he told Coppie, who smiled at him with a shy, painted smile. "The children kept coming, but they never said."

"Poor man," said Will absently, watching him with a child's uncommitted look.

The nurse's eyes were bright and wet. She reached for the hypodermic, but the doctor shook his head.

"Wait," he said, and walked to the bed. He stood on tiptoe to peer into the dying man's face. "No, no use. Too old. Can't survive organ transplant, certainty of cytic shock. No feasible therapy." The nurse's eyes were now flowing. The doctor said to her, with patience but not very much patience, "No alternative. Only kept him going this long from gratitude."

The nurse sobbed, "Isn't there *anything* we can do for him?"

"Yes." The doctor gestured, and the lights on the diagnostic dials winked out. "We can let him die."

Little Pat hiked herself up on a chair, much too large for her, and dangled her feet. "Be nice to get rid of this furniture, anyway," she said. "Well, nurse? He's dead. Don't wait." The nurse looked rebelliously at the doctor, but the doctor only nodded. Sadly the nurse went to the door and admitted the adults who had waited outside. The four of them surrounded the body and bore it gently through the door. Before it closed the nurse looked back and wailed: "He loved you!"

The children did not appear to notice. After a

moment Pat said reflectively, "Sorry about the book. Should have opened it."

"He didn't notice," said Will, wiping his hands. He had touched the old man's fingers.

"No. Hate crying, though."

The doctor said, "Nice of you. Helped him, I think." He picked up the phone and ordered a demolition crew for the house. "Monument?"

"Oh, yes," said another child. "Well. Small one, anyway."

The doctor, who was nine, said, "Funny. Without him, what? A few hundred thousand dollars and the Foundation makes a flexible world, no more rigid adults, no more—" He caught himself narrowly. The doctor had observed before that he had a tendency to over-identify with adults, probably because his specialty had been geriatrics. Now that Elphen DeBeckett was dead, he no longer had a specialty.

"Miss him somehow," said Celine frankly, coming over to look over Will's shoulder at the quaint old murals on the wall. "What the nurse said, true enough. He loved us."

"And clearly we loved him," piped Freddy, methodically sorting through the contents of the dead man's desk. "Would have terminated him with the others otherwise, wouldn't we?"

# Nightmare with Zeppelins

The Zeppelin dirigible balloons bombed London again last night and I got little sleep what with the fire brigades clanging down the street and the antiaircraft guns banging away. Bad news in the morning post. A plain card from Emmie to let me know that Sam's gone, fast and without much pain. She didn't say, but I suppose it was the flu, which makes him at least the fifth of the old lib-lab boys taken off this winter. And why not? We're in our seventies and eighties. It's high time.

Shaw said as much the other day when I met him on the steps of the Museum reading room, he striding in, I doddering out. In that brutal, flippant way of his, he was rather funny about how old Harry Lewes was standing in the way of youngsters like himself, but I can't bring myself to put his remarks down; they would be a little too painful to contemplate.

Well, he's quite recovered from that business with his foot that gave us all such a fright. Barring the 'flu, he may live to my age, and about 1939 bright youngsters now unborn will be watching like hawks for the smallest sign of rigidity, of eccentricity, and saying complacently: "Grand old boy, G.B.S. Such a pity he's going the least bit soft upstairs." And I shall by then be watching from Olympus, and chuckling.

Enough of him. He has the most extraordinary way of getting into everybody's conversation, though it is true that my own conversation does wander, these bad days. I did not think that the second decade of the twentieth century would be like this, though, as I have excellent reason to be, I am glad it is not worse.

I am really quite unhappy and uncomfortable as I sit here at the old desk. Though all the world knows I don't hold with personal service for the young and healthy, I am no longer a member of either of those classes. I do miss the ministrations of Bagley, who at this moment is probably lying in a frozen trench and even more uncomfortable than I. I can't seem to build as warm a fire as he used to. The coals won't go right. Luckily, I know what to do when I am unhappy and uncomfortable: work.

Anyway, Wells is back from France. He has been talking, he says, to some people at the Cavendish Laboratory, wherever that is. He told me we must make a "radium bomb." I wanted to ask: "Must we, Wells? Must we, *really?*"

He says the great virtue of a radium bomb is that it explodes *and keeps on exploding*—for hours, days, weeks. The italics are Wells's—one could hear them in his rather high-pitched voice—and he is welcome to them.

I once saw an explosion which would have interested Wells and, although it did not *keep on exploding*, it was as much of an explosion as I ever care to see.

I thought of telling him so. But, if he believed me, there would be a hue and a cry—I wonder, was I ever once as *consecrated* as he?—and if he did not, he might all the same use it for the subject of one of his "scientific" romances. After I am gone, of course, but surely that event cannot be long delayed, and in any case that would spoil it. And I want the work. I do not think I have another book remaining—forty-one fat volumes will have to do—but this can hardly be a book.

A short essay; it must be short if it is not to become an autobiography and, though I have re-sisted few temptations in my life, I mean to fight that one off to the end. That was another jeer of Shaw's. Well, he scored off me, for I confess that some such thought had stirred in my mind.

My lifelong struggle with voice and pen against social injustice had barely begun in 1864, and yet I had played a part in three major work stoppages, published perhaps a dozen pamphlets and was the editor and principal contributor of the still-remem-bered *Labour's Voice*. I write with what must look like immodesty only to explain how it was that I came to the attention of Miss Carlotta Cox. I was working with the furious energy of a very young man who has discovered his vocation, and no doubt Miss Cox mistook my daemon—now long gone, alas!—for me.

Miss Cox was a member of that considerable group of ruling-class Englishmen and women who devote time, thought and money to improving the lot of the workingman. Everybody knows of good Josiah Wedge-wood, Mr. William Morris, Miss Nightingale; they were the great ones. Perhaps I alone today remem-ber Miss Cox, but there were hundreds like her and pray God there will always be.

She was then a spinster in her sixties and had

spent most of her life giving away her fortune. She
had gone once in her youth to the cotton mills whence
that fortune had come, and knew after her first horrified
look what her course must be. She instructed her
man of business to sell all her shares in that Inferno
of sweated labour and for the next forty years, as she
always put it, attempted to make restitution.

She summoned me, in short, to her then-celebrated
stationer's shop and, between waiting on purchasers
of nibs and foolscap, told me her plan. I was to go to
Africa.

Across the Atlantic, America was at war within
herself. The rebellious South was holding on, not
with any hope of subduing the North, but in the
expectation of support from England.

England herself was divided. Though England had
abolished slavery on her own soil almost a century
earlier, still the detestable practice had its apologists,
and there were those who held the rude blacks in-
capable of assuming the dignities of freedom. I was
to seek out the Dahomeys and the Congolese on
their own grounds and give the lie to those who
thought them less than men.

"Tell England," said Miss Cox, "that the so-called
primitive Negroes possessed great empires when our
fathers lived in wattle huts. Tell England that the
black lawgivers of Solomon's time are true representatives of their people, and that the monstrous cari-
cature of the plantation black is a venal creation of an
ignoble class!"

She spoke like that, but she also handed me a
cheque for two hundred and fifty pounds to defray
my expenses of travel and to subsidize a wide distri-
bution of the numbers of *Labour's Voice* which would
contain my correspondence.

Despite her sometimes grotesque manner, Miss Cox's project was not an unwise one. Whatever enlightenment could be bought at a price of two hundred and fifty pounds was a blow at human slavery. Nor, being barely twenty, was I much distressed by the thought of a voyage to strange lands.

In no time at all, I had turned the direction of *Labour's Voice* over to my tested friends and contributors Mr. Samuel Blackett and Miss Emma Chatto (they married a month later) and in a week I was aboard a French "composite ship," iron of frame and wooden of skin, bound for a port on the Dark Continent, the home of mystery and enchantment.

So we thought of it in those days and so, in almost as great degree, do we think of it today, though I venture to suppose that, once this great war is over, those same creations of Count Zeppelin which bombed me last night may dispel some of the mystery, exorcise the enchantment and bring light into the darkness. May it be so, though I trust that whatever discoveries these aeronauts of tomorrow may bring will not repeat the discovery Herr Faesch made known to me in 1864.

The squalor of ocean travel in those days is no part of my story. It existed and I endured it for what seemed like an eternity, but at last I bade farewell to *Le Flamant* and all her roaches, rats and stench. Nor does it become this memoir to discuss the tragic failure of the mission Miss Cox had given me.

(Those few who remember my *Peoples of the Earth* will perhaps also remember the account given in the chapter I entitled "Africa Journeyings." Those, still fewer, whose perception revealed to them an unaccountable gap between the putrid sore throat with which I was afflicted at the headwaters of the Congo and my leave taking on the Gold Coast will find herewith the chronicle of the missing days).

It is enough to say that I found no empires in 1864. If they had existed, and I believe they had, they were vanished with Sheba's Queen. I did, however, find Herr Faesch. Or he found me.

How shall I describe Herr Faesch for you? I shan't, Shaw notwithstanding, permit myself so hackneyed a term as "hardy Swiss"; I am not so far removed from the youthful spring of creation as that. Yet Swiss he was, and surely hardy as well, for he discovered me (or his natives did) a thousand miles from a community of Europeans, deserted by my own bearers, nearer to death than ever I have been since. He told me that I tried thrice to kill him, in my delirium; but he nursed me well and I lived. As you see.

He was a scientific man, a student of Nature's ways, and a healer, though one cure was beyond him. For, sick though I was, he was more ravaged by destructive illness than I. I woke in a firelit hut with a rank poultice at my throat and a naked savage daubing at my brow, and I was terrified; no, not of the native, but of the awful cadaverous face, ghost-white, that frowned down at me from the shadows.

That was my first sight of Herr Faesch.

When, a day later, I came able to sit up and to talk, I found him a gentle and brave man, whose English was every bit as good as my own, whose knowledge surpassed that of any human I met before or since. But the mark of death was on him. In that equatorial jungle, his complexion was alabaster. Ruling the reckless black warriors who served him, his strength yet was less than a child's. In those steaming afternoons when I hardly dared stir from my cot for fear of stroke, he wore gloves and a woolen scarf at his neck.

We had, in all, three days together. As I regained my health, his health dwindled.

He introduced himself to me as a native of Geneva, that colorful city on the finest lake of the Alps. He listened courteously while I told him of my own errand and did me, and the absent Miss Cox, the courtesy of admiring the spirit which prompted it—though he was not sanguine of my prospects of finding the empires.

He said nothing of what had brought him to this remote wilderness, but I thought I knew. Surely gold. Perhaps diamonds or some other gem, but I thought not; gold was much more plausible.

I had picked up enough of the native dialect to catch perhaps one word in twenty of what he said to his natives and they to him—enough, at any rate, to know that when he left me in their charge for some hours, that first day, he was going to a hole in the ground. It could only be a mine, and what, I asked myself, would a European trouble to mine in the heart of unexplored Africa but gold?

I was wrong, of course. It was not gold at all.

Wells says that they are doing astonishing things at the Cavendish Laboratory, but I do think that Herr Faesch might have astonished even Wells. Certainly he astonished me. On the second day of my convalescence, I found myself strong enough to be up and walking about.

Say that I was prying. Perhaps I was. It was oppressively hot—I dared not venture outside—and yet I was too restless to lie abed waiting for Herr Faesch's return. I found myself examining the objects on his camp table and there were, indeed, nuggets. But the nuggets were not gold. They were a silvery metal, blackened and discolored, but surely without gold's yellow hue; they were rather small, like irregular lark's eggs, and yet they were queerly heavy. Perhaps there was a score of them, aggregating about a pound or two.

I rattled them thoughtfully in my hand, and then observed that across the tent, in a laboratory jar with a glass stopper, there were perhaps a dozen more—yes, and in yet another place in that tent, in a pottery dish, another clutch of the things. I thought to bring them close together so that I might compare them. I fetched the jar and set it on the table; I went after the pellets in the pottery dish.

Herr Faesch's voice, shaking with emotion, halted me. "Mr. Lewes!" he whispered harshly. "Stop, sir!"

I turned, and there was the man, his eyes wide with horror, standing at the flap of the tent. I made my apologies, but he waved them aside.

"No, no," he croaked, "I know you meant no harm. But I tell you, Mr. Lewes, you were very near to death a moment ago."

I glanced at the pellets. "From these, Herr Faesch?"

"Yes, Mr. Lewes. From those." He tottered into the tent and retrieved the pottery dish from my hands. Back to its corner it went; then the jar, back across the tent again. "They must not come together. No, sir," he said, nodding thoughtfully, though I had said nothing with which he might have been agreeing, "they must not come together."

He sat down. "Mr. Lewes," he whispered, "have you ever heard of uranium?" I had not. "Or of pitchblende? No? Well," he said earnestly, "I assure you that you will. These ingots, Mr. Lewes, are uranium, but not the standard metal of commerce. No, sir. They are a rare variant form, indistinguishable by the most delicate of chemical tests from the ordinary metal, but possessed of characteristics which are—I shall merely say 'wonderful,' Mr. Lewes, for I dare not use the term which comes first to mind."

"Remarkable," said I, feeling that some such response was wanted.

He agreed. "Remarkable indeed, my dear Mr. Lewes! You really cannot imagine how remarkable. Suppose I should tell you that the mere act of placing those few nuggets you discovered in close juxtaposition to each other would liberate an immense amount of energy. Suppose I should tell you that if a certain critical quantity of this metal should be joined together, an explosion would result. Eh, Mr. Lewes? What of that?"

I could only say again, "Remarkable, Herr Faesch." I knew nothing else to say. I was not yet one-and-twenty, I had had no interest in making chemists' stinks, and much of what he said was science to me, which was worse than Greek, for I should have understood the Greek tolerably well. Also a certain apprehension lingered in my mind. That terrible white face, those fired eyes, his agitated speech—I could not be blamed, I think. I believed he might be mad. And though I listened, I heard not, as he went on to tell me what his discovery might mean.

The next morning he thrust a sheaf of manuscript at me. "Read, Mr. Lewes!" he commanded me and went off to his mine; but something went wrong. I drowsed through a few pages and made nothing of them except that he thought in some way his nuggets had affected his health. There was a radiant glow in the mine, and the natives believed that glow meant sickness and in time death, and Herr Faesch had come to agree with the natives. A pity, I thought absently, turning in for a nap.

A monstrous smashing sound awakened me. No one was about. I ran out, thrusting aside the tent flap and there, over a hill, through the interstices of the trees, I saw a huge and angry cloud. I don't know how to describe it; I have never since seen its like, and pray God the world never shall again until the end of time.

Five miles away it must have been, but there was heat from it; the tent itself was charred. Tall it was—I don't know how tall, stretching straight and thin from the ground to a toadstool crown shot with lightnings.

The natives came after a time, and though they were desperately afraid, I managed to get from them that it was Herr Faesch's mine that had blown up, along with Herr Faesch and a dozen of themselves. More than that, they would not say.

And I never saw one of them again. In a few days, when I was strong enough, I made my way back to the river and there I was found and helped—I have never known by whom. Half dazed, my fever recurring, I remember only endless journeying, until I found myself near a port.

Yes, there was explosion enough for any man.

That whippersnapper Wells! Suppose, I put it to you, that some such "radium bomb" should be made. Conceive the captains of Kaiser Will's dirigible fleet possessed of a few nuggets apiece such as those Herr Faesch owned half a century ago. Imagine them cruising above the city of London, sowing their dragon's-teeth pellets in certain predetermined places, until in time a sufficient accumulation was reached to set the whole thing off. Can you think what horror it might set free upon the world?

And so I have never told this story, nor ever would if it were not for those same Zeppelin dirigible balloons. Even now I think it best to withhold it until this war is over, a year or two perhaps. (And that will probably make it posthumous—if only to accommodate Shaw—but no matter.)

I have seen a great deal. I know what I know, and I feel what I feel; and I tell you, this marvelous decade that stretches ahead of us after this present war will open new windows on freedom for the human race. Can it be doubted? Poor Bagley's letters from the trenches tell me that the very *poilus* and Tommies are determined to build a new world on the ruins of the old.

Well, perhaps Herr Faesch's nuggets will help them, these wiser, nobler children of the dawn who are to follow us. They will know what to make of them. One thing is sure: Count Zeppelin has made it impossible for Herr Faesch's metal ever to be used for war. Fighting on the ground itself was terrible enough; this new dimension of warfare will end it. Imagine sending dirigibles across the skies to sow such horrors! Imagine what monstrous brains might plan such an assault! Merciful heaven. They wouldn't dare.

# The Quaker Cannon

Lieutenant John Kramer did crossword puzzles during at least eighty per cent of his waking hours. His cubicle in Bachelor Officers Quarters was untidy; one wall was stacked solid with newspapers and magazines to which he subscribed for their puzzle pages. He meant, from week to week, to clean them out but somehow never found time. The ern, or erne, a sea eagle, soared vertically through his days and by night the ai, a three-toed sloth, crept horizontally. In edes, or Dutch communes, dyers retted ecru, quaffing ades by the tun, and thought was postponed.

John Kramer was in disgrace and, at thirty-eight, well on his way to becoming the oldest first lieutenant in the North American (and Allied) Army. He had been captured while unconscious as an aftermath of the confused fighting around Tsingtao. A few exquisitely unpleasant months passed and he then delivered three TV lectures for the yutes. In them he announced his total conversion to Neo-Utilitarianism, denounced the North American (and Allied) military command as a loathsome pack of war-waging, anti-utilitarian mad dogs, and personally admitted the waging of viral warfare against the United Utilitarian Republics.

The yutes, or Utilitarians, had been faithful to their principles. They had wanted Kramer only for what he could do for them, not for his own sweet self, and when they had got the juice out of him they exchanged him. A month later he came out of his fog at Fort Bradley, Utah, to find himself being court-martialed.

He was found guilty as charged, and sentenced to a reprimand. The lightness of the sentence was something to be a little proud of, if not very much. It stood as a grudging tribute to the months he had held out against involutional melancholia in the yute Blank Tanks. For exchanged PW's, the severity of their courts-martial was in inverse proportion to the duration of their ordeal in Utilitarian hands. Soldiers who caved in after a couple of days of sense-starvation could look forward only to a firing squad. Presumably a returned soldier dogged (or rigid) enough to be driven into hopeless insanity without cooperating would have been honorably acquitted by his court, but such a case had not yet come up.

Kramer's "reprimand" was not the face-to-face bawling-out suggested to a civilian by the word. It was a short letter with numbered paragraphs which said (1) you are reprimanded, (2) a copy of this reprimand will be placed in your service record. This tagged him forever as a foul ball, destined to spend the rest of his military life shuffling from one dreary assignment to another, without hope of promotion or reward.

He no longer cared. Or thought he did not; which came to the same thing.

He was not liked in the Officers Club. He was bad company. Young officers passing through Bradley on their way to glory might ask him, "What's it *really* like in a Blank Tank, Kramer?" But beyond answering, "You go nuts," what was there to talk about? Also he did not drink, because when he drank he went on to become drunk, and if he became drunk he would cry.

So he did a crossword puzzle in bed before breakfast, dressed, went to his office, signed papers, did puzzles until lunch, and so on until the last one in bed at night. Nominally he was Commanding Officer of the 561st Provisional Reception Battalion. Actually he was (with a few military overtones) the straw boss of a gang of clerks in uniform who saw to the arrival, bedding, feeding, equipping, inoculation and transfer to a training unit of one thousand scared kids per week.

On a drizzle-swept afternoon Kramer was sounding one of those military overtones. It was his appointed day for a "surprise" inspection of Company D of his battalion. Impeccable in dress blues, he was supposed to descend like a thunderbolt on this company or that, catching them all unaware, striding arrogantly down the barracks aisle between bunks, white-gloved and eagle-eyed for dust, maddened at the sight of disarray, vengeful against such contraband as playing cards or light reading matter. Kramer knew, quite well, that one of his orderly room clerks always telephoned the doomed company to warn that he was on his way. He did not particularly mind it. What he minded was unfair definitions of key words, and ridiculously variant spellings.

The permanent-party sergeant of D Company bawled "Tench-*hut!*" when Kramer snapped the door open and stepped crisply into the barracks. Kramer froze his face into its approved expression of controlled

annoyance and opened his mouth to give the noncom
his orders. But the sergeant had miscalculated. One of
the scared kids was still frantically mopping the aisle.

Kramer halted. The kid spun around in horror,
made some kind of attempt to present arms with the
mop and failed. The mop shot from his soapy hands
like a slung baseball bat, and its soggy gray head
schlooped against the lieutenant's dress-blue chest.

The kid turned white and seemed about to faint on
the damp board floor. The other kids waited to see
him destroyed.

Kramer was mildly irritated. "At ease," he said.
"Pick up that mop. Sergeant, confound it, next time
they buzz you from the orderly room don't cut it so
close."

The kids sighed perceptibly and glanced covertly at
each other in the big bare room, beginning to suspect it might not be too bad after all. Lieutenant
Kramer then resumed the expression of a nettled bird
of prey and strode down the aisle. Long ago he had
worked out a "random" selection of bunks for special
attention and now followed it through habit. If he
had thought about it any more, he would have supposed that it was still spy-proof; but every noncom in
his cadre had long since discovered that Kramer
stopped at either every second bunk on the right and
every third on the left, or every third bunk on the
right and every second on the left—depending on
whether the day of the month was odd or even. This
would not have worried Kramer if he had known it;
but he never even noticed that the men beside the
bunks he stopped at were always the best-shaved,
best-policed and healthiest-looking in each barracks.

Regardless, he delivered a certain quota of mean-
ingless demerits which were gravely recorded by the
sergeant. Of blue-eyed men on the left and brown-

eyed men on the right (this, at least, had not been penetrated by the noncoms) he went on to ask their names and home towns. Before discovering crossword puzzles he had memorized atlases, and so he had something to say about every home town he had yet encountered. In this respect at least he considered himself an above-average officer, and indeed he was.

It wasn't the Old Army, not by a long shot, but when the draft age went down to fifteen some of the Old Army's little ways had to go. One experimental reception station in Virginia was trying out a Barracks Mother system. Kramer, thankful for small favors, was glad they hadn't put him on that project. Even here he was expected, at the end of the inspection, to call the "men" around him and ask if anything was bothering them. Something always was. Some gangling kid would scare up the nerve to ask, gee, lieutenant, I know what the Morale Officer said, but exactly *why* didn't we ever use the megaton-head missiles in spite of the treaties, and another would want to know how come Lunar Base was such a washout, tactically speaking, sir. And then he would have to rehearse the dry "recommended discussion themes" from the briefing books; and then, finally, one of them, nudged on by others, would pipe up, "Lieutenant, what's it *like* in the Blank Tanks?" And he would know that already, forty-eight hours after induction, the kids all knew about what Lieutenant John Kramer had done.

But today he was spared. When he was halfway through the rigmarole the barracks phone rang and the sergeant apologetically answered it.

He returned from his office-cubicle on the double, looking vaguely frightened. "Compliments of General Grote's secretary, sir, and will you please report to him at G-1 as soon as possible."

"Thank you, sergeant. Step outside with me a moment." Out on the duckboard walk, with the drizzle trickling down his neck, he asked: "Sergeant, who is General Grote?"

"Never heard of him, sir."

Neither had Lieutenant Kramer.

He hurried to Bachelor Officers Quarters to change his sullied blue jacket, not even pausing to glance at the puzzle page of the *Times*, which had arrived while he was at "work." Generals were special. He hurried out again into the drizzle.

Around him and unnoticed were the artifacts of an Army base at war. Sky-eye search radars popped from their silos to scan the horizons for a moment and then retreat, the burden of search taken up by the next in line. Helicopter sentries on guard duty prowled the barbed-wire perimeter of the camp. Fort Bradley was not all reception center. Above-ground were the barracks, warehouses and rail and highway termini for processing recruits—ninety thousand men and all their goods—but they were only the skin over the fort itself. They were, as the scared kids told each other in the dayrooms, naked to the air. If the yutes ever *did* spring a megaton attack, they would become a thin coating of charcoal on the parade ground, but they would not affect the operation of the *real* Fort Bradley a bit.

The *real* Fort Bradley was a hardened installation beneath many yards of reinforced concrete, some miles of rambling warrens that held the North American (and Allied) Army's G-1. Its business was people: the past, present and future of every soul in the Army.

G-1 decided that a fifteen-year-old in Duluth was unlikely to succeed in civilian schools and drafted him.

G-1 reduced his Army tests and civilian records to symbols, consulted its stored tables of military requirements and assigned him, perhaps, to Machinist Training rather than Telemetering School. G-1 yanked a platoon leader halfway around the world from Formosa and handed him a commando for a raid on the yutes' Polar Station Seven. G-1 put foulball Kramer at the "head" of the 561st PRB. G-1 promoted and allocated and staffed and rewarded and punished.

Foulball Kramer approached the guardbox at the elevators to the warrens and instinctively squared his shoulders and smoothed his tie.

General Grote, he thought. He hadn't *seen* a general officer since he'd been commissioned. Not close up. Colonels and majors had court-martialed him. He didn't know who Grote was, whether he had one star or six, whether he was Assignment, Qualifications, Training, Evaluation, Psychological—or Disciplinary.

Military Police looked him over at the elevator head. They read him like a book. Kramer wore his record on his chest and sleeves. Dull gold bars spelled out the overseas months—for his age and arm, the Infantry, not enough. "Formosa," said a green ribbon, and "the storming of the beach" said a small bronze spearpoint on it. A brown ribbon told them "Chinese Mainland," and the stars on it meant that he had engaged in three of the five mainland campaigns—presumably Canton, Mukden and Tsingtao, since they were the first. After that, nothing. Especially not the purple ribbon that might indicate a wound serious enough to keep him out of further fighting.

The ribbons, his age and the fact that he was still a first lieutenant were grounds enough for the MP's to despise him. An officer of thirty-eight should be a captain at least. Many were majors and some were colonels. "You can go down, Lieutenant," they told the patent foulball, and he went down to the interminable concrete tunnels of G-1.

A display machine considered the name *General Grote* when he typed it on its keyboard, and told him with a map where the general was to be found. It was a longish walk through the tunnels. While he walked past banks of clicking card-sorters and their servants he pondered other information the machine had gratuitously supplied: GROTE, Lawrence W, Lt Gen, 0-459732, Unassigned.

It did not lessen any of Kramer's puzzles. A three-star general, then. He couldn't *possibly* have anything to do with disciplining a lousy first-john. Lieutenant generals ran Army Groups, gigantic ad hoc assemblages of up to a hundred divisions, complete with air forces, missile groups, amphibious assault teams, even carrier and missile-sub task forces. The fact of his rank indicated that, whoever he was, he was an immensely able and tenacious person. He had gone through at least a twenty-year threshing of the wheat from the chaff, all up the screening and evaluation boards from second lieutenant to, say, lieutenant colonel, and then the murderous grind of accelerated courses at Command and General Staff School, the fanatically rigid selection for the War College, an obstacle course designed not to train the substandard up to competence but to keep them out. It was just this side of impossible for a human being to become a lieutenant general. And yet a few human beings in every generation did bulldoze their way through that little gap between the impossible and the almost impossible.

And such a man was unassigned?

\*      \*      \*

Kramer found the office at last. A motherly, but sharp-eyed, WAC major told him to go right in.

John Kramer studied his three-star general while going through the ancient rituals of reporting-as-ordered. General Grote was an old man, straight, spare, white-haired, tanned. He wore no overseas bars. On his chest were all the meritorious service ribbons his country could bestow, but none of the decorations of the combat soldier. This was explained by a modest sunburst centered over the ribbons. General Grote was, had always been, General Staff Corps. A desk man.

"Sit down, Lieutenant," Grote said, eyeing him casually. "You've never heard of me, I assume."

"I'm afraid not, sir."

"As I expected," said Grote complacently. "I'm not a dashing tank commander or one of those flying generals who leads his own raids. I'm one of the people who moves the dashing tank commanders and flying generals around the board like chess pieces. And now, confound it, I'm going to be a dashing combat leader at last. You may smoke if you like."

Kramer obediently lit up.

"Dan Medway," said the general, "wants me to start from scratch, build up a striking force and hit the Asian mainland across the Bering Strait."

Kramer was horrified twice—first by the reference to The Supreme Commander as "Dan" and second by the fact that he, a lieutenant, was being told about high strategy.

"Relax," the general said. "Why you're here, now. You're going to be my aide."

Kramer was horrified again. The general grinned.

"Your card popped out of the machinery," he said, and that was all there was to say about that, "and so you're going to be a highly privileged character and everybody will detest you. That's the way it is with aides. You'll know everything I know. And vice versa; that's the important part. You'll run errands for me, do investigations, serve as hatchet man, see that my pajamas are pressed without starch and make coffee the way I like it—coarse grind, brought to the boil for just a moment in an old-fashioned coffee pot. Actually what you'll do is what I want you to do from day to day. For these privileges you get to wear a blue fourragère around your left shoulder which marks you as a man not to be trifled with by colonels, brigadiers or MP's. That's the way it is with aides. And, I don't know if you have any outside interests, women or chess or drinking. The machinery didn't mention any. But you'll have to give them up if you do."

"Yes, sir," said Kramer. And it seemed wildly possible that he might never touch pencil to puzzle again. With something to *do*—

"We're Operation Ripsaw," said the general. "So far, that's me, Margaret out there in the office and you. In addition to other duties, you'll keep a diary of Ripsaw, by the way, and I want you to have a summary with you at all times in case I need it. Now call in Margaret, make a pot of coffee, there's a little stove thing in the washroom there, and I'll start putting together my general staff."

It started as small and as quietly as that.

# II

It was a week before Kramer got back to the 561st long enough to pick up his possessions, and then he left the stacks of *Timeses* and *Saturday Reviews* where they lay, puzzles and all. No time. The first person to hate him was Margaret, the motherly major. For all her rank over him, she was a secretary and he was an aide with a fourragère who had the general's willing ear. She began a policy of nonresistance that was noncooperation, too; she would not deliberately obstruct him, but she would allow him to poke through the files for ten minutes before volunteering the information that the folder he wanted was already on the general's desk. This interfered with the smooth performance of Kramer's duties, and of course the general spotted it at once.

"It's nothing," said Kramer when the general called him on it. "I don't like to say anything."

"Go on," General Grote urged. "You're not a soldier any more; you're a rat."

"I think I can handle it, sir."

The general motioned silently to the coffee pot and waited while Kramer fixed him a cup, two sugars, no cream. He said: "Tell me everything, always. All the dirty rumors about inefficiency and favoritism. Your suspicions and hunches. Anybody that gets in your way—or more important, in mine. In the underworld they shoot stool-pigeons, but here we give them blue cords for their shoulders. Do you understand?"

Kramer did. He did not ask the general to intercede with the motherly major, or transfer her; but he did handle it himself. He discovered it was very easy. He simply threatened to have her sent to Narvik.

With the others it was easier. Margaret had resented him because she was senior in Operation Ripsaw to him, but as the others were sucked in they found him there already. Instead of resentment, their attitude toward him was purely fear.

The next people to hate him were the aides of Grote's general staff because he was a wild card in the deck. The five members of the staff—Chief, Personnel, Intelligence, Plans & Training and Operations—proceeded with their orderly, systematic jobs day by day, building Ripsaw . . . until the inevitable moment when Kramer would breeze in with, "Fine job, but the general suggests—" and the unhorsing of many assumptions, and the undoing of many days' work. That was his job also. He was a bird of ill omen, a coiled snake in fair grass, a hired killer and a professional betrayer of confidences—though it was not long before there were no confidences to betray, except from an occasional young, new officer who hadn't learned his way around, and those not worth betraying. That, as the general had said, was the way it was with aides. Kramer wondered sometimes if he liked what he was doing, or liked himself for doing it. But he never carried the thought through. No time.

Troops completed basic training or were redeployed from rest areas and entrained, emplaned, embussed or embarked for the scattered staging areas of Ripsaw. Great forty-wheeled trucks bore nuclear cannon up the Alcan Highway at a snail's pace. Air groups and missile sections launched on training exercises over Canadian wasteland that closely resembled tundra, with grid maps that bore names like Maina Pylgin and Kamenskoe. Yet these were not Ripsaw, not yet, only the separate tools that Ripsaw would someday pick up and use.

Ripsaw itself moved to Wichita and a base of its own when its headquarters staff swelled to fifteen hundred men and women. Most of them hated Kramer.

It was never perfectly clear to Kramer what his boss had to do with the show. Kramer made his coffee, carried his briefcase, locked and unlocked his files, delivered to him those destructive tales and delivered for him those devastating suggestions, but never understood just why there had to be a Commanding General of Ripsaw.

The time they went to Washington to argue an allocation of seventy rather than sixty armored divisions for Ripsaw, for instance, General Grote just sat, smiled and smoked his pipe. It was his chief of staff, the young and brilliant major general Cartmill, who passionately argued the case before D. Beauregard Medway, though when Grote addressed his superior it still was as "Dan." (They did get the ten extra divisions, of course.)

Back in Wichita, it was Cartmill who toiled around the clock coordinating. A security lid was clamped down early in the game. The fifteen hundred men and women in the Wichita camp stayed in the Wichita camp. Commerce with the outside world, except via coded messages to other elements of Ripsaw, was a capital offense—as three privates learned the hard way. But through those coded channels Cartmill reached out to every area of the North American (and Allied) world. Personnel scoured the globe for human components that might be fitted into Ripsaw. Intelligence gathered information about that tract of Siberia which they were to invade, and the waters they were to cross. Plans & Training slaved at methods of effecting the crossing and invasion efficiently, with the least (or at any rate the optimum least, consistent with requirements of speed, security and so on) losses in men and materiel. Operations studied and restudied the various ways the crossing and invasion might go right or wrong, and how a good turn of fortune could be exploited, a bad turn minimized. General Cartmill was in constant touch with all of them, his fingers on every cord in the web. So was John Kramer.

Grote ambled about all this with an air of pleased surprise.

Kramer discovered one day that there had been books written about his boss—not best sellers with titles like *"Bloody Larry" Grote, Sword of Freedom*, but thick, gray mimeographed staff documents, in Chinese and Russian, for top-level circulation among yute commanders. He surprised Grote reading one of them—in Chinese.

The general was not embarrassed. "Just refreshing my memory of what the yutes think I'm like so I can cross them up by doing something different. Listen: 'Characteristic of this officer's philosophy of attack is varied tactics. Reference his lecture, *Lee's 1862 Campaigns*, delivered at Fort Leavenworth Command & General Staff School, attached. Opposing commanders should not expect a force under him to do the same—' Hmm. *Tsueng*, water radical. '—under him to press the advance the same way twice.' Now all I have to do is make sure we attack by the book, like Grant instead of Lee, slug it out without any brilliant variations. See how easy it is, John? How's the message center?"

Kramer had been snooping around the message center at Grote's request. It was a matter of feeding out cigarettes and smiles in return for an occasional incautious word or a hint; gumshoe work. The message center was an underground complex of encoders, decoders, transmitters, receivers and switchboards. It was staffed by a Signal Corps WAC battalion in three shifts around the clock. The girls were worked hard—though a battalion should have been enough for the job. Messages went from and to the message center linking the Wichita brain with those

seventy divisions training now from Capetown to
Manitoba, a carrier task force conducting exercises in
the Antarctic, a fleet of landing craft growing every
day on the Gulf of California. The average time-lag
between receipt of messages and delivery to the
Wichita personnel at destination was 12.25 minutes.
The average number of erroneous transmissions detected per day was three. Both figures General Grote
considered intolerable.

"It's Colonel Bucknell that's lousing it up, General. She's trying too hard. No give. Physical training
twice a day, for instance, and a very hard policy on
excuses. A stern attitude's filtered down from her to
the detachments. Everybody's chewing out subordinates to keep themselves covered. The working girls
call Bucknell 'the monster.' Their feeling is the Army's
impossible to please, so what the hell."

"Relieve her," Grote said amiably. "Make her mess
officer; Ripsaw chow's rotten anyway." He went back
to his Chinese text.

And suddenly it all began to seem as if it really
might someday rise and strike out across the Strait.
From Lieutenant Kramer's Ripsaw Diary:

> At AM staff meeting CG RIPSAW xmitted
> order CG NAAARMY designating RIPSAW D
> day 15 May next. Gen CARTMILL observed
> this date allowed 45 days to form troops in
> final staging areas assuming RIPSAW could be
> staged in 10 days. CG RIPSAW stated that a
> 10-day staging seemed feasible. Staff concurred.
> CG RIPSAW so ordered. At 1357 hours CG
> NAAARMY concurrence received.

They were on the way.

As the days grew shorter Grote seemed to have less and less to do, and curiously so did Kramer. He had not expected this. He had been aide-de-camp to the general for nearly a year now, and he fretted when he could find no fresh treason to bring to the general's ears. He redoubled his prowling tours of the kitchens, the BOQ, the motor pools, the message center, but not even the guard mounts or the shine on the shoes of the soldiers at Retreat parade was in any way at fault. Kramer could only imagine that he was missing things. It did not occur to him that, as at last they should be, the affairs of Ripsaw had gathered enough speed to keep them straight and clean, until the general called him in one night and ordered him to pack. Grote put on his spectacles and looked over them at Kramer. "D plus five," he said, "assuming all goes well, we're moving this headquarters to Kiska. I want you to take a look-see. Arrange a plane. You can leave tomorrow."

It was, Kramer realized that night as he undressed, Just Something to Do. Evidently the hard part of his job was at an end. It was now only a question of fighting the battle, and for that the field commanders were much more important than he. For the first time in many months he thought it would be nice to do a crossword puzzle, but instead fell asleep.

It was an hour before leaving the next day that Kramer met Ripsaw's "cover."

The "cover" was another lieutenant general, a bristling and wiry man named Clough, with a brilliant combat record staked out on his chest and sleeves for the world to read. Kramer came in when his buzzer sounded, made coffee for the two generals and was aware that Grote and Clough were old pals and that the Ripsaw general was kidding the pants off his guest.

"You always were a great admirer of Georgie Patton," Grote teased. "You should be glad to follow in his footsteps. Your operation will go down in history as big and important as his historic cross-Channel smash into Le Havre."

Kramer's thoughts were full of himself—he did not much like getting even so close to the yutes as Kiska, where he would be before the sun set that night—but his ears pricked up. He could not remember any cross-Channel smash into Le Havre. By Patton or anybody else.

"Just because I came to visit your show doesn't mean you have to rib me, Larry," Clough grumbled.

"But it's such a pleasure, Mick."

Clough opened his eyes wide and looked at Grote. "I've generaled against Novotny before. If you want to know what I think of him, I'll tell you."

Pause. Then Grote, gently: "Take it easy, Mick. Look at my boy there. See him quivering with curiosity?"

Kramer's back was turned. He hoped his blush would subside before he had to turn around with the coffee. It did not.

"Caught red-faced," Grote said happily, and winked at the other general. Clough looked stonily back. "Shall we put him out of his misery, Mick? Shall we fill him in on the big picture?"

"Might as well get it over with."

"I accept your gracious assent." Grote waved for Kramer to help himself to coffee and to sit down. Clearly he was unusually cheerful today, Kramer thought. Grote said: "Lieutenant Kramer, General Clough is the gun-captain of a Quaker cannon which covers Ripsaw. He looks like a cannon. He acts like a cannon. But he isn't loaded. Like his late idol George Patton at one point in his career, General Clough is the commander of a vast force which exists on paper and in radio transmissions alone."

Clough stirred uneasily, so Grote became more serious. "We're brainwashing Continental Defense Commissar Novotny by serving up to him his old enemy as the man he'll have to fight. The yute radio intercepts are getting a perfect picture of an assault on Polar Nine being prepared under old Mick here. That's what they'll prepare to counter, of course. Ripsaw will catch them flatfooted."

Clough stirred again but did not speak.

Grote grinned. "All right. We *hope*," he conceded. "But there's a lot of planning in this thing. Of course, it's a waste of the talent of a rather remarkably able general—" Clough gave him a lifted-eyebrow look— "but you've got to have a real man at the head of the fake army group or they won't believe it. Anyway, it worked with Patton and the Nazis. Some unkind people have suggested that Patton never did a better bit of work than sitting on his knapsack in England and letting his name be used."

"All full of beans with a combat command, aren't you?" Clough said sourly. "Wait'll the shooting starts."

"Ike never commanded a battalion before the day he invaded North Africa, Mick. He did all right."

"Ike wasn't up against Novotny," Clough said heavily. "I can talk better while I'm eating, Larry. Want to buy me a lunch?"

General Grote nodded. "Lieutenant, see what you can charm out of Colonel Bucknell for us to eat, will you? We'll have it sent in here, of course, and the best girls she's got to serve it." Then, unusually, he stood up and looked appraisingly at Kramer.

"Have a nice flight," he said.

# III

Kramer's blue fourragère won him cold handshakes but a seat at the first table in the Hq Officers Mess in Kiska. He didn't have quite enough appetite to appreciate it.

Approaching the island from the air had taken appetite away from him, as the GCA autocontroller rocked the plane in a carefully calculated zigzag in its approach. They were, Kramer discovered, under direct visual observation from any chance-met bird from yute eyries across the Strait until they got below five hundred feet. Sometimes the yutes sent over a flight of birds to knock down a transport. Hence the zigzags.

Captain Mabry, a dark, tall Georgian who had been designated to make the general's aide feel at home, noticed Kramer wasn't eating, pushed his own tray into the center strip and, as it sailed away, stood up. "Get it off the pad, shall we? Can't keep the Old Man waiting."

The captain took Mabry through clanging corridors to an elevator and then up to the eyrie. It was only a room. From it the spy-bird missiles—rockets, they were really, but the services liked to think of them as having a punch, even though the punch was only a television camera—were controlled. To it the birds returned the pictures their eyes saw.

Brigadier Spiegelhauer shook Kramer's hand. "Make yourself at home, Lieutenant," he boomed. He was short and almost skeletally thin, but his voice was enormous. "Everything satisfactory for the general, I hope?"

"Why, yes, sir. I'm just looking around."

"Of course," Spiegelhauer shouted. "Care to monitor a ride?"

"Yes, sir." Mabry was looking at him with amusement, Kramer saw. Confound him, what right did *he* have to think Kramer was scared—even if he was? Not a physical fear; he was not insane. But . . . scared.

The service life of a spy-bird over yute territory was something under twenty minutes, by then the homing heads on the ground-to-air birds would have sniffed out its special fragrance and knocked it out. In that twenty-minute period it would see what it could see. Through its eyes the observers in the eyrie would learn just that much more about yute dispositions—so long as it remained in direct line-of-sight to the eyrie, so long as everything in its instrumentation worked, so long as yute jamming did not penetrate its microwave control.

Captain Mabry took Kramer's arm. "Take 'er off the pad," Mabry said negligently to the launch officer. He conducted Kramer to a pair of monitors and sat before them.

On both eight-inch screens the officers saw a diamond-sharp scan of the inside of a silo plug. There was no sound. The plug lifted off its lip without a whisper, dividing into two semicircles of steel. A two-inch circle of sky showed. Then, abruptly, the circle widened; the lip irised out and disappeared; the gray surrounded the screen and blanked it out, and then it was bright blue, and a curl of cirrocumulus in one quadrant of the screen.

Metro had promised no cloud over the tactical area, but there was cloud there. Captain Mabry frowned and tapped a tune on the buttons before him; the cirrocumulus disappeared and a line of gray-white appeared at an angle on the screen. "Hori-

zon," said Mabry. "Labble to make you seasick,
Lootenant." He tapped some more and the image
righted itself. A faint yellowish stain, not bright against
the bright cloud, curved up before them and burst
into spidery black smoke. "Oh, they are *anxious*,"
said Mabry, sounding nettled. "General, weather has
busted it again. Cain't see a thing."

Spiegelhauer bawled angrily, "I'm going to the
weather station," and stamped out. Kramer knew
what he was angry about. It was not the waste of a
bird; it was that he had been made to lose face
before the general's aide-de-camp. There would be a
bad time for the Weather Officer because Kramer
had been there that day.

The telemetering crew turned off their instruments.
The whining eighteen-inch reel that was flinging tape
across a row of fifteen magnetic heads, recording the
picture the spy-bird took, slowed and droned and
stopped. Out of instinct and habit Kramer pulled out
his rough diary and jotted down *Brig. Spiegelhauer—
Permits bad wea. sta. situation?* But it was little
enough to have learned on a flight to Kiska, and
everything else seemed going well.

Captain Mabry fetched over two mugs of hot cocoa. "Sorry," he said. "Cain't be helped, I guess."

Kramer put his notebook away and accepted the
cocoa.

"Beats U-2in'," Mabry went on. "Course, you don't
get to see as much of the country."

Kramer could not help a small, involuntary tremor.
For just a moment there, looking out of the spy-
bird's eyes, he had imagined himself actually in the
air above yute territory and conceived the possibility
of being shot down, parachuting, internment, the
Blank Tanks, "Yankee! Why not be good fellow? You
*proud* you murderer?"

"No," Kramer said, "you don't get to see as much of the country." But he had already seen all the yute country he ever wanted.

Kramer got back in the elevator and descended rapidly, his mind full. Perhaps a psychopath, a hungry cat or a child would have noticed that the ride downward lasted a second or two less than the ride up. Kramer did not. If the sound echoing from the tunnel he walked out into was a bit more clangorous than the one he had entered from, he didn't notice that either.

Kramer's mind was occupied with the thought that, all in all, he was pleased to find that he had approached this close to yute territory, and to yute Blank Tanks, without feeling *particularly* afraid. Even though he recognized that there was nothing to be afraid of, since of course the yutes could not get hold of him here.

Then he observed that the door Mabry opened for him led to a chamber he knew he had never seen before.

They were standing on an approach stage and below them forty-foot rockets extended downward into their pit. A gantry-bridge hung across space from the stage to the nearest rocket, which lay open, showing a clumsily padded compartment where there should have been a warhead or an instrument capsule.

Kramer turned around and was not surprised to find that Mabry was pointing a gun at him. He had almost expected it. He started to speak. But there was someone else in the shadowed chamber, and the first he knew of *that* was when the sap struck him just behind the ear.

It was all coming true: "Yankee! Why not be honest man? You *like* murder babies?" Kramer only shook his head. He knew it did no good to answer. Three years before he had answered. He knew it also did no good to keep quiet; because he had done that too. What he knew most of all was that nothing was going to do him any good because the yutes had him now, and who would have thought Mabry would have been the one to do him in?

They did not beat him at this point, but then they did not need to. The nose capsule Mabry had thrust him into had never been designed for carrying passengers. With ingenuity Kramer could only guess at Mabry had contrived to fit it with parachutes and watertight seals and flares so the yute gunboat could find it in the water and pull out their captive alive. But he had taken 15- and 20-G accelerations, however briefly. He seemed to have no serious broken bones, but he was bruised all over. Secretly he found that almost amusing. In the preliminary softening up, the yutes did not expect their captives to be in physical pain. By being in pain he was in some measure upsetting their schedule. It was not much of a victory but it was all he had.

Phase Two was direct questioning: What was Ripsaw exactly? How many divisions? Where located? Why had Lieutenant-General Grote spent so much time with Lieutenant-General Clough? When Mary Elizabeth Grote, before her death, entertained the Vietnamese UNESCO delegate's aunt in Sag Harbor, had she known her husband had just been passed over for promotion to brigadier? And was resentment over that the reason she had subsequently donated twenty-five dollars to a mission hospital in Laos? What were the Bering Straits rendezvous points for missile submarines supporting Ripsaw? Was the transfer of Lieutenant Colonel Carolyn S. Bucknell from Message Center Battalion C.O. to Mess Officer a cover for some CIC complexity? What air support was planned for D plus one? D plus two? Did Major Somebody-or-other's secret drinking account for the curious radio intercept in clear logged at 0834 on 6 October? Or was "Omobray for my eadhay" the code designation for some nefarious scheme to be launched against the gallant, the ever-victorious forces of Neo-Utilitarianism?

Kramer was alternately cast into despondency by the amount of knowledge his captors displayed and puzzled by the psychotic irrelevance of some of the questions they asked him. But most of all he was afraid. As the hours of Phase Two became days, he became more and more afraid—afraid of Phase Three—and so he was ready for Phase Three when the yutes were ready for him.

Phase Three was physical. They beat the living behell out of First Lieutenant John Kramer, and then they shouted at him and starved him and kicked him and threw him into bathtubs filled half with salt and water and half with shaved ice. And then they kicked him in the belly and fed him cathartics by the ounce and it went on for a long time; but that was not the bad thing about Phase Three. Kramer found himself crying most of the time, when he was conscious. He did not *want* to tell them everything he knew about Ripsaw—and thus have them be ready when it came, poised and prepared, and know that maybe 50,000 American lives would be down the drain because the surprise was on the wrong side. But he did not know if he could help himself. He was in constant pain. He thought he might die from the pain. Sometimes people did. But he didn't think much about the pain, or the fear of dying, or even about what would happen if—no, *when* he cracked.

What he thought about was what came next. For the bad thing about Phase Three was Phase Four.

He remembered. First they would let him sleep. (He had slept very well that other time, because he hadn't known exactly what the Blank Tanks were like. He didn't think he would sleep so well this time.) Then they would wake him up and feed him quickly, and bandage his worst bruises, and bandage his ears, with cotton tampons dipped in vaseline jelly plugged into them, and bandage his eyes, with light-tight adhesive around them, and bandage his mouth, with something like a boxer's toothguard inside so he couldn't even bite his tongue, and bandage his arms and legs, so he couldn't even move them or touch them together. . . .

And then the short superior-private who was kicking him while he thought all this stopped and talked briefly to a noncom. The two of them helped him to a mattress and left him. Kramer didn't want to sleep, but he couldn't help himself; he slipped off, crying weakly out of his puffed and bloody eyes, because he didn't want to sleep, he wanted to die.

Ten hours later he was back in the Blank Tanks.

Sit back and listen. What do you hear?

Perhaps you think you hear nothing. You are wrong. You discount the sound of a distant car's tires, or the crackle of metal as steam expands the pipes. Listen more carefully to these sounds; others lie under them. From the kitchen there is a grunt and hum as the electric refrigerator switches itself on. You change position; your chair creaks, the leather of your shoes slip-slides with a faint sound. Listen more carefully still and hear the tiny roughness in the main bearing of the electric clock in the next room, or the almost inaudible hum of wind in a television antenna. Listen to yourself: Your heartbeat, your pulse in your chin. The rumble of your belly and the faint grating of your teeth. The susurrus of air entering your nostrils. The rub of thumb against finger.

In the Blank Tanks a man hears nothing at all.

The pressure of the tampons in the ear does not allow stirrup to strike anvil; teeth cannot touch teeth, hands cannot clap, he cannot make a noise if he tries to, or hear it if he did.

That is deafness. The Blank Tanks are more than deafness. In them a man is blind, even to the red fog that reaches through closed eyelids. There is nothing to smell. There is nothing to taste. There is nothing to feel except the swaddling-cloths, and through time the nerve ends tire and stop registering this constant touch.

It is something like being unborn and something like never having been at all. There is nothing, absolutely nothing, and although you are not dead you are not alive either. And there you stay.

Kramer was ready for the Blank Tank and did not at once panic. He remembered the tricks he had employed before. He swallowed his own sputum and it made a gratifying popping sound in his inner ear; he hummed until his throat was raw and gasped through flaring nostrils until he became dizzy. But each sound he was able to produce lasted only a moment. He might have dropped them like snowflakes onto wool. They were absorbed and they died.

It was actually worse, he remembered tardily, to produce a sound because you could not help but listen for the echo and no echo came. So he stopped.

In three years he *must* have acquired some additional resources, he thought. Of course. He had! He settled down to construct a crossword puzzle in his head. Let 1 Across be a tropical South American bird, *hoatzin*. Let 1 Down be a medieval diatonic series of tones, *hexacord*. Let 2 Down be the Asiatic wild ass, or *onagin*, which might make the first horizontal word under 1 Across be, let's see, E - N - . . . well, why not the ligature of couplets in verse writing, or *enjambment*. That would make 3 Down— He began to cry, because he could not remember 1 Across.

Something was nagging at his mind, so he stopped crying and waited for it to take form, but it would not. He thought of General Grote, by now surely aware that his aide had been taken; he thought of the consternation that must be shuddering through all the tentacles of Ripsaw. It was not actually going to be so hard, he thought pathetically, because he didn't actually have to *hold out* against the Blank Tanks, he only had to *wait*. After D day, or better, say, D plus 7, it wouldn't much matter what he told them. Then the divisions would be across. Or not across. Breakthrough or failure, it would be decided by then and he could talk.

He began to count off Ripsaw's division officers to himself, as he had so often seen the names on the morning reports. Catton of the XLIst Armored, with Colonels Bogart, Ripner and Bletterman. M'Cleargh of the Highland & Lowland, with Brigadiers Douglass and McCloud. Leventhal of the Vth Israeli, with Koehne, Meier and—he stopped, because it had occurred to him that he might be speaking aloud. He could not tell. All right. Think of something else.

But what?

There was nothing dangerous about sensory deprivation, he lied. It was only a rest. Nobody was hurting him. Looked at in the right way, it was a chance to do some *solid* thinking like you never got

time for in real life—strike that. In *outside* life. For
instance, what about freshing up on French irregular
verbs? Start with avoir. Tu as, vous avez, nous avons.
Voi avete, noi abbiamo, du habst . . . Du habst? How
did that get in there? Well, how about poetry?

> It is an Ancient Mariner, and he stops the next of
>     kin.
> The guests are met, the feast is set, and sisters
>     under the skin
> Are rag and bone and hank of hair, and beard
>     and glittering eye
> Invite the sight of patient Night, etherized under
>     the sky.
> I should have been a ragged claw; I should have
>     said 'I love you';
> But—here the brown eyes lower fell—I hate to
>     go above you.
> If Ripsaw fail and yutes prevail, what price
>     Clough's Quaker cannon?
> So Grote—

Kramer stopped himself, barely in time. Were
there throat mikes? Were the yutes listening in?

He churned miserably in his cotton bonds, because, as near as he could guess, he had probably
been in the Blank Tank for less than an hour. D day,
he thought to himself, praying that it was only to
himself, was still some six weeks away and a week
beyond that was seven. Seven weeks, forty-nine days,
eleven hundred and, um, seventy-six hours, sixty-six
thousand minutes plus. He had only to wait those
minutes out, what about the diary?, and then he
could talk all he wanted. Talk, confess, broadcast,
anything, what difference would it make then?

He paused, trying to remember. That furtive

thought had struggled briefly to the surface but he had lost it again. It would not come back.

He tried to fall asleep. It should have been easy enough. His air was metered and the $CO_2$ content held to a level that would make him torpid; his wastes catheterized away; water and glucose valved into his veins; he was all but *in utero,* and unborn babies slept, didn't they? Did they? He would have to look in the diary, but it would have to wait until he could remember what thought it was that was struggling for recognition. And that was becoming harder with every second.

Sensory deprivation in small doses is one thing; it even has its therapeutic uses, like shock. In large doses it produces a disorientation of psychotic proportions, a melancholia that is all but lethal; Kramer never knew when he went loopy.

# IV

He never quite knew when he went sane again, either, except that one day the fog lifted for a moment and he asked a WAC corporal, "When did I get back to Utah." The corporal had dealt with returning yute prisoners before. She said only: "It's Fort Hamilton, sir. Brooklyn."

He was in a private room, which was bad, but he wore a maroon bathrobe, which was good—at least it meant he was in a hospital instead of an Army stockade. (Unless the private room meant he was in the detention ward of the hospital.)

Kramer wondered what he had done. There was no way to tell, at least not by searching his memory. Everything went into a blurry alternation of shouting relays of yutes and the silence of the Blank Tanks.

He was nearly sure he had finally told the yutes everything they wanted to know. The question was, when? He would find out at the court-martial, he thought. Or he might have jotted it down, he thought crazily, in the diary.

Jotted it down in the . . . ?

*Diary!*

*That* was the thought that had struggled to come through to the surface!

Kramer's screams brought the corporal back in a hurry, and then two doctors who quickly prepared knockout needles. He fought against them all the way.

"Poor old man," said the WAC, watching him twitch and shudder in unconsciousness. (Kramer had just turned forty.) "Second dose of the Blank Tanks for him, wasn't it? I'm not surprised he's having nightmares." She didn't know that his nightmares were not caused by the Blank Tanks themselves, but by his sudden realization that his last stay in the Tanks was totally unnecessary. It didn't matter what he told the yutes, or when! They had had the diary all along, for it had been on him when Mabry thrust him in the rocket; and all Ripsaw's secrets were in it!

The next time the fog lifted for Kramer it was quick, like the turning on of a light, and he had distorted memories of dreams before it. He thought he had just dreamed that General Grote had been with him. He was alone in the same room, sun streaming in a window, voices outside. He felt pretty good, he thought tentatively, and had no time to think more than that because the door opened and a ward boy looked in, very astonished to find Kramer looking back at him.

"Holy heaven," he said. "Wait there!"

He disappeared. Foolish, Kramer thought. Of course he would wait. Where else would he go?

And then, surprisingly, General Grote did indeed walk in.

"Hello, John," he said mildly, and sat down beside the bed, looking at Kramer. "I was just getting in my car when they caught me."

He pulled out his pipe and stuffed it with tobacco, watching Kramer. Kramer could think of nothing to say. "They said you were all right, John. Are you?"

"I—think so." He watched the general light his pipe. "Funny," he said. "I dreamed you were here a minute ago."

"No, it's not so funny; I was. I brought you a present."

Kramer could not imagine anything more wildly improbable in the world than that the man whose combat operation he had betrayed should bring him a box of chocolates, bunch of flowers, light novel or whatever else was appropriate. But the general glanced at the table by Kramer's bed.

There was a flat, green-leather-covered box on it. "Open it up," Grote invited.

Kramer took out a glittering bit of metal depending from a three-barred ribbon. The gold medallion bore a rampant eagle and lettering he could not at first read.

"It's your D.S.M.," Grote said helpfully. "You can pin it on if you like. I tried," he said, "to make it a Medal of Honor. But they wouldn't allow it, logically enough."

"I was expecting something different," Kramer mumbled foolishly.

Grote laughed. "We smashed them, boy," he said gently. "That is, Mick did. He went straight across

Polar Nine, down the Ob with one force and the
Yenisei with another. General Clough's got his forward command in Chebarkul now, loving every minute of it. Why, I was in Karpinsk myself last week—
they let me get that far—of course, it's a rest area. It
was a brilliant, bloody, backbreaking show. Completely successful."

Kramer interrupted in sheer horror: "Polar *Nine?*
But that was the cover—the Quaker cannon!"

General Grote looked meditatively at his former
aide. "John," he said after a moment, "didn't you
ever wonder why the card-sorters pulled you out for
my staff? A man who was sure to crack in the Blank
Tanks, because he already had?"

The room was very silent for a moment.

"I'm sorry, John. Well, it worked—had to, you
know; a lot of thought went into it. Novotny's been
relieved. Mick's got his biggest victory, no matter
what happens now; he was the man that led *the*
invasion."

The room was silent again.

Carefully Grote tapped out his pipe into a metal
wastebasket. "You're a valuable man, John. Matter of
fact, we traded a major general to get you back."

Silence.

Grote sighed and stood up. "If it's any consolation
to you, you held out four full weeks in the Tanks.
Good thing we'd made sure you had the diary with
you. Otherwise our Quaker cannon would have been
a bust."

He nodded good-bye and was gone. He was a
good officer, was General Grote. He would use a
weapon in any way he had to, to win a fight; but if
the weapon was destroyed, and had feelings, he would
come around to bring it a medal afterwards.

Kramer contemplated his Distinguished Service

Medal for a while. Then he lay back and considered ringing for a Sunday *Times*, but fell asleep instead.

Novotny was now a sour, angry corps commander away off on the Baltic periphery because of him; a million and a half NAAARMY troops were dug in the heart of the enemy's homeland; the greatest operation of the war was an unqualified success. But when the nurse came in that night, the Quaker cannon—the man who had discovered that the greatest service he could perform for his country was to betray it—was moaning in his sleep.

# *The 60/40 Stories*

**W**hen Cyril Kornbluth and I first began to write stories together, we didn't know exactly how writers were supposed to collaborate. For that matter, we didn't really know how writers were supposed to write, either. Like most fledgling authors at that unripe stage (neither of us was old enough to vote), we studied every scrap of data on the subject we could find. What we learned was more confusing than helpful. Marcel Proust locked himself in a cork-lined room. Thorne Smith set up a card table with a portable typewriter and a bottle of whiskey on his front lawn, took off all his clothes and began to type. Ernest Hemingway wrote everything out by hand, crossed out, interlined and corrected and gave the result to someone to type. Since we didn't have the cork-lined room, the front lawn or the person to type manuscripts for us, none of that seemed applicable. And if information on how a writer wrote was sparse and confusing, the information on how they collaborated simply did not exist.

So we devised a procedure of our own. . . . Well, that's not quite accurate. Candor compels me to admit that I was the one who devised it; Cyril didn't really like it that much, but he went along, and so we produced about a dozen of what we called "the sixty-forty stories."

The procedure was quite formal. I conceived an idea for a story and wrote out an "action chart" to show what should happen in each "take" of 600 words or so. The length of the unit was not arbitrary. It was determined by the number of words on an average pulp-magazine page. It was a rule in many of the great pulp-fiction publishing factories that, to keep the lip-moving readers interested, every page needed a typographical break in the form of a skipped line and a large initial letter—otherwise, they thought, the unbroken type would be too daunting. Writers who were professionally expert enough to know this would so construct their stories that breaks in the action took place at such intervals. If they didn't, the editors would generally stick a break in on every page anyway.

Having written the action chart, I would turn it over to Cyril. He would convert it into a "first draft" —which was exactly what it sounds like it was—and return it to me for final rewrite and sale. Since I was by then a full-fledged science-fiction magazine editor (though not a very good one, and with a minute budget), most of the sales were to myself. Which is, of course, why Cyril agreed to the system in the first place, since the sixty-forty system got its name from the fact that I took 60% of the proceeds and Cyril got forty.

That division was not perfectly satisfactory to Cyril, though I didn't at the time realize quite how much it graveled him. (Years later, reminiscing together over a few drinks, he mentioned off-handedly that it had occurred to him once or twice to push me under a subway train.) As we gained confidence we began to write stories with others or even by ourselves. The whole sixty-forty period lasted only about two years, and then we didn't collaborate again until we wrote *The Space Merchants,* ten years later.

The sixty-forty stories were mechanically constructed, and by and large they were pretty bad. I don't think it was entirely the fault of the system, though. I think we simply had not learned how to write well. Once in a while we had fairly good ideas, and simply lacked the skill to do them justice. More often the ideas were hackneyed or silly to begin with, and to rescue them from their triviality we committed that most common of fledgling writers' faults: lacking the ability to do justice to the medium, we resorted to kidding it.

Still, not all of them were *altogether* awful. Of the lot, there are a couple that I am willing to risk reviving (though with a considerable amount of revision and editing), and here they are: "Mars-Tube" and "Trouble in Time."

# Trouble in Time

To begin at the beginning, everybody knows that scientists are crazy. I may be either mistaken or prejudiced, but this seems especially true of mathematico-physicists. In a small town like Colchester gossip spreads fast and furiously, and one evening the word was passed around that an outstanding example of the species Doctissimus Dementiae had finally lodged himself in the old frame house beyond the dog pound on Court Street, mysterious crates and things having been unloaded there for weeks previous.

Abigail O'Liffey, a typical specimen of the low type that a fine girl like me is forced to consort with in a small town, said she had seen the Scientist. "He had broad shoulders," she said dreamily, "and red hair, and a scraggly little mustache that wiggled up and down when he chewed gum."

"What would you expect it to do?"

She looked at me dumbly. "He was wearing a kind of garden coat," she said. "It was like a painter's, only it was all burned in places instead of having paint on it. I'll bet he discovers things like Paul Pasteur."

"*Louis* Pasteur," I said. "Do you know *his* name, by any chance?"

"Whose—the Scientist's? Clarissa said one of the expressmen told her husband it was Cramer or something."

"Never heard of him," I said. "Good night." And I slammed the screen door. Cramer, I thought—it was the echo of a name I knew, and a big name at that. I was angry with Clarissa for not getting the name more accurately, and with Abigail for bothering me about it, and most of all with the Scientist for stirring me out of my drowsy existence with remembrances of livelier and brighter things not long past.

So I slung on a coat and sneaked out the back door to get a look at the mystery man, or at least his house. I slunk past the dog pound, and the house sprang into sight like a Christmas tree—every socket in the place must have been in use, to judge from the flood of light that poured from all windows. There was a dark figure on the unkempt lawn; when I was about ten yards from it and on the verge of turning back, it shouted at me: "Hey, you! Can you give me a hand?"

I approached warily; the figure was wrestling with a crate four feet high and square. "Sure," I said.

The figure straightened. "Oh, so he's a she," it said. "Sorry, lady. I'll get a hand truck from inside."

"Don't bother," I assured it. "I'm glad to help." And I took one of the canvas slings as it took the other, and we carried the crate in, swaying perilously. "Set it here, please," he said, dropping his side of the crate. It *was* a he, I saw in the numerous electric bulbs' light, and from all appearances the Scientist, Cramer, or whatever his name was.

I looked about the big front parlor, bare of furniture but jammed with boxes and piles of machinery.

"That was the last piece," he said amiably, noting my gaze. "Thank you. Can I offer you a scientist's drink?"

"Not—ethyl?" I cried rapturously.

"The same," he assured me, vigorously attacking a crate that tinkled internally. "How do you know?"

"Past experience. My alma mater was the Housatonic University, School of Chemical Engineering."

He had torn away the front of the crate, laying bare a neat array of bottles. "What's a C.E. doing in this stale little place?" he asked, selecting flasks and measures.

"Sometimes she wonders," I said bitterly. "Mix me an Ethyl Martini, will you?"

"Sure, if you like them. I don't go much for the fancy swigs myself. Correct me if I'm wrong." He took the bottle labeled $C_2H_5OH$. "Three cubic centimeters?"

"No—you don't start with the ethyl!" I cried. "Put four minims of fusel oil in a beaker." He complied. "Right—now a tenth of a grain of saccharine saturated in theine barbiturate ten percent solution." His hands flew through the pharmaceutical ritual. "And *now* pour in the ethyl slowly, and stir, don't shake."

He held the beaker to the light. "Want some color in that?" he asked, immersing it momentarily in liquid air from a double thermos.

"No," I said. "What are you having?"

"A simple fusel highball," he said, expertly pouring and chilling a beakerful, and brightening it with a drop of a purple dye that transformed the colorless drink into a sparkling beverage. We touched beakers and drank deep.

"That," I said gratefully when I had finished coughing, "is the first real drink I've had since graduating three years ago. The stuff has a nostalgic appeal for me."

He looked blank. "It occurs to me," he said, "that I ought to introduce myself. I am Stephen Trainer, late of Mellon, late of Northwestern, late of Cambridge, sometime fellow of the Sidney School of Technology. Now you tell me who you are and we'll be almost even."

I collected my senses and announced, "Miss Mabel Evans, late in practically every respect."

"I am pleased to make your acquaintance, Miss Evans," he said. "Won't you sit down?"

"Thank you," I murmured. I was about to settle on one of the big wooden boxes when he cried out at me.

"For God's sake—not there!"

"And why not?" I asked, moving to another. "Is that your reserve stock of organic bases?"

"No," he said. "That's part of my time machine."

I looked at him. "Just a nut, huh?" I said pityingly. "Just another sometimes capable fellow gone wrong. He thinks he knows what he's doing, and he even had me fooled for a time, but the *idée fixe* come out at last, and we see the man for what he is—mad as a hatter. Nothing but a time-traveler at the bottom of that mass of flesh and bone." I felt sorry for him, in a way.

His face grew as purple as the drink in his hand. As though he too had formed the association, he drained it and set it down. "Listen," he said. "I only know one style of reasoning that parallels yours in its scope and utter disregard of logic. Were you ever so unfortunate as to be associated with that miserable charlatan, Dr. George B. Hopper?"

"My physics professor at Housatonic," I said, "and whaddya make of that?"

"I am glad of the chance of talking to you," he said in a voice suddenly hoarse. "It's no exaggeration to say that for the greater part of my life I've wanted to come across a pupil of that scientific fraud, Hopper."

"Actually," I said, "I thought he was kind of nice-looking."

"Nice-looking!" he bellowed. "My dear young woman! He's a jerk! I know the man well. I've sat under him and over him in various faculties. We even went to Cambridge together—it disgusted both of us. And now at last you've put yourself into my hands, and so you are going to learn the truth about physics."

I watched his hands carefully, but he didn't seem to be moving either of them in my direction. "So go on with your lecture," I muttered.

He looked at me glassily. "I *am* going on with my lecture," he said. "Listen closely. You've heard of Albert Einstein?"

"I never personally dated him, but sure."

"A great man. Great, great, great. Said time is relative."

"I've heard that," I conceded. "Relative to what?"

"Relative to velocity," he said triumphantly, and beamed at me, delighted with himself for having made the point so clear.

It didn't seem clear to me. I thought there should be more. I waited for it, but he just kept on beaming until I nudged him and he made a grab for the decanter.

"Yes?" I said.

"Yes what?" he rejoined.

"Yes, if time is relative to velocity, so what?"

"Oh," he said, nodding, "I see what you mean." He thought for a moment. "Oh, I remember," he announced. "You go faster, time goes slower. You go a *lot* faster—as fast as light—and time stops completely. You with me so far?"

"No."

"That's good," he said gratefully, reaching again for the decanter. He missed and reached again grimly, his fist opening and closing and finally snapping shut on its neck. "Would you care to join me in partaking once again?" he asked graciously.

"Oh, granted," I said politely, trying to figure out what those little pinwheels were that seemed to be going around in my head.

"Right," he said, pouring and drinking. "Now. This is the important point. See, if you go *faster* than light, then you *travel* in time."

"Oh, yeah, sure," I said, swallowing. "To where?"

He shrugged. "The future, of course. I mean, honestly, my dear young woman, that's a stupid question. What would be the point of going into the past, for heaven's sake? You've *been* in the past. Would be *dull*. A whole waste of my brilliant machine. Like going back to where you lived when you were a kid. Nostalgia stuff. Kind of thing poets might do. Or historians. Not *scientists*, always breaking ground, new frontiers, remorseless march of progress, steely-eyed investigators of the ultimate unknown—"

"Sweetie," I said, "your needle's stuck. Turn it off a minute."

"Oh, sorry," he apologized. "Get carried away. So you go into the future, not the past."

"You said that already," I interrupted.

"Did I?" he asked with a delighted smile. "I'm brighter than I thought." He waggled his head fuzzily. I wondered why he looked so suddenly much taller than I, and realized abruptly that I was lying full length on the floor. I shuddered at the very thought of what my aunt would say to that.

"Help me up, will you?" I begged.

"Certainly," he said, not making a move to do so. "Did you have any other questions?"

"Sure," I said, grabbing at his arm to pull myself back to a seat. "I'll remember them in a minute."

He looked doubtful. "I hope I can remember the answers," he muttered, indicating thought by a Homeric configuration of his eyebrows, cheeks, forehead and chin.

I refilled both glasses, pondering, and then got it. "Oh, yeah," I said. "I question your basic premise. There's nothing I can put my finger on, but I believe it's not quite dry behind the ears."

He glared at me. "You talk like that old moron Hopper," he said. I shrugged. He snarled, "All right! You can question as much as you like, but it works. I'll show you the gimmicks."

We clambered to our feet. "There," he said, pointing to the box I had nearly sat upon, "there lies the scientific wizardry that provides us with the key to all the ages." And he took up a crowbar and jimmied the top off the crate.

I carefully lifted out the most miscellaneous collection of junk ever seen outside a modern art museum. "What, for example," I asked, gingerly dangling a canvas affair at arm's length, "does this thing do?"

"One wears it as a belt," he explained. I put the thing on and found that it resolved itself into a normal Sam Browne belt with all sorts of oddments of things hanging from it. One compartment was marked *Salicylic acid,* another *Gadenolite,* another *Pemmican.* "What's this stuff?"

"Necessary supplies," he said dreamily. "You need the rare earths because they enhance the flux of chronons, and the pemmican in case you get hungry."

"And the salicylic acid? That's aspirin. Are you expecting a hangover in the future?"

He gave me a frosty glare. "Do you think I'd use this thing *sober?*"

"And—" I was reaching for the compartment marked *Entropy gradient*. He squawked in sudden panic.

"Oh, no! Don't touch those! You have no *idea* what forces you would be releasing. So do you want to try it or not?"

I blinked. It was a new idea, but under the circumstances it seemed a fairly good one. The circumstances were pretty drunk.

"Will you save some ethyl for when I get back?"

He looked at me in astonishment. "Get back?" he repeated questioningly. Then he shook his head. "All in its proper time," he said. "Now. I have but to plug this into a wall socket and, providing you get on the time-wheel, out you go like a light—*pouf*."

"Don't be silly," I said. "In the first place, I'm practically out now. In the second place, I don't care whether I go out *pouf* or out *splash*—though the latter is more customary in my case—and in the third place I don't believe your silly old machine works anyway. I dare you to make me go *pouf*. I just dare you."

"Okay," he said. "There's the time-wheel. Get on it."

The time-wheel reminded me of a small, hand-turned merry-go-round. I got on it with a good will and he made it turn. I was just beginning to wonder why he had been so vague about the question of getting back when he plugged in the lead to the wall socket, and I went out like a light—*pouf*.

There are few things more sobering than time-travel. On going *pouf* I closed my eyes, as was natural. Possibly I screamed a little, too. All I know is when I opened my eyes they were bleary and aching, and certainly nowhere very near the old house past the dog-pound on Court Street. The locale appeared to be something like Rockefeller Center, only without fountains.

I was standing on polished stones—beautifully polished stones which seemed to set the keynote of the surroundings. Everything was beautiful and everything was polished. Before me was a tall, tall building. It was a dark night, and there seemed to be a great lack of illumination in this world of tomorrow.

I followed my nose into the building. The revolving door revolved without much complaint, and did me the favor of turning on the lights of the lobby.

There were no people there; there were no people anywhere in sight. I tried to shout, and the ghastly echo from the still darkened sections made me tremble to my boots. I didn't try again, but very mousily looked about for an elevator or something. The something turned out to be a button in a vast column, labeled in plain English, "Slavies' ring."

I rang, assuring myself that doing so was no confession of inferiority, but merely the seizing of an offered opportunity. All the lobby lights went out, then, but the column was glowing like mother-of-pearl before a candle. A sort of door opened, and I walked through. "Why not?" I asked myself grimly.

I seemed to be standing on a revolving staircase—but one that actually revolved! It carried me up like a gigantic corkscrew at a speed that was difficult to determine. It stopped after a few minutes, and another door opened. I stepped through and said "Thank you" nicely to the goblins of the staircase, and shuddered again as the door slammed murderously fast and hard.

Lights went on again at my landing place—I was getting a bit more familiar with this ridiculous civilization. Was everybody away at Bermuda for the summer? I wondered. Then I chattered my teeth.

Corpses! Hundreds of them! I had had the bad taste, I decided, to land in the necropolis of the world of tomorrow.

On slabs of stone they lay in double rows, great lines of them stretching into the distance of the huge chamber into which I had blundered. Morbid curiosity moved me closer to the nearest stiff. I had taken a course in embalming to get my C.E., and I pondered on the advances of that art.

Something hideously like a bed lamp clicked on as I bent over the mummified creature. God above! With a rustling like the pages of an ancient book it moved—flung its arms over its eyes!

I'm afraid I may have screamed. But almost immediately I realized that the terror had been of my own postulation. Corpses do not move. This thing had moved—therefore it was not a corpse, and I had better get hold of myself unless I was determined to go batty.

It was revolting but necessary that I examine the thing. From its fingers thin, fine silver wires led into holes in the slab. I rolled it over, not heeding its terrible groans, and saw that a larger strand penetrated the neck, apparently in contact with its medulla oblongata. Presumably it was sick—this was a hospital. I rambled about cheerfully, scanning cryptic dials on the walls, wondering what would happen next, if anything.

There was a chair facing the wall; I turned it around and sat down.

"Greetings, unknown friend," said an effeminate voice.

"Greetings right back at you," said I, courtesy having always been my most outstanding trait.

"You have seated yourself in a chair; please be advised that you have set into motion a sound track that may be of interest to you."

The voice came from a panel in the wall that had lit up with opalescent effects.

"My name," said the panel, "is unimportant. You will probably wish to know first, assuming that this record is ever played, that there are duplicates artfully scattered throughout this city, so that whoever visits us will hear our story."

"Clever, aren't you?" I said sourly. "Suppose you stop fussing around and tell me what's going on around here."

"I am speaking," said the panel, "from the Fifth Century of Bickerstaff."

"Whatever that means," I said.

"Or, by primitive reckoning, 2700 A.D."

"Thanks."

"To explain, we must begin at the beginning. You may know that Bickerstaff was a poor Scotch engineer who went and discovered atomic power. I shall pass over his early struggles for recognition, merely stating that the process he invented was economical and efficient beyond anything similar in history.

"With the genius of Bickerstaff as a prod, humanity blossomed forth into its fullest greatness. Poetry and music, architecture and sculpture, letters and graphics became the principal occupations of mankind."

The panel coughed. "I myself," it said, modestly struggling with pride, "was a composer of no little renown in this city.

"However, there was one thing wrong with the Bickerstaff Power Process. That is, as Bickerstaff was to mankind, so the element yttrium was to his process. It was what is known as a catalyst, a substance introduced into a reaction for the purpose of increasing the speed of the reaction."

I, a chemical engineer, listening to that elementary rot! I didn't walk away. Perhaps he was going to say something of importance.

"In normal reactions the catalyst is not changed either in quantity or in quality, since it takes no real part in the process. However, the Bickerstaff process subjected all matter involved to extraordinary heat, pressure, and bombardment, and so the supply of yttrium has steadily vanished.

"Possibly we should have earlier heeded the warnings of nature. It may be the fault of no one but ourselves that we have allowed our race to become soft and degenerate in the long era of plenty. Power, light, heat—for the asking. And then we faced twin terrors: shortage of yttrium—and the Martians."

Abruptly I sat straight. Martians! I didn't see any of *them* around.

"Our planetary neighbors," said the panel, "are hardly agreeable. It came as a distinct shock to us when their ships landed this year—*my* year, that is—as the bearers of a message.

"Flatly we were ordered: Get out or be crushed. We could have resisted, we could have built warmachines, but what was to power them? Our brainmen did what they could, but it was little enough.

"They warned us, did the Martians. They said that we were worthless, absolutely useless, and they deserved the planet more than we. They had been watching our planet for many years, they said, and we were unfit to own it.

"That is almost a quotation of what they said. Not a translation, either, for they spoke English and indeed all the languages of Earth perfectly. They had observed us so minutely as to learn our tongues!

"Opinion was divided as to the course that lay before us. There were those who claimed that by hoarding the minute supply of yttrium remaining to us we might be able to hold off the invaders when they should come. But while we were discussing the idea the supply was all consumed.

"Some declared themselves for absorption with the Martian race on its arrival. Simple laws of biogenetics demonstrated effectively that such a procedure was likewise impossible.

"A very large group decided to wage guerrilla warfare, studying the technique from Clausewitz's 'Theory and Practise.' Unfortunately, the sole remaining copy of this work crumbled into dust when it was removed from its vault.

"And then . . .

"A man named Selig Vissarion, a poet of Odessa, turned his faculties to the problem, and evolved a device to remove the agonies of waiting. Three months ago—*my* time, remember—he proclaimed it to all mankind.

"His device was—the Biosomniac. It so operates that the sleeper—the subject of the device, that is—is thrown into a deep slumber characterized by dreams of a pleasurable nature. And the slumber is one from which he will never, without outside interference, awake.

"The entire human race, as I speak, is now under the influence of the machine. All but me, and I am left only because there is no one to put me under. When I have done here—I shall shoot myself.

"For this is our tragedy: Now, when all our yttrium is gone, we have found a device to transmute metals. Now we could *make* all the yttrium we need, except that . . .

"*The device cannot be powered except by the destruction of the atom.*

"And so, unknown friend, farewell. You have heard our history. Remember it, and take warning. Be warned of sloth, beware of greed. Farewell, my unknown friend."

And, with that little sermon, the shifting glow of the panel died and I sat bespelled. It was all a puzzle to me. If the Martians were coming, why hadn't they arrived? Or had they? At least I saw none about me.

I looked at the mummified figures that stretched in great rows the length of the chamber. These, then, were neither dead nor ill, but sleeping. Sleeping against the coming of the Martians. I thought. My chronology was fearfully confused. Could it be that the invaders from the red planet had not yet come, and that I was only a year or two after the human race had plunged itself into sleep? That must be it.

And all for the want of a little bit of yttrium!

Absently I inspected the appendages of the time-travelling belt. They were, for the most part, compact boxes labeled with the curt terminology of engineering. "Converter," said one. "Entropy gradient," said another. And a third bore the cryptic word, "Gadenolite." That baffled my chemical knowledge. Vaguely I remembered *something* I had done back in Housatonic with the stuff. It was a Scandinavian rare earth, as I remember, containing tratia, eunobia, and several oxides. And one of them, I slowly remembered—

Then I said it aloud, with dignity and precision: "One of the compounds present in this earth in large proportions is yttrium dioxide."

Yttrium dioxide? Why, that was—

*Yttrium!*

It was one of those things that was just too good to be true. Yttrium! Assuming that the Martians hadn't come yet, and that there really was a decent amount of the metal in the little box on my belt . . .

Quite the little heroine, I, I thought cheerfully, and strode to the nearest sleeper. "Excuse me," I said.

He groaned as the little reading lamp flashed on. "Excuse me," I said again.

He didn't move. Stern measures seemed to be called for. I shouted in his ear, "Wake up, you!" But he wouldn't.

I wandered among the sleepers, trying to arouse some, and failing in every case. It must be those little wires, I thought gaily as I bent over one of them.

I inspected the hand of the creature, and noted that the silvery filaments trailing from the fingers did not seem to be imbedded very deeply in the flesh. Taking a deep breath I twisted one of the wires between forefinger and thumb, and broke it with ease.

The creature groaned again, and—opened its eyes!

"Good morning," I said feebly.

It didn't answer me, but sat up and stared from terribly sunken pits for a full second. It uttered a little wailing cry. The eyes closed again, and the creature rolled from its slab, falling heavily to the floor. I felt for the pulse; there was none. Beyond doubt this sleeper slept no longer—I had killed him.

I walked away from the spot, realizing that my problem was not as simple as it might have been. A faint glow lit up the hall, and the lights above flashed out. The new radiance came through the walls of the building.

It must be morning, I thought. I had had a hard night, and a strange one. I pressed the "Slavies' ring" again, and took the revolving staircase down to the lobby.

The thing to do now was to find some way of

awakening the sleepers without killing them. That meant study. Study meant books, books meant library. I walked out into the polished stone plaza and looked for libraries.

There was some fruitless wandering about and stumbling into several structures precisely similar to the one I had visited; finally down the vista of a broad, gleaming street I saw the deep-carven words, "Stape Books Place," on the pediment of a traditionally squat, classic building. I set off for it, and arrived too winded by the brisk walk to do anything more than throw myself into a chair.

A panel in the wall lit up and an effeminate voice began, "Greetings, unknown friend. You have seated yourself in a chair; please be advised—"

"Go to hell," I said shortly, rose, and left the panel to go through a door inscribed "Books of the Day."

It turned out to be a conventional reading room whose farther end was a maze of stacks and shelves. Light poured in through large windows, and I felt homesick for old Housatonic. If the place had been a little more dusty I'd never have known it from the Main Tech Library.

A volume I chose at random proved to be a work on anthropology: "A General Introduction to the Study of Decapilation Among the Tertiates of Gondwana as Contrasted with the Primates of Eurasia." I found one photograph—in color—of a hairless monkey, shuddered, and restored the volume.

The next book was "The Exagmination into the incamination for the resons of his Works in the pregreSs," which also left me stranded. It appeared to be a critique of the middle work of one James Joyce, reprinted from the original edition of Paris, 1934 A.D.

I chucked the thing into a corner and rummaged among the piles of pamphlets that jammed a dozen shelves. "Rittenhouse's Necrology"—no. "Statistical Isolates Relating to Isolate Statisticals"—likewise no. "The Cognocrat Manifest"—I opened it and found it a description of a superstate which had yet to be created. "Construction and Operation of the Biosomniac"—that was it!

I seated myself at one of the polished tables and read through the slim pamphlet rapidly once, then tore out some of its blank pages to take notes on. "The arrangement of the regulating dials is optional," I copied onto the paper scraps, and sketched the intricate system of Bowden wires that connected the bodies with the controls. That was as much of a clue as I could get from the little volume, but it indicated in its appendix more exhaustive works. I looked up "Vissarion," the first on the list.

"Monarch! may many moiling mockers make
my master more malicious marry mate—"

it said. Mankind, artist to the last, had yet found time to compose an epic poem on the inventor of the Biosomniac. I flung the sappy thing away and took down the next work on the list, "Chemistry of the Somniac." It was a sound treatise on the minute yet perceptible functionings of the subject under the influence of the Vissarion device. More notes and diagrams, collated with the information from the other book.

"The vitality of the sleeper is more profoundly affected by the operations of the Alphate dial . . . It is believed that the Somniac may be awakened by a suitable manipulation of the ego-flow so calculated as to shock the sleeper to survive a severing of the quasi-amniotic wiring system."

I rose and tucked the notes into my belt. That was enough for me! I'd have to experiment, and most likely make a few mistakes, but in a few hours men would be awake to grow hard and strong again after their long sleep, to pluck out their wires themselves, and to take my yttrium and with it build the needed war-machines against the Martians. No more sleep for Earth! And perhaps a new flowering of life when the crisis of the invaders was past?

"The compleat heroine—quite!" I chortled aloud as I passed through the door. I glanced at the glowing panel, but it glowed no longer—the unknown speaker had said his piece and was done. Onward and outward to save the world, I thought.

"Excuse me," said a voice.

I spun around and saw a fishy individual staring at me through what seemed to be a small window.

"What are you doing awake?" I asked excitedly.

He laughed softly. "That, my dear young lady, is just what I was about to ask you."

"Come out from behind that window," I said nervously. "I can hardly see you."

"Don't be silly," he said sharply. "I'm quite a few million miles away. I'm on Mars. In fact, I'm a Martian."

I looked closer. He *did* seem sort of peculiar, but hardly the bogeyman that his race had been cracked up to be. "Then you will please tell me what you want," I said. "I'm a busy woman with little time to waste on Martians." Brave words. I knew it would take him a while to get from Mars to where I was; by that time I would have everyone awake and stinging.

"Oh," he said casually. "I just thought you might like a little chat. I suppose you're a time-traveler."

"Just that."

"I thought so. You're the fourth—no, the fifth—this week. Funny how they always seem to hit on this year. My name is Alfred, John Alfred."

"How do you do?" I said politely. "And I'm Mabel Evans of Colchester, Vermont. Year, 1940. But why have you got a name like an Earthman?"

"We all have," he answered. "We copied it from you Terrestrials. It's your major contribution to our culture."

"I suppose so," I said bitterly. "Those jellyfish didn't have much to offer anybody except poetry and bad sculpture. I hardly know why I'm reviving them and giving them the yttrium to fight you blokes off."

He looked bored, as nearly as I could see. "Oh, have you some yttrium?"

"Yes."

"Much?"

"Enough for a start. Besides, I expect them to pick up and acquire some independence once they get through their brush-up with Mars. By the way—when will you invade?"

"We plan to *colonize*," he said, delicately emphasizing the word, "beginning about two years from now. It will take that long to get everything in shape to move."

"That's fine," I said enthusiastically. "We should have plenty of time to get ready, I think. What kind of weapons do you use? Death-rays?"

"Of course," said the Martian. "And heat rays, and molecular collapse rays, and disintegrator rays, and resistance rays—you just name it and we have it in stock, lady."

He was a little boastful. "Well," I said, "you just wait until we get a few factories going—then you'll see what high-speed, high-grade production can be. We'll have everything you've got—double."

"All this, of course," he said with a smug smile, "after you wake the sleepers and give them your yttrium?"

"Of course. Why shouldn't it be?"

"Oh, I was just asking. But I have an idea that you've made a fundamental error."

"Error, my neck," I said. "What do you mean?"

"Listen closely, please," he said. "Your machine—that is, your time-traveller—operates on the principle of time-dilation, does it not?"

"Oh, sure," I said, nodding my head emphatically. That was a mistake. I hardly heard him as he went on:

"So at the speed of light time stands still, while *past* the speed of light it goes in the opposite direction?"

I said loftily, "That's a rather crude and approximate description of the process, but what about it?"

He gave me a smug smile. "Just this. Your machine can't work."

I looked down at myself to see if I were really there. As far as I could tell, I was. "What are you talking about?" I demanded.

"Simply this, Miss Evans. What you describe might happen, according to theory, if you exceeded the speed of light. Unfortunately, the same theory says that is impossible."

"Impossible?" I queried, with a sinking feeling.

"Impossible. Meaning you can't do it." He looked at me gloatingly. Then he continued, slowly and remorselessly: "Your theory is fallacious. Ergo, your machine doesn't work. If your machine doesn't work, you couldn't have used it to get here. There is no other way for you to have gotten here. Therefore . . . *you are not here!* and so the projected *colonization* will proceed on schedule!"

And the light flashed in my head. Of course! that was what I had been trying to think of back in the house. The weakness in Trainer's logic!

Then I went *pouf* again, my eyes closed, and I thought to myself, "Since the machine didn't work and couldn't have worked, I didn't travel in time. So I must be back with Trainer."

I opened my eyes. I was.

"You moron," I snapped at him as he stood goggle-eyed, his hand on the wall socket. "Your machine doesn't work!"

He stared at me blankly. "It must work. You were gone. I saw it with my own eyes."

I said tolerantly, "But you can't have, because it was impossible. The Martian made that very clear."

"So then where were you, impossibly?"

"I seemed to be impossibly in 2700 A.D."

"How was it," he inquired, reaching for a fresh flask of ethyl.

"Very, very silly. I'm glad the machine didn't work." He offered me a beaker and I drained it. "I'd hate to think that I'd really been there." I took off the belt and stretched my aching muscles.

"Do you know, Mabel," he said, looking at me hard, "I think I'm going to like this town."

# Mars-Tube

Ray Stanton set his jaw as he stared at the molded lead seal on the door of the Martian museum. The seal was not really lead; nothing on Mars was exactly like its Earthly counterparts. And perhaps the institution was not a museum, either, as much as it was a—what would you call it? Maybe a cenotaph? Or a time capsule? Or a biographical sketch. . . .

Or a suicide note.

"Read it," ordered Annamarie Hudgins, the expedition's information-locating specialist (she did not like being called "librarian.") Obediently Stanton deciphered its inscription, his tongue stumbling over the unfamiliar sibilants of the Martian language as he read it aloud before translating:

"To the . . . strangers from the third planet . . . who have won their . . . bitter . . . triumph . . . we of Mars charge you . . . not to wantonly destroy . . . that which you will find . . . within this door . . . our codified learning . . . may serve you . . . better than we ourselves . . . might have done."

Stanton rubbed his jaw. "That's it," he said. "Something like that, anyway."

165

"Only something?" the girl demanded.

Stanton shrugged; there was plenty of Martian voice and written text to learn from, but not all the concepts seemed entirely translatable. He felt ashamed of being an Earthman as he read the soft indictment. "Pathetic," he whispered. "Those poor damned people."

"We don't even know if they were people," said Annamarie practically. She was a slim, dark girl, not the sort of person you would have expected on the first manned expedition to Mars—the first that had avoided being wiped out by the Martians, anyway.

"We know they built cities and machines and left them running for us, even though we were killing them all off. That's close enough to people for me. Maybe better than people."

She said scornfully, "To work, Stanton," and dolefully he began copying the inscription into his notebook. It was true that they didn't know much first-hand about the Martians. They had never seen a living one. They never would; there weren't any more.

In defense of the human race, you could point out that the Martians had begun the war by killing off the first human expedition. But when the humans ended it, they did so totally. It had raged in space, rocket ship against fleet of rocket ships, for decades before the hard-pressed human research establishments had come up with the final solution to the Martian problem. But after that there were no Martians alive in space, or anywhere else.

"It could have been different," Stanton grumbled as he broke the seal.

"But it wasn't," said Annamarie testily. "Get on with it, Stanton. We're supposed to study this thing and get back, not worship it. Open the door."

Stanton shook his head somberly, but copied the

seal's inscription into his voluminous black archeologist's notebook. Then he tore off the seal and tentatively pushed the door. It swung open easily, and an automatic switch snapped on the hidden lights as the first two human beings entered the building.

Both Stanton and Annamarie had seen many marvels in their first days on the red planet, for every secret place was now open to human eyes. All of the Martian cities still worked—heating systems, lighting, elevators, subways. There were even Martian robots still functioning, though at exactly what they functioned the explorers seldom knew. The most popular hypothesis was that they were a sort of janitor or handyman, keeping the complex mechanisms going for their vanished creators. The robots paid no attention to the new human proprietors and when, early, members of the expedition had trapped and dismantled a few, they had simply gone dead, their power sources shorted out, their mechanisms still.

There were no robots visible here but, as the lights slowly blossomed over the colossal hall of the library, Stanton staggered back in amazement that so much stately glory could be built into one room.

"Oh, my God," he whispered.

"Oh, buck up, Stanton," snapped the girl. "The war was a crying shame, but mourning the dead won't bring them back."

"I know . . . but look!"

"You look," she said. "I have work to do."

The synthetic slabs of gem-like rose crystal that the Martians had reserved for their most awesome sanctuaries were flashing from every wall and article of furnishing, winking with soft ruby lights. One of the typically Martian ramps led up in a gentle curve from their left. The practical Annamarie at once commenced to mount it, heading for the reading-rooms that would be found above. Stanton followed more slowly, pausing to examine the symbolic ornamentation in the walls.

"We must have guessed right, Annamarie," he observed, catching up with her. "This one's the central museum-library for sure. Take a look at the wall-motif."

Annamarie glanced at a panel just ahead, a bas-relief done in the rose crystal. "Because of the *ultima* symbol, you mean?"

"Yes, and because—well, look." The room in which they found themselves was less noble than the other, but considerably more practical. It was of radical design, corridors converging like the spokes of a wheel on a focal point where they stood. Inset in the floor—they were almost standing on it—was the *ultima* symbol, the quadruple linked circles which indicated preeminence. Stanton peered down a corridor lined with racks of wire spools. He picked up a spool and stared at its title-tag.

"Where do you suppose we ought to start?" he asked.

"Anywhere at all," Annamarie replied. "We've got lots of time, and no way of knowing what to look for. What's the one in your hands?"

"It seems to say 'The Under-Eaters'—whatever that may mean." Stanton juggled the tiny "book" undecidedly. "That phrase seems familiar somehow. What is it?"

"Couldn't say. Put it in the scanner and we'll find out." Stanton obeyed, pulling a tiny reading-machine from its cubicle. The delicacy with which Stanton threaded the fragile wire into its proper receptacle was something to watch. The party had ruined a hundred spools of records before they'd learned how to adjust the scanners, and Stanton had learned caution.

Stanton and his companion leaned back against the book-racks and watched the fluorescent screen of the scanner. A touch of the lever started its operation. There was a soundless flare of light on the screen as the wire made contact with the scanning apparatus, then the screen filled with the curious wavering peak-and-valley writing of the Martian graphic language.

By the end of the third "chapter" the title of the book was still almost as cryptic as ever. A sort of preface had indicated that "Under-Eaters" was a name applied to a race of underground demons who feasted on the flesh of living Martians. Whether these really existed or not Stanton had no way of telling. The Martians had made no literary distinction between fact and fiction, as far as could be learned. It had been their opinion that anything except pure thought-transference was only approximately true, and that it would be useless to distinguish between an intentional and an unintentional falsehood.

But the title had no bearing on the context of the book, which was a kind of pseudo-history with heavily allusive passages. It was a treatment of the Earth-Mars war: seemingly it had been published only a few months before the abrupt end to hostilities. One rather tragic passage, so Stanton thought, read:

"A special meeting of the tactical council was called on (an untranslatable date) to discuss the so-called new disease on which the attention of the enemy forces has been concentrating. This was argued against by (a high official) who demonstrated conclusively that the Martian intellect was immune to nervous diseases of any foreign order, due to its high development through telepathy as cultivated for (an untranslatable number of) generations. A minority report submitted that this very development itself would render the Martian intellect more liable to succumb to unusual strain. (A medical authority) suggested that certain forms of insanity were contagious by means of telepathy, and that the enemy-spread disease might be of that type."

Stanton cursed softly: "Damn Moriarity and his rocket ship. Damn Sweeney for getting killed and damn and double-damn the World Congress for declaring war on Mars!" He felt like a murderer, though he knew he was no more than a slightly pacifistic young exploring archaeologist. Annamarie nodded sympathetically but pointed at the screen. Stanton looked again and his imprecations were forgotten as he brought his mind to the problem of translating another of the strangely referential passages:

"At this time the Under-Eaters launched a bombing campaign on several of the underground cities. A number of subterranean caves were linked with the surface through explosion craters and many of the sinister creations fumbled their way to the surface. A corps of technologists prepared to reseal the tunnels of the Revived, which was done with complete success, save only in (an untranslatable place-name) where several Under-Eaters managed to wreak great havoc before being slain or driven back to their tunnels. The ravages of the Twice-Born, however, were trivial compared to the deaths resulting from the mind diseases fostered by the flying ships of the Under-Eaters, which were at this time . . ."

The archaeologist frowned. There it was again. Part of the time "Under-Eaters" obviously referred to the Earthmen, the rest of the time it equally obviously did not. The text would limp along in styleless, concise prose and then in would break an obscure reference to the "Creations" or "Twice-Born" or "Raging Glows."

"Fairy tales for the kiddies," said Annamarie Hudgins, snapping off the scanner.

Stanton replied indirectly: "Put it in the knapsack. I want to take it back and show it to some of the others. Maybe they can tell me what it means." He swept a handful of other reading-bobbins at random into the knapsack, snapped it shut, and straightened. "Lead on, Mac-Hudgins," he said. "Let's get back to the subway."

Of the many wonders of the red planet, the one that the exploration party had come to appreciate most was the colossal system of subways which connected each of the underground cities of Mars.

With absolute precision the web of tunnels and gliding cars still functioned, and would continue to do so until the central controls were found by some Earthman and the vast propulsive mechanisms turned off.

The Mars-Tube was electrostatic in principle. The perfectly round tunnels through which the subway sped were studded with hoops of charged metal. The analysis of the metal hoops and the generators for the propulsive force had been beyond Earthly science, at least as represented by the understaffed exploring party.

Through these hoops sped the single-car trains of the Mars-Tube, every four minutes through every hour of the long Martian day. The electrostatic emanations from the hoops held the cars nicely balanced against the pull of gravity; save only when they stopped for the stations, the cars never touched anything more substantial than a puff of air. The average speed of the subway, stops not included, was upwards of five hundred miles an hour. There were no windows in the cars, for there would have been nothing to see through them but the endless tunnel wall slipping smoothly and silently by.

So easy was the completely automatic operation that the men from Earth could scarcely tell when the car was in motion, except by the signal panel that dominated one end of the car with its blinking lights and numerals.

Stanton led Annamarie to a station with ease and assurance. There was only one meaning to the tear-drop-shaped guide signs of a unique orange color that were all over Mars. Follow the point of a sign like that anywhere on Mars and you'd find yourself at a Mars-Tube station—or what passed for one.

Since there was only one door to a car, and that opened automatically whenever the car stopped at a station, there were no platforms. Just a smaller or larger anteroom with a door also opening automatically, meeting the door of the tube-car.

A train eventually slid in, and Stanton ushered Annamarie through the sliding doors. They swung themselves gently onto one of the excessively broad seats and immediately opened their notebooks. Each seat had been built for a single Martian, but accommodated two Terrestrials with room to spare.

At perhaps the third station, Annamarie, pondering the implications of a passage in the notebook, looked up for an abstracted second—and froze. "Ray," she whispered in a strangled tone. "When did that come in?"

Stanton darted a glance at the forward section of the car, which they had ignored when entering. Something—something animate—was sitting there, quite stolidly ignoring the Terrestrials. "A Martian," he whispered to himself, his throat dry.

It had the enormous chest and hips, the waspish waist and the coarse, bristly hairs of the Martians. But the Martians were all dead—

"It's only a robot," he cried more loudly than was necessary, swallowing as he spoke. "Haven't you seen enough of them to know what they look like by now?"

"What's it doing here?" gulped Annamarie, not over the fright.

As though it were about to answer her question itself, the thing's metallic head turned, and its blinking eyes swept incuriously over the humans. For a long second it stared, then the dull glow within its eye-sockets faded, and the head turned again to the front. The two had not set off any system of reflexes in the creature.

"I never saw one of them in the subway before," said Annamarie, passing a damp hand over her sweating brow.

Stanton was glaring at the signal panel that dominated the front of the car. "I know why, too," he said. "I'm not as good a linguist as I thought I was— not even as good as I ought to be. We're on the wrong train—I read the code-symbol wrong."

Annamarie giggled. "Then what shall we do—see where this takes us or go back?"

"Get out and go back, of course," grumbled Stanton, rising and dragging her to her feet.

The car was slowing again for another station. They could get out, emerge to the surface, cross over, and take the return train to the library.

Only the robot wouldn't let them.

For as the car was slowing, the robot rose to its feet and stalked over to the door. "What's up?" Stanton whispered in a thin, nervous voice. Annamarie prudently got behind him.

"We're getting out here anyhow," she said. "Maybe it won't follow us."

But they didn't get out. For when the car had stopped, and the door relays clicked, the robot shouldered the humans aside and stepped to the door.

But instead of exiting himself, the robot grasped the edge of the door in his steel tentacles, clutched it with all his metal muscles straining, and held it shut!

"Damned if I can understand it," said Stanton. "It was the most uncanny thing—it held the door completely and totally shut there, but it let us get out as peaceful as playmates at the next stop. We crossed over to come back, and while we were waiting for a return car I had time to dope out the station number. It was seventh from the end of the line, and the branch was new to me. So we took the return car back to the museum. The same thing happened on the trip back—robot in the car; door held shut."

"Go on," said Ogden Josey, Roëntgenologist of the expedition. "What happened then?"

"Oh. We just went back to the library, took a different car, and here we are."

"Interesting," said Josey. "Only I don't believe it a bit."

"No?" Annamarie interrupted, her eyes narrowing. "Want to take a look?"

"Sure."

"How about tomorrow morning?"

"Fine," said Josey. "You can't scare me. Now how about dinner?"

He turned and led the way across the vast plaza.

This was Earth Central—no one had yet found out what the Martians had called it. It was where the eighty members of the first post-war human expedition to Mars made their home. From it they launched their exploration parties and to it they returned with their reports.

Neither Stanton nor Annamarie Hudgins was, properly speaking, an explorer. Their duties were closer to home. They didn't mind this. For one thing, there were no decaying Martian cadavers on this part of the planet; that strange race, once it learned it was dying, had migrated to a few remote places on the planet to expire. Why? No one could guess. Perhaps it was simple neatness; they didn't want their conquerors to find their world untidy with corrupting flesh. The parties who visited the Martian hecatombs, gas-masked and sealed-suited, did valuable work but were not envied. Nor were the ones who descended into the deeper levels where the mysterious Martian power generators throbbed and glittered. No one knew what worrisome radiation might come from the vast machines, and those who investigated them were watched carefully for whatever harm might come.

The expedition's base was a huge, rotunda-like affair that might have been designed for anything by the Martians—no one dared guess what. It was given its present capacity by the explorers because it contained things that looked like tables and other things that were close enough to chairs, and enough of both to meet the needs of a regiment. As Josey entered, Stanton and Annamarie lagged behind.

"What are you planning, exactly, for tomorrow?" Stanton inquired. "I don't see the point of taking Josey with us when we go to look the situation over again."

"He'll come in handy," Annamarie promised. "He's a good shot."

"A good shot?" squawked Stanton. "What do you expect we'll have to shoot at?"

But Annamarie was already inside the building.

## II.

"Hey, Sand-Man!" hissed Annamarie.

"Be right there," sleepily said Stanton. "This is the strangest date I ever had." He appeared a moment later dressed in the roughest kind of exploring garb.

The girl raised her brows. "Expect to go mountain-climbing?" she asked.

"I had a hunch," he said amiably.

"So?" she commented. "I get them too. One of them is that Josey is still asleep. Go rout him out."

Stanton grinned and disappeared into Josey's cubicle, emerging with him a few moments later. "He was sleeping in his clothes," Stanton explained. "Filthy habit."

"Never mind that. Are we all heeled?" Annamarie proudly displayed her own pearl-handled pipsqueak of a mild paralyzer. Josey produced a heat-pistol, while Stanton patted the holster of his five-pound blaster.

"Okay then. We're off."

The Martian subway service was excellent every hour of the day. Despite the earliness, the trip to the central museum station took no more time than usual—a matter of minutes.

Stanton stared around for a second to get his bearings, then pointed. "The station we want is over there—just beyond the large pink monolith. Let's go."

The first train in was the one they wanted. They stepped into it, Josey leaping over the threshold like a startled fawn. Nervously he explained, "I never know when one of those things is going to snap shut on my—my cape." He yelped shrilly: 'What's *that*?"

"Ah, I see the robots rise early," said Annamarie, seating herself as the train moved off. "Don't look so disturbed, Josey—we told you one would be here, even if you didn't believe us."

"We have just time for a spot of breakfast before things should happen," announced Stanton, drawing canisters from a pouch on his belt. "Here—one for each of us." They were filled with a syrup that the members of the Earth expedition carried on trips such as this—concentrated amino acids, fibrinogen, minerals, and vitamins, all in a sugar solution.

Annamarie Hudgins shuddered as she downed the sticky stuff, then lit a cigarette. As the lighter flared the robot turned his head to precisely the angle required to center and focus its eyes on the flame, then eyes-fronted again.

"Attracted by light and motion," Stanton advised scientifically. "Stop trembling, Josey. There's worse to come. Say, is this the station?"

"It is," said Annamarie. "Now watch. These robots function smoothly and fast—don't miss anything."

The metal monster, with a minimum of waste motion, was doing just that. It had clumped over to the door; its monstrous appendages were fighting the relays that were to drive the door open, and the robot was winning. The robots were built to win—powerful, even by Earthly standards.

Stanton rubbed his hands briskly and tackled the robot, shoving hard. The girl laughed sharply. He turned, his face showing injury. "Suppose you help," he suggested with some anger. "I can't move this by myself."

"All right—heave!" gasped the girl, complying.

"Ho!" added Josey unexpectedly, adding his weight.

"No use," said Stanton. "No use at all. We couldn't move this thing in seven million years." He wiped his brow. The train started, then picked up speed. All three were thrown back as the robot carelessly nudged them out of its way as it returned to its seat.

"I think," said Josey abruptly, "we'd better go back by the return car and see about the other side of the station."

"No use," said the girl. "There's a robot on the return, too."

"Then let's walk back," urged Josey. By which time the car had stopped at the next station. "Come on," said Josey, stepping through the door with a suspicious glance at the robot.

"No harm in trying," mused Stanton as he followed with the girl. "Can't be more than twenty miles."

"And that's easier than twenty Earth miles," cried Annamarie. "Let's go."

"I don't know what good it will do though," remarked Stanton, ever the pessimist. "These Martians were thorough. There's probably a robot at every entrance to the station, blocking the way. *If* they haven't sealed up the entrances entirely."

There was no robot at the station, they discovered several hours and about eight miles later. But the entrance to the station that was so thoroughly and mysteriously guarded was—no more. Each entrance was sealed; only the glowing teardrop pointers remained to show where the entrance had been.

"Well, what do we do now?" groaned Josey, rubbing an aching thigh.

Stanton did not answer directly. "Will you look at that," he marvelled, indicating the surrounding terrain. The paved ground beneath them was seamed with cracks. The infinitely tough construction concrete of the Martians was billowed and rippled, stuck through with jagged ends of metal reinforcing I-beams. The whole scene gave the appearance of total devastation—as though a natural catastrophe had come along and wrecked the city first; then the survivors of the disaster, petulantly, had turned their most potent forces on what was left in sheer disheartenment.

"Must have been bombs," suggested the girl.

"Must have been," agreed the archaeologist. "Bombs and guns and force beams and Earth—Marsquakes, too."

"You didn't answer his question, Ray," reminded Annamarie. "He said: 'What do we do now'?"

"I was just thinking about it," he said, eyeing one of the monolithic buildings speculatively. "Is your Martian as good as mine? See if you can make out what that says."

"That" was a code-symbol over the sole door to the huge edifice. "I give up," said Annamarie with irritation. "What does it say?"

"Powerhouse, I think."

"Powerhouse? Powerhouse for what? All the energy for lighting and heating the city comes from the big underground ones. The only thing they need power for here—the only thing— Say!"

"That's right," grinned Stanton. "It must be for the Mars-Tube. Do you suppose we could find a way of getting from that building into the station?"

"There's only one way to find out," Annamarie parroted, looking for Josey for confirmation. But Josey was no longer around. He was at the door to the building, shoving it open. The others hastened after him.

## III.

"Don't wiggle, Annamarie," whispered Josey plaintively. "You'll fall on me."

"Shut up," she answered tersely. "Shut up and get out of my way." She swung herself down the Martian-sized manhole with space to spare. Dropping three feet or so from her hand-hold on the lip of the pit, she alighted easily. "Did I make much noise?" she asked.

"Oh, I think Krakatoa has been louder when it went off," Stanton replied bitterly. "But those things seem to be deaf."

The three stood perfectly still for a second, listening tensely for sounds of pursuit. They had stumbled into a nest of robots in the powerhouse, apparently left there by the thoughtful Martian race to prevent entrance to the mysteriously guarded subway station via this route. What was in that station that required so much privacy? Stanton wondered. Something so deadly dangerous that the advanced science of the Martians could not cope with it, but was forced to resort to quarantining the spot where it showed itself? Stanton didn't know the answers, but he was very quiet as a hidden upsurge of memory strove to assert itself. Something that had been in the bobbin-books . . . "The Under-Eaters." That was it. Had they anything to do with this robot *cordon sanitaire*?

The robots had not noticed them, for which all three were duly grateful. Ogden nudged the nearest to him—it happened to be Annamarie—and thrust out a bony finger. "Is *that* what the Mars-Tube looks like from inside?" he hissed piercingly.

As their eyes became acclimated to the gloom—they dared use no lights—the others made out the lines of a series of hoops stretching out into blackness on either side ahead of them. No lights anywhere along the chain of rings; no sound coming from it.

"Maybe it's a deserted switch line, one that was

abandoned. That's the way the Tube ought to look, all right, only with cars going along it," Stanton muttered.

"Hush!" it was Annamarie. "Would that be a car coming—from the left, way down?"

Nothing was visible, but there was the faintest of sighing sounds. As though an elevator car, cut loose from its cable, were dropping down its shaft far off there in the distance. "It sounds like a car," Stanton conceded. "What do you think, Og— Hey! Where's Josey?"

"He brushed me, going toward the Tube. Yes—there he is! See him? Bending over between those hoops!"

"We've got to get him out of there! Josey!" Stanton cried, forgetting about the robots in the light of this new danger. "Josey! Get out of the Tube! There's a train coming!"

The dimly visible figure of the Roëntgenologist straightened and turned toward the others querulously. Then as the significance of that rapidly mounting *hiss-s-s-s* became clear to him, he leaped out of the tube, with a vast alacrity. A split second later the hiss had deepened to a high drone, and the bulk of a car shot past them, traveling eerily without visible support, clinging to and being pushed by the intangible fields of force that emanated from the metal hoops of the Tube.

Stanton reached Josey's form in a single bound. "What were you trying to do, imbecile?" he grated. "Make an early widow of your prospective fiancee?"

Josey shook off Stanton's grasp with dignity. "I was merely trying to establish that that string of hoop was the Mars-Tube, by seeing if the powerleads were connected with the rings. It—uh, it was the Tube; that much is proven," he ended somewhat lamely.

"Brilliant man!" Stanton started to snarl, but Annamarie's voice halted him. It was a very small voice.

"You loudmouths have been very successful in attracting the attention of those animated pile-drivers," she whispered with the very faintest of breaths. "If you will keep your lips zipped for the next little while maybe the robot that's staring at us over the rim of the pit will think we're turbogenerators or something and go away. Maybe!"

Josey swiveled his head up and gasped. "It's there—it's coming down!" he cried. "Let's leave here!"

The three backed away toward the tube, slowly, watching the efforts of the machine-thing to descend the precipitous wall. It was having difficulties, and the three were beginning to feel a bit better, when—

Annamarie, turning her head to watch where she was going, saw and heard the cavalcade that was bearing down on them at the same time and screamed shrilly. "Good Lord—the cavalry!" she yelled. "Get out your guns!"

A string of a dozen huge, spider-shaped robots of a totally new design were charging down at them, running swiftly along the sides of the rings of the Tube, through the tunnel. They carried no weapons, but the three soon saw why—from the ugly snouts of the egg-shaped bodies of the creatures protruded a black cone. A blinding flash came from the cone of the first of the new arrivals; the aim was bad, for overhead a section of the cement roof flared ghastly white and commenced to drop.

Annamarie had her useless paralyzer out and firing before she realized its uselessness against metal beings with no nervous systems to paralyze. She hurled it at the nearest of the new robots in a highly futile gesture of rage.

But the two men had their more potent weapons out and firing, and were taking a toll of the spider-like monstrosities. Three or four of them were down, partially blocking the path of the oncoming others; another was missing all its metal legs along one side of its body, and two of the remainder showed evidence of the accuracy of the Earthmen's fire.

But the odds were still extreme, and the built-in blasters of the robots were coming uncomfortably close.

Stanton saw that, and shifted his tactics. Holstering his heavy blaster, he grabbed Annamarie and shoved her into the Mars-Tube, crying to Josey to follow. Josey came slowly after them, turning to fire again and again at the robots, but with little effect. A quick look at the charge-dial on the butt of his heat-gun showed why; the power was almost exhausted.

He shouted as much to Stanton. "I figured that would be happening—now we run!" Stanton cried back, and the three sped along the Mars-Tube, leaping the hoops as they came to them.

"What a time for a hurdle race!" gasped Annamarie, bounding over the rings, which were raised about a foot from the ground. "You'd think we would have known better than to investigate things that're supposed to be private."

"Save your breath for running," panted Josey. "Are they following us in here?"

Stanton swivelled his head to look, and a startled cry escaped him. "They're following us—but look!"

The other two slowed, then stopped running altogether and stared in wonder. One of the robots had charged into the Mars-Tube—and had been levitated! He was swinging gently in the air, the long metal legs squirming fiercely, but not touching anything.

"How— ?"

"They're metal!" Annamarie cried. "Don't you see— they're metal, and the hoops are charged. They must have some of the same metal as the Tube cars are made of in their construction—the force of the hoops acts on them, too!"

That seemed to be the explanation. . . . "Then we're safe!" gasped Josey, staggering about, looking for a place to sit.

"Not by a long shot! Get moving again!" And Stanton set the example.

"You mean because they can still shoot at us?" Josey cried, following Stanton's dog-trot nonetheless. "But they can't aim the guns—they seem to be built in, only capable of shooting directly forward."

"Very true," gritted Stanton. "But have you forgotten that this subway is in use? According to my calculations, there should be another car along in about thirty seconds or less—and please notice, there isn't any bypath any more. It stopped back a couple of hundred feet. If we get caught here by a car, we get smashed. So—unless you want to go back and sign an armistice with the robots . . . ? I thought not—so we better keep going. Fast!"

The three were lucky—very lucky. For just when it seemed certain that they would have to run on and on until the bullet-fast car overtook them, or go back and face the potent weapons of the guard robots, a narrow crevice appeared in the side of the tunnel wall. The three bolted into it and slumped to the ground.

*CRASH!*

"What was that?" cried Annamarie.

"That," said Josey slowly, "was what happens to a robot when the fast express comes by. Just thank God it wasn't us."

Stanton poked his head gingerly into the Mars-Tube and stared down. "Say," he muttered wonderingly, "when we wreck something we do it good. We've ripped out a whole section of the hoops—by proxy, of course. When the car hit the robot they were both smashed to atoms, and the pieces knocked out half a dozen of the suspension rings. I would say, offhand, that this line has run its last train."

"Where do you suppose this crevice leads?" asked Annamarie, forgetting the damage that couldn't be undone.

"I don't know. The station ought to be around here somewhere—we were running toward it. Maybe this will lead us into the station if we follow it. If it doesn't, maybe we can drill a tunnel from here to the station with my blaster."

Drilling wasn't necessary. A few feet in, the scarcely passable crevice widened into a broad fissure, through which a faint light came from a wall-chart showing the positions and destinations of the trains. The chart was displaying the symbol of a Zeta train—the train that would never arrive.

"Very practical people, we are," Annamarie remarked with irony. "We didn't think to bring lights."

"We never needed them anywhere else on the planet—we can't be blamed too much. Anyway, the code-panel gives us a little light."

By the steady, dim red glow cast by the code-panel, the three could see the anteroom fairly clearly. It was disappointing. For all they could tell, there was no difference between this and any other station on the whole planet. But why all the secrecy? The dead Martians surely had a reason for leaving the guard-robots so thick and furious. But what was it?

Stanton pressed an ear to the wall of the anteroom. "Listen!" he snapped. "Do you hear— ?"

"Yes," said the girl at length. "Scuffling noises—a sort of gurgling too, like running water passing through pipes."

"Look there!" wailed Josey.

"Where?" asked the archaeologist naturally. The dark was impenetrable. Or was it? There was a faint glimmer of light, not a reflection from the code-panel, that shone through a continuation of the fissure. It came, not from a single source of light, but from several, eight or ten at least. The lights were bobbing up and down. "I'd swear they were walking!" marvelled Ray.

"Ray," shrieked the girl faintly. As the lights grew nearer, she could see what they were—pulsing domes of a purplish glow that ebbed and flowed in tides of dull light. The light seemed to shine from behind a sort of membrane, and the outer surfaces of the membrane were marked off with faces—terrible, savage faces, with carnivorous teeth projecting from mouths that were like ragged slashes edged in writhing red.

"Ray!" Annamarie cried again. "Those lights— they're the luminous heads of living creatures!"

"God help us—you're right!" Stanton whispered. The patterns of what he had read in the bobbin-books began to form a whole in his mind. It all blended in—"Under-Eaters," "Fiends from Below," "Raging Glows." Those weirdly cryptic creatures that were now approaching. And—"Good Lord!" Stanton ejaculated, feeling squeamishly sick. "Look at them— they look like human beings!"

\* \* \*

It was true. The resemblance was not great, but the oncoming creatures did have such typically Terrestrial features as hairless bodies, protruding noses, small ears, and so forth, and did not have the unmistakable hourglass silhouette of the true Martians.

"Maybe that's why the Martians feared and distrusted the first Earthmen they saw. They thought we were related to these—things!" Stanton said thoughtfully.

"Mooning over it won't help us now," snapped Annamarie. "What do we do to get away from them? They make me nervous!"

"We don't do anything to get away. What could we do? There's no place to go. We'll have to fight—get out your guns!"

"Guns!" sneered Josey. "What guns? Mine's practically empty, and Annamarie threw hers away!"

Stanton didn't answer, but looked as though a cannonshell had struck him amidships. Grimly he drew out his blaster. "Then this one will have to do all of us," was all he said. "If only these accursed blasters weren't so unmanageable—there's at least an even chance that a bad shot will bring the roof down on us. Oh, well—I forgot to mention," he added casually, "that, according to the records, the reason that the true Martians didn't like these things was that they had the habit of *eating* their victims. Bearing that in mind, I trust you will not mind my chancing a sudden and unanimous burial for us all." He drew the blaster and carefully aimed it at the first of the oncoming group. He was already squeezing the trigger when Josey grabbed his arm. "Hold on, Ray!" Josey whispered. "Look what's coming."

The light-headed ones had stopped their inexorable trek toward the Terrestrials. They were bunched fearfully a few yards within the fissure, staring beyond the three humans, into the Mars-Tube.

Three of the spider-robots, the Tube-tenders, were there. Evidently the destruction of one of their number, and the consequent demolition of several of the hoops, had short-circuited this section of the track so that they could enter it and walk along without fear.

There was a deadly silence that lasted for a matter of seconds. The three from Earth cowered as silently as possible where they were, desirous of attracting absolutely no attention from either side. Then—Armageddon!

The three robots charged in, abruptly, lancing straight for the luminous-topped bipeds in the crevasse. Their metal legs stamped death at the relatively impotent organic creatures, trampling their bodies until they died. But the cave-dwellers had their methods of fighting, too; each of them carried some sort of instrument, hard and heavy-ended, with which they wreaked havoc on the more delicate parts of the robots.

More and more "Raging Glows" appeared from the crevasse, and it seemed that the three robots, heavily outnumbered, would go down to a hard-fought but inevitable "death"—if that word could be applied to a thing whose only life was electromagnetic. Already there were better than a score of the strange bipeds in the cavern, and destruction of the metal creatures seemed imminent.

"Why don't the idiotic things use their guns?" Annamarie shuddered.

"Same reason I didn't—the whole roof might come down. Don't worry—they're doing all right. Here come some more of them."

True enough. From the Mars-Tube emerged a running bunch of the robots—ten or more of them.

The slaughter was horrible—a carnage made even more unpleasant by the fact that the dimness of the cavern concealed most of the details. The fight was in comparative silence, broken only by the faint metallic clattering of the workings of the robots, and an occasional thin squeal from a crushed biped. The cave-dwellers seemed to have no vocal organs.

The robots were doing well enough even without guns. Their method was simply to trample and bash the internal organs of their opponents until the opponent had died. Then they would kick the pulped corpse out of the way and proceed to the next.

The "Hot-Heads" had had enough. They broke and ran back down the tunnel from which they had come. The metal feet of the robots clattered on the rubble of the tunnel floor as they pursued them at maximum speed. It took only seconds for the whole of the ghastly running fight to have traveled so far from the humans as to be out of sight and hearing. The only remnants to show it had ever existed were the mangled corpses of the cave-dwellers, and one or two wrecked robots.

Stanton peered after the battle to make sure it was gone. Then, mopping his brow, he slumped to a sitting position and emitted a vast "Whew!" of relief. "I have seldom been so sure I was about to become dead," he said pensively. "Divide and rule is what I always say—let your enemies fight it out among themselves. Well, what do we do now? My curiosity is sated—let's go back."

"That," said the girl sternly, "is the thing we are most not going to do. If we've come this far we can go a little farther. Let's go on down this tunnel and see what's there. It seems to branch off down farther; we can take the other route from that of the robots."

Josey sighed. "Oh, well," he murmured resignedly. "Always game, that's me. Let's travel."

"It's darker than I ever thought darkness could be, Ray," Annamarie said tautly. "And I just thought of something. How do we know *which* is the other route—the one the robots didn't take?"

"A typical question," snarled Stanton. "So you get a typical answer: I don't know. Or, to phrase it differently, we just have to put ourselves in the robots' place. If you were a robot, where would you go?"

"Home," Ogden answered immediately. "Home and to bed. But these robots took the tunnel we're in. So let's turn back and take the other one."

"How do you know?"

"Observation and deduction. I observed that I am standing in something warm and squishy, and I deduced that it is the corpse of a recent lighthead."

"No point in taking the other tunnel, though," Annamarie's voice floated back. She had advanced a few steps and was hugging the tunnel wall. "There's an entrance to another tunnel here, and it slopes back the way we came. I'd say, offhand, that the other tunnel is just an alternate route."

"Noise," said Stanton. "Listen."

There was a scrabbling, chittering, quite indescribable sound, and then another one. Suddenly, terrific squalling noises broke the underground silence and the three ducked as they sensed something swooping down on them and gliding over their heads along the tunnel.

"What was that?" yelped Josey.

"A cat-fight, I think," said Stanton. "I could hear two distinct sets of vocables, and there were sounds of battle. Those things could fly, glide, or jump—

probably jump. I think they were a specialized form of tunnel life adapted to living, breeding, and fighting in a universe that was long, dark, and narrow. Highly specialized."

Annamarie giggled hysterically. "Like the bread-and-butterfly that lived on weak tea with cream in it."

"Something like," Stanton agreed.

Hand in hand, they groped their way on through the utter blackness. Suddenly there was a grunt from Josey, on the extreme right. "Hold it," he cried, withdrawing his hand to finger his damaged nose. "The tunnel seems to end here."

"Not end," said Annamarie. "Just turns to the left. And take a look at what's there!"

The men swerved and stared. For a second no one spoke; the sudden new vista was too compelling for speech.

"Ray!" finally gasped the girl. "It's incredible! It's *incredible!*"

There wasn't a sound from the two men at her sides. They had rounded the final bend in the long tunnel and come out into the flood of light they had seen. The momentary brilliance staggered them and swung glowing spots before their eyes.

Then, as the effects of persistence of vision faded, they saw what the vista actually was. It was a great cavern, the hugest they'd ever seen on either planet— and by tremendous odds the most magnificent.

The walls were not of rock, it seemed, but of slabs of liquid fire—liquid fire which, their stunned eyes soon saw, was a natural inlay of incredible winking gems.

Opulence was the rule of this drusy cave. Not even so base a metal as silver could be seen here; gold was the basest available. Platinum, iridium, little pools of shimmering mercury dotted the jewel-studded floor of the place. Stalactites and stalagmites were purest rock-crystal.

Flames seemed to glow from behind the walls colored by the emerald, ruby, diamond, and topaz. "How can such a formation occur in nature?" Annamarie whispered. No one answered.

" 'There are more things in heaven and under it—' " raptly misquoted Josey. Then, with a start, "What act's that from?"

It seemed to bring the others to. "Dunno," chorused the archaeologist and the girl. Then, the glaze slowly vanishing from their eyes, they looked at each other.

"Well," breathed the girl.

In an abstracted voice, as though the vision of the jewels had never been seen, the girl asked, "How do you suppose the place is lighted?"

"Radioactivity," said Josey tersely. There seemed to be a tacit agreement—if one did not mention the gems neither would the others. "Radioactive minerals and maybe plants. All this is natural formation. Weird, of course, but here it is."

There was a feeble, piping sound in the cavern.

"Can this place harbor life?" asked Stanton in academic tones.

"Of course," said Josey, "any place can." The thin, shrill piping was a little louder, strangely distorted by echoes.

"Listen," said the girl urgently. "Do you hear what I hear?"

"Of course not," cried Stanton worriedly. "It's just my—I mean our imagination. I can't be hearing what I think I'm hearing."

Josey had pricked his ears up. "Calm down, both of you," he whispered. "If you two are crazy—so am I. That noise is something—somebody—singing Gil-

bert and Sullivan. 'A Wand'ring Minstrel, I', I believe the tune is."

"Yes," said Annamarie hysterically. "I always liked
that number." Then she reeled back into Stanton's
arms, sobbing hysterically.

"Slap her," said Josey, and Stanton did, her head
rolling loosely under the blows. She looked up at
him.

"I'm sorry," she said, the tears still on her cheeks.

"I'm sorry, too," echoed a voice, thin, reedy, and
old; "and I suppose you're sorry. Put down your guns.
Drop them. Put up your hands. Raise them. I really
am sorry. After all, I don't *want* to kill you."

## IV.

They turned and dropped their guns almost immediately, Stanton shrugging off the heavy power-pack
harness of his blaster as Josey cast down his useless
heat-pistol. The creature before them was what one
would expect as a natural complement to this cavern.
He was weird, pixyish, dressed in fantastic points
and tatters, stooped, wrinkled, whiskered, and palely
luminous. *Induced radioactivity*, Stanton thought.

"Hee," he giggled. "Things!"

"We're men," said Josey soberly. "Men like—like
you." He shuddered.

"Lord," marvelled the pixy to himself, his gun not
swerving an inch. "What won't they think of next!
Now, now, you efts—you're addressing no puling
creature of the deep. I'm a man and proud of it.
Don't palter with me. You shall die and be reborn
again—eventually, no doubt. I'm no agnostic, efts.
Here in this cavern I have seen—oh the things I
have seen." His face was rapturous with holy bliss.

"Who are you?" asked Annamarie.

The pixy started at her, then turned to Josey with a questioning look. "Is your friend all right?" the pixy whispered confidentially. "Seems rather effeminate to me."

"Never mind," the girl said hastily. "What's your name?"

"Marshall Ellenbogan," said the pixy surprisingly. "Second Lieutenant in the United States Navy. But," he snickered, "I suspect my commission's expired."

"If you're Ellenbogan," said Stanton, "then you must be a survivor from the first Mars expedition. The one that started the war."

"Exactly," said the creature. He straightened himself with a sort of somber dignity. "You can't know," he groaned, "you never could know what we went through. Landed in a desert. Then we trekked for civilization—all of us, except three kids that we left in the ship. I've often wondered what happened to them." He laughed. "Civilization! Cold-blooded killers who tracked us down like vermin. Killed Kelly, Keogh. Moley. Jumped on us and killed us—like that." He made a futile attempt to snap his fingers. "But not me—not Ellenbogan—I ducked behind a rock and they fired on the rock and rock and me both fell into a cavern. I've wandered—Lord! how I've wandered. How long ago was it, efts?"

The lucid interval heartened the explorers. "Fifty years, Ellenbogan," said Josey. "What did you live on all that time?"

"Moss-fruits from the big white trees. Meat now and then, eft, when I could shoot one of your light-headed brothers." He leered. "But I won't eat you. I haven't tasted meat for so long now . . . Fifty years. That makes me seventy years old. You efts never live for more than three or four years, you don't know how long seventy years can be."

"We aren't efts," snapped Stanton. "We're human beings same as you. I swear we are! And we want to take you back to Earth where you can get rid of that poison you've been soaking into your system! Nobody can live in a radium-impregnated cave for fifty years and still be healthy. Ellenbogan, for God's sake be reasonable!"

The gun did not fall or waver. The ancient creature regarded them shrewdly, his head cocked to one side. "Tell me what happened," he said at length.

"There was a war," said the girl. "It was about you and the rest of the expedition—armed this time, because the kids you left in the ship managed to raise Earth for a short time when they were attacked, and they told the whole story. The second expedition landed, and—well, it's not very clear. We only have the ship's log to go by, but it seems to have been about the same with them. Then the Earth governments raised a whole fleet of rocket ships, with everything in the way of guns and ray-projectors they could hold installed. And the Martians broke down the atomic-power process from one of the Earth ships they'd captured, and they built a fleet. And there was a war, the first interplanetary war in history. For neither side ever took prisoners. There's some evidence that the Martians realized they'd made a mistake at the beginning after the war had been going only about three years, but by that time it was too late to stop. And it went on for fifty years, with rocketships getting bigger and faster and better, and new weapons being developed . . . Until finally we developed a mind-disease that wiped out the entire Martian race in half a year. They were telepathic, you know, and that helped spread the disease."

"Good for them," snarled the elder. "Good for the treacherous, devilish, double-dealing rats . . . And what are you people doing here now?"

"We're an exploring party, sent by the new all-Earth confederation to examine the ruins and salvage what we can of their knowledge. We came on you here quite by accident. We haven't got any evil intentions. We just want to take you back to your own world. You'll be a hero there. Thousands will cheer you—millions. Ellenbogan, put down your gun. Look—we put ours down!"

"Hah!" snarled the pixy, retreating a pace. "You had me going for a minute. But not any more!" With a loud click, the pixy thumbed the safety catch of his decades-old blaster. He reached back to the power pack he wore across his back, which supplied energy for the weapon, and spun the wheel to maximum output. The power-jack was studded with rubies which, evidently, he had hacked with diamonds into something resembling finished, faceted stones.

"Wait a minute, Ellenbogan," Stanton said desperately. "You're the king of these parts, aren't you? Don't you want to keep us for subjects?"

"Monarch of all I survey, eft. Alone and undisputed." His brow wrinkled. "Yes, eft," he sighed, "you are right. You efts are growing cleverer and cleverer—you begin almost to understand how I feel. Sometimes a king is lonely—sometimes I long for companionship—on a properly deferential plane, of course. Even you efts I would accept as my friends if I did not know that you wanted no more than my blood. I can never be the friend of an eft. Prepare to die."

Josey snapped: "Are you going to kill the girl, too?"

"Girl?" cried the pixy in amazement. "What girl?"

His eyes drifted to Annamarie Hudgins. "Bless me," he cried, his eyes bulging. "Why, so he is! I mean, she is! That would explain it, of course, wouldn't it?"

"Of course," said Stanton. "But you're not going to kill her, are you?"

"If she were an eft," mused the pixy, "I certainly would. But I'm beginning to doubt that she is. In fact, you're probably all almost as human as I am. However—" He mistily surveyed her.

"Girl," he asked dreamily, "do you want to be a queen?"

"Yes, sir," said Annamarie, preventing a shudder. "Nothing would give me more pleasure."

"So be it," said the ancient, with great decision. "So be it. The ceremony of coronation can wait till later, but you are now ex officio my consort."

"That is splendid," cried Annamarie, "simply splendid." She essayed a chuckle of pleasure, but which turned out to be a dismal choking sound. "You've—you've made me positively the happiest woman under—der Mars."

She walked stiffly over to the walking monument commemorating what had once been a man, and kissed him gingerly on the forehead. The pixy's seamed face glowed for more reasons than the induced radioactivity as Stanton stared in horror.

"The first lesson of a queen is obedience," said the pixy fondly, "so please sit there and do not address a word to these unfortunate former friends of yours. They are about to die."

"Oh," pouted Annamarie. "You are cruel, Ellenbogan."

He turned anxiously, though keeping the hair-trigger weapon full on the two men. "What troubles you, sweet?" he demanded. "You have but to ask and it shall be granted. We are lenient to our consort."

The royal "we" already, thought Stanton. He wondered if the ancient would be in the market for a coat of arms. Three years of freehand drawing in his high school in Cleveland had struck Stanton as a dead waste up till now; suddenly it seemed that it might save his life.

"How," Annamarie was complaining, "can I be a *real* queen without any subjects?"

The pixy was immediately suspicious, but the girl looked at him so blandly that his ruffles settled down. He scratched his head with the hand that did not hold the blaster. "True," he admitted. "I hadn't thought of that. Very well, you may have a subject. One subject."

"I think two would be much nicer," Annamarie said a bit worriedly, though she retained the smile.

"One!"

"Please—two?"

"One! One is enough. Which of these two shall I kill?"

Now was the time to start the sales-talk about the coat-of-arms, thought Stanton. But he was halted in mid-thought, the words unformed, by Annamarie's astonishing actions. Puckering her brow so very daintily, she stepped over to the pixy and slipped an arm about his waist. "It's hard to decide," she remarked languidly, staring from one to the other, still with her arm about the pixy. "But I think—

"Yes. I think—kill *that* one." And she pointed at Stanton.

Stanton didn't stop to think about what a blaster could do to a promising career as artist by appointment to Mars's only monarch. He jumped—lancing straight as a string in the weak Martian gravity, directly at the figure of the ancient. He struck and bowled him over. Josey, acting a second later, landed on top of him, the two piled onto the pixy's slight figure. Annamarie, wearing a twisted smile, stepped aside and watched quite calmly.

Oddly enough, the pixy had not fired the blaster.

After a second, Stanton's voice came smotheredly from the wriggling trio. He was addressing Josey. "Get up, you oaf," he said. "I think the old guy is dead."

Josey clambered to his feet, then knelt again to examine Ellenbogan. "Heart failure, I guess," he said briefly. "He was pretty old."

Stanton was gently prodding a swelling eye. "Your fault, idiot," he glared at Josey. "I doubt that one of your roundhouse swings touched Ellenbogan. And as for you, friend," he sneered, turning to Annamarie, "you have my most heartfelt sympathies. Not for worlds would I have made you a widow so soon. I apologize," and he bowed low, recovering himself with some difficulty.

"Did it ever occur to you," Annamarie said tautly— Stanton was astounded as he noticed she was trembling with a nervous reaction—"did it ever occur to you that maybe you owe me something? Because if I hadn't disconnected his blaster from the power-pack, you would be—"

Stanton gaped as she turned aside to hide a flood of sudden tears, which prevented her from completing the sentence. He dropped to one knee and ungently turned over the old man's body. Right enough—the lead between power-pack and gun was dangling loose, jerked from its socket. He rose again and, staring at her shaking figure, stepped unsteadily toward her.

Josey, watching them with scientific impersonality, upcurled a lip in the beginnings of a sneer. Then suddenly the sneer died in birth, and was replaced by a broad smile. "I've seen it coming for some time," more loudly than was necessary, "and I want to be the first to congratulate you. I hope you'll be very happy," he said. . . .

A few hours later, they stared back at the heap of earth under which was the body of the late Second Lieutenant Ellenbogan, U.S.N., and quietly made their way toward the walls of the cavern. Choosing a different tunnel mouth for the attempt, they began the long trek to the surface. Though at first Stanton and Annamarie walked hand-in-hand, it was soon arm-in-arm, then with arms around each other's waists, while Josey trailed sardonically behind.

*Epilogue to*
# The Space Merchants

**A** few years after World War II was over, I bought a house in Red Bank, New Jersey, and settled down to write for a living. While I was in the process of doing so, Cyril came east for a visit. He had been living in Chicago and doing news work for a wire service, but that was beginning to get a little stale. So he brought his new family east and we began to collaborate seriously.

I had begun a satirical science-fiction novel about the future of advertising, which Horace Gold wanted to publish in his magazine, *Galaxy*. It was about one-third complete when I showed it to Horace and, because I was still in the process of converting to full-time writing (I had been running my literary agency), I could not see a way of completing it in time to meet Horace's publishing schedule. So I gave the fragment to Cyril and asked if he wanted to? And he said sure.

Cyril wrote the next third, based on the rough notes and ideas I had. For the final third we tried something new. We talked over in general what we thought should happen. Then we flipped a coin. The loser went up to the third floor, where we kept the typewriters and desks, and wrote the first four pages of the conclusion to the novel. Then that one came downstairs, signaled to the other; who then went up and wrote the next four pages. And so on, and so on, turn and about, until the rough draft was finished.

Of course, that "rough draft" was sometimes, oh, boy, you'd better believe it, *rough*. But as drafts go it was really good. It was structurally complete. It needed rewriting, editing, tying together, neatening up—it needed what any manuscript needs to go from preliminary draft to published book. But the hard work was done; and so, for the rest of Cyril's life, when we collaborated (there were six more novels after that one), that was how we did it.

We called the novel *Fall Campaign*, but Horace was having none of that. "The title stinks," he explained, "so I am changing it to *Gravy Planet*." A while later Ian Ballantine agreed to bring it out in book form from his then brand-new publishing company, Ballantine Books, and they wanted to change the name, too. They called it *The Space Merchants*.

*The Space Merchants* caught on to an extent greater than any of us had expected. (Especially greater than had been expected by any of the half-dozen publishing houses that had rejected it before Ian Ballantine came along.) It has stayed in print for more than thirty years, in something around forty languages (Hebrew last year, and now being translated into Chinese).

It was the first novel I ever published. Many writers will testify how unpleasant it is when your first novel disappears without a trace. That's true, but it's not altogether a joy, either, when your first novel does conspicuously better than your second, third and tenth. For a good many years after 1953, as new books came out, I braced myself for the standard review that began, "While not up to the standards of *The Space Merchants*, the new Pohl (or Pohl-Kornbluth, or whatever) is nevertheless . . ." (It took twenty-five years before the standard review began saying, "While not up to the standards of *Gateway*, the new Pohl is nevertheless . . .")

*The Space Merchants* is the story of one Mitch Courtenay, copysmith Star Class, in the employ of Earth's largest advertising agency. As the advertising agencies have taken over the total domination of all human behavior, this means Courtenay is high in the councils of power, far more potent than any mere President of the United States. What spoils it for him is his dawning perception that the ad agencies are despoiling the planet and enslaving the human race. The agency he has been working for, Fowler Schocken Associates, has begun a mammoth campaign to sell the planet Venus to the human race as a sort of virgin Hawaii, ripe for colonization and full of the promise of riches. Of course, it isn't; it's a hell-hole of screeching hurricane winds, waterless and furnace-hot. When Courtenay discovers that his wife, Kathy, is a member of the outlawed underground band of Conservationists, he changes sides. He is helped by the President of the United States, a little man whose principal function is as a figurehead; the President is allowed to address the Congress now and then, though, and uses that opportunity to make it possible for Courtenay to steal the Venus spaceship. With the small band of Conservationists, Courtenay and his wife take off for Venus, where they can start anew.

The novel *The Space Merchants* stops there. So did the original version of the magazine serial, *Gravy*

*Planet*, when we turned it in. But Horace Gold was having none of that, either. "You haven't ended it right," he explained. "You have to show the landing on Venus and what it's like there. So go back to Red Bank, you two, and write a new ending."

So we did as Horace decreed, adding a few thousand words to the serial version. These chapters didn't appear in the book. Nor do they play any part in the long-delayed sequel, *The Merchants' War*, when I got around to writing it thirty years later; they went in a direction I didn't want to take. In fact, they have never been in print anywhere since the final serial installment of *Gravy Planet* came off the newsstands more than three decades ago.

But here they are. . . .

# Gravy Planet

## XX

So we landed on Venus. After the wild excitement wore off I felt like sitting down and writing a postcard to the little man back in Washington:

"Dear Mr. President, now I know what you mean. On special occasions they sometimes let me in, too. Sincerely, Mitchell ('Superfluous') Courtenay."

We torpedoed Venus's billowy cloud layers, roared incandescently down in the tangential orbiting approach, minced the final few hundred meters to the landing—and I discovered that Venus had instantaneously changed me. I wasn't a Star Class Copysmith any more. I wasn't a hero or an indispensable leader.

I was a bum.

They were nice enough about it. They said things like: "No, thanks, I can handle it myself," and, "Would you mind stepping back, Mr. Courtenay?" when what they should have said was: "Get the hell out of the way." And I wondered how long it would take before they began to put it that way.

You know what it's like being a lost soul?

It's wandering through a spaceship with busy people rushing here and there carrying incomprehensible things. It's people talking urgently and efficiently to each other and you understand maybe one word in three. It's offering a suggestion or trying to help and getting a blank stare and polite refusal.

It's Kathy: "Not right now, Mitch darling. Why don't you—" And her voice trailed off because there wasn't any good end to that sentence. The only appropriate, constructive, positive thing I could do was drop dead. But nobody said so. They would carry me on the books, a hero whose brief hour of service rendered, when balanced against the long years that followed, might or might not show a tiny net profit. You never could tell with ex-heroes, but you can't just gas them . . .

They were nice about letting me come along when fourteen of the really important people donned spacesuits and set foot on Venus. (Note for historians: it was completely unceremonious. We just went out the lock into the lee of the ship, anchored by cables. Nobody noticed who of the fifteen was first to step out—and be yanked by the burning wind as far as the cable slack would let him, or her.)

I reached for my wife and the wind sent her bobbing on the end of her cable out of my grasp. Nor did she notice me, a hulking and brutish figure in an oversized suit, trying to claw my way to her along the grab-irons welded to the hull. She had eyes only for the planet I had given her, the orange-lit, sandstorming inferno.

When they reeled us in and we took off our armor, I felt as though I had been flailed with anchor chains from Easter to Christmas. Aching, I turned to Kathy. She was briskly rubbing her surgeon's fingers and conferring with somebody named Bartlow in words that sounded like these: "—then we'll clam the ortnick for seven frames and woutch green until sembril gills?"

"Yes," Bartlow said, nodding.

"Splendid. When the grimps quorn with the fibers, Bronson can fline dimethyloxypropyloluene with the waterspouts—"

I hung around and Kathy finally noticed me with a "Hello, dear" and plunged back into the important stuff. After a while I wandered off. I got in the way of the crews dismantling the ship's internal bulkheads. Then I got in the way of the commissary women, then in the way of the engineers who were already modifying our drive reactor to an AC electric pile. When I got in the way of the medics who were patching up passengers banged around in the landing, I took a sleepy-pill. My dreams were not pleasant.

Kathy was crouched over the desk when I woke up, pawing through stacks of green, pink and magenta-covered folders. I yawned. "You been up all night?"

She said absently, "Yes."

"Anything I can do to help?"

"No."

I rescued one of the folders from the floor. *Medical Supplies Flow Chart, 3d to 5th Colony Year, No Local Provisioning Assumed* was the heading. The one under it covered: *Permissible Reproductive Rate, 10th Colony Year.*

"That's real planning," I said. "Got one covering forecasted life-expectancy of third-generation colonists born of blue-eyed mothers and left-handed fathers?"

"Please, Mitch," she said impatiently. "I've got to

find the planning schedules for the first two months. Naturally we planned far ahead."

I dressed and wandered out to the chowline. The man ahead of me, still wearing the soft padded undershoes that went with donning a heat suit, was telling his friends about Venus. Not more than a tenth of the colonists had seen their new planet close up as yet: he had a large and fascinated audience.

"So we located the spot for the drilling unit," he said. "We moored it to a rock taller than me. We started bracing the unit. What happens? *Plop*. The damn rock explodes."

"Rocks don't explode," objected somebody.

"So I thought too, friend. But it did. Then the wind catches the drill and you should've seen that thing take off. Lucky we hadn't cast off the cables to the ship yet; it'd still been going. As it is, back to the shop. A whole day's work shot."

I listened through the story and the questions.

When he was hurrying off to another incomprehensible job, I said to him: "Wait a minute. I want to talk to you."

"Sure, Mr. Courtenay. What can I do for you?"

"Most of this stuff I don't get, but I understand a rock drill. You're a foreman. Can you put me on your crew?"

"You *sure* you understand a rock drill, Mr. Courtenay? It ain't easy to change a carbide tip out there in the wind. You got to unscrew the camber-flamber and wuldge it to the imbrie before the wind gets it, and that takes—"

There we were again. But this time I said: "I can handle it."

"That's great, Mr. Courtenay. I can use another man. Weiss, I guess you don't know him, he got smacked by a piece of flying something or other, so I'm one short." He measured me with his eye. "You can use his suit. It wasn't hurt a bit."

An ugly little chill went through me. "What about Weiss?"

"The work-suits are too rigid. Something hits you hard, it goes *clang* hard enough to bust your ear-drums, drive your eyes into your head and rupture membranes all through your body. But the suit lives through it. Well, we go out with a replacement drill at 1730, Port Fourteen aft. I'll see you there, Mr. Courtenay."

I was there and proud of it.

The drilling crew was big and tough—shock troops. They knew my name and face, of course, and were reserved. As we got into the armored work-suits, one of them asked apologetically: "Sure you can handle this detail, Mr. Courtenay? It's rough out there—"

I felt my blood pounding with anger I shouldn't put into words. He was only trying to be helpful. There was no use yelling at him that I was a man and could swing my weight with men, that I wasn't just a copysmith and as obsolete as the dinosaur. I nodded and we stepped out.

*Whoosh!* The wind hurled us five yards.

*Crack!* The cables held.

Three seconds outside and I was fighting for breath.

"Goddam it!" I gasped, hating my weakness.

I had forgotten that work-suits were wired for sound. The foreman's voice said inside my helmet: "Mr. Courtenay, please keep the circuit clear for orders. Guire! Slack off! More—hold it! Winters, haul your cable—hold it. Mr. Courtenay, work your way over to Winters and lay hold."

Clawing along the storm-swept rocks, I reached

Winters and grabbed the cable. I wondered dimly if the suit's oxygen supply was functioning, if the dryer was working. It didn't feel as if they were. I could hardly breathe and I was soaked with sweat.

I made a feeble pretense of helping Winters, who had the build of a granite crag, jockey the drill.

It was like flying a kite—if it took five men to fly a kite, and if the kite had to be kept at ground level, and if the kite perpetually threatened to fly you instead of vice versa.

After two minutes outside, my leg and arm muscles were quivering uncontrollably from the mere effort of standing up and keeping balanced. It was the tremor of flexor pulling against extensor, the final fatigue that comes just before you let go, forgetting everything except that you can't keep it up any longer, that you'll die if you keep it up for another split-second.

But I hung on for one minute more, streaming sweat, sobbing air into my lungs and maybe—maybe—helping a little with a few extra foot-pounds of heave-ho on the cable when it was ordered.

And then I let go, a little less than half-conscious, and the wind got me. My cable streamed and I dangled at the end of it, unable to do anything but listen to the voices in my helmet.

"Mr. Courtenay, can you make it back to the ship?"

"He don't answer. He must have blacked out."

"Stinking luck! Almost get the drill positioned and then—damn the stinking luck! Winters, work your way to him and see if he's all right."

"Hell, what can I see? Phone them to reel him in is all we can do."

"Winchman! Reel in Number Five. He's blacked out."

The cable thrummed and I began to scrape along the ground to the port.

And still they talked. "We can do it with four if it kills us, men. You all game?"

I heard the ragged chorus of yesses as I scraped helplessly over the rocks, like a fish on a hook.

"Shouldn't have let him come out at all," one of the crew said.

Shame was crowded out by terror. My suit clanged against something and motion stopped. A rock, I saw dazedly. A big rock. The six ring-bolts to which my cable was lashed began to creak and strain.

The fools at the winch, I realized with clear, pure horror, had not noticed I was snagged.

"Stop!" I screamed into the helmet. But I did not have a phone line through my cable to the ship.

The foreman understood instantly. *"Winchman! Ease off! He's snagged!"* The ring-bolts ceased to strain. "Mr. Courtenay, can you clear yourself or—or should we come to help you?" He was only human. There was bitterness in his voice.

I said rustily: "I can clear myself. Thanks."

But I didn't have to. The big, solid rock I had snagged on began to disappear. I don't mean it vanished, either with or without a thunderclap. Nor did it grow transparent and finally become invisible. But it began to melt from the top, like a ball of string unraveling or like an apple being peeled for a banquet before it's divided into servings—and yet it was something like gradually turning into powder and blowing away. Naturally, it isn't easy to describe.

It was the first Venusian anybody had ever seen.

# XXI

They got me into the ship and patched me up. Kathy didn't tend me in the hospital—she was a surgeon and administrator, and all I had was R.N. stuff like bruises and scrapes, but plenty of them.

In three days I was discharged with the entire hospital staff suspecting I was psychotic. I could go them one better. I *knew* I was.

Item: I would wash and wash, but I never felt clean.

Item: Suicidal tendencies. I wanted to go into the nuclear reactor room so bad I could taste it—and the reactor room was sudden death.

Item: Claustrophobia. The giant ship wasn't big enough for me. I wanted to go outside, into that flailing inferno.

The first night out of the hospital, I sat up in bed waiting and waiting for Kathy to come back from a staff meeting. I was dog-tired, but I didn't dare sleep. I had once found myself halfway to the reactor room before I stubbed my toe and woke up.

She came in, blinking and red-eyed at 0245. "Still awake?" she yawned at me, plumping onto her hammock.

"Kathy," I said hoarsely. "I'm cracking up."

She looked at me without much interest. "Did I ever tell you I read a paper on malingering to the New York Academy of Medicine?"

I got up mechanically and started for the reactor room, grabbed hold of myself, turned around and sat down. I told her where I had been going.

She turned nasty. "Not you. I know you better than most doctors get to know their patients. I also know the exact science of psychiatry and I know that a person with your mental configuration could not possibly have the symptoms you describe. No more than two plus two can equal five. I presume you feel rejected—which, God knows, you have every right to—and are consciously trying to hoodwink me into thinking you're an interesting case that needs my personal attention."

"Bitch," I said.

She was too tired to be angry. "If I thought there were the smallest possible chance that your alleged symptoms are real and do spring from your unconscious, I'd treat you. But there isn't any such chance. I have to conclude that you're consciously trying to divert my energy from the job I have to do. And under the circumstances that is a despicable thing."

"Bitch," I said again, and got up and went out to go to the reactor room.

My feet moved as though they didn't belong to me, and I still felt the dirt on me that no soap and water or alcohol had been able to remove.

She had meant every word of it. She knew her trade. And it *was* an exact science. She thoroughly believed that I couldn't have the symptoms I had. If she'd said it about somebody else, I would have taken her word for it unquestioningly. Only I had the symptoms—

*Or were they symptoms?*

I stopped in the corridor, though my legs wanted to go on carrying me into the reactor room.

AGRONOMY SECTION, a sign over a door said. I went in. There was no microscope. I looked through three more rooms before I found one—and a knife that would do as a scalpel.

I meant only to flick a pinpoint specimen off the

base of my thumb, but in my dull intoxication I gashed a minor blood vessel. I found some reasonably sterile-looking gauze and wound it around my hand.

I dropped the ragged little crumb of meat into the oil-lens objective, tapped it to shake free the bubbles, levered it into a turret chosen at random. There was some difficulty in getting the light source to function—I couldn't make out what I was supposed to do with the knob marked "polarizer"—but finally the stage appeared through the eyepiece, bathed in a greenish glow.

I saw:

Life.

Clustered around the fabric of epidermis that loomed in the eyepiece like a decayed glacier were massive chunks of rock, the random dust particles of any atmosphere, the faint accretion that no washing will completely remove from the human skin. They were featureless, irregular blobs, most of them.

But not all.

Among the dust fragments were a dozen or so living things, sea-urchin-shaped. Under the flaring light of the microscope, they seemed spurred to action. The spines of one touched the spines of another; they flexed and locked. A third blundered into the linked pair, and they became a Laocoön trio.

They were no protozoans or bacilli of Earth. They glowed; they were utterly alien. And as I watched, the trio became six, then ten globes locked together. And at once the character of the action changed: The clustered spheroids seemed to beat their flagella in unison, driving the mass, like eggs trailing from a spawning trout, about the field of vision. Purposefully, the massed ten ran down the other globes and absorbed them, till all were joined.

That was the second time anyone had seen a Venusian.

This time, though, it was with awareness.

*I* didn't want to go into the reactor room. *I* didn't want to go outside. The Venusian did and somehow we had become . . . tangled.

Kathy, with the reflexes of a doctor, woke easily when I shook her shoulder. She stared fixedly at me.

"Come along," I said. "I want to show you something under a microscope. And I can't begin to tell you what it is because you won't believe me until you see it."

"You, with a microscope," she said scornfully.

But she came.

She looked, blinked, looked again. At last, not moving from the eyepiece, she said softly: "Good God! What in the world are they?"

"Now you prepare a slide from my skin," I told her.

She did, in seconds, and stared at it through the microscope. I knew the—cells?—were going through their outlandish linkup behavior.

"I'm sorry, Mitch," she said doubtfully. "Some sort of pathogenic organism, causing a paranoid configuration—" She swallowed. "I didn't mean to be unfair."

"It's all right." Forgiven, she was in my arms. "But they're—it's not a pathogenic organism. It's a Venusian." I told her about the rock that vanished. "Some of it got carried in with me on the suit, I suppose, and got on me, or into me—I don't know. *But I feel intelligence*. I can sort of isolate it, now that I can tell which is it and which is me. I can think of the reactor room in two ways. When it's me thinking, I know it's deadly. When it's *it* thinking, there's—hunger? Yes, I think hunger."

"It lives on plutonium? No, there isn't any on Venus. It has to be manufactured."

I was exploring, thinking of the reactor room, what was in it, what it looked like, what happened there, and noting my—no, its—no, call them *the* reactions that followed.

"Energy," I said softly. "Not material. It wants to be irradiated."

And I thought of the outside. The wind meant nothing to it. The heat meant mild comfort, like air to me or water to a minnow.

But lightning, free electrons and cosmic rays—ah, that was really living!

"Energy," I whispered.

And I thought of the rocks of Venus, the rocks that sometimes exploded and sometimes unwound like balls of string.

"Love," I said almost inaudibly. "Community. The whole that is greater than the sum of its parts. Without hate, without fear—"

Kathy told me later that I pitched forward onto my face in an old-fashioned faint.

# XXII

Well, the grass is still not green. But Kathy and I walked the hundred yards from the ship's skeleton to our hut this morning with only oxygen masks on. The wind was no more than gale force, and it keeps dropping in velocity every week.

Once we found that the Venusians, those incongruous flurries of silicate life, were capable of something resembling thought, we learned what they needed and what they could do.

They needed energy. We gave them energy, from the hot-gas ends of our giant Hilsch tubes. Maxwell's mythical demon picked the hottest molecules from Venus's air and flung them at the Venusians, who rejoicingly sucked them dry of high-level heat and used the energy so they could reproduce even more prolifically to absorb still more energy.

The water roared down from the cooling upper atmosphere like an ocean falling out of the sky. Now we have seas, and the poisoned atmosphere is being locked in chemical bonds with the soil and the rocks.

We've saved a decade at least, the planners say. And the Venusians are doing it for us. They're feasting themselves into famine on the energy we ripped out of the air for them. They'll never vanish completely, of course; as the amount of available energy grows less and less, they'll reduce their numbers and we'll have more and more of the planet for our use, but we'll keep some of them alive out of sheer gratitude.

We cannibalized the ship for our huts and shops, leaving only the giant structural members that we'll be able to work with later—melt them down, I suppose, or cut them up into useful shapes. It's a tidy little community, each couple with a plot of ground and furniture that doesn't have to be rolled or folded out of the way. We're scouting the terrain for sources of metals and minerals, which won't be senselessly scooped out of the ground, manufactured, used and thrown away; they'll be restored to the soil or scrupulously collected and reworked. We can't grow anything yet, but already we have plans for the protection of the rich loam we'll create.

It's a Conservationist world, all right, and it makes

sense . . . you take what you need from the planet and put it back when you're through. On Earth, that's the worst kind of radicalism, of course. Being a copysmith, trained in semantics, I keep wondering how I could get my concepts so tangled that I mistook the epitome of conservatism for wild-eyed sabotage, when I know now that any kind of purposeless destruction is almost physical anguish for a Conservationist.

You don't have to be a prophet to see how Venus is developing into a self-sustaining economy. Kathy figured it out: By the time our first-born is of age, Fowler Schocken's commercials will have come true.

# The Final Stories

**A**fter Cyril's death, and even after I had completed and published the first few stories in this collection (along with one or two not included), I still had a few fragments that I didn't know what to do with. They were too good to throw away, but how to handle them escaped me.

One had to do with fourteenth-century England, one with a parent-teacher's meeting at a school for handicapped children, one was a light-hearted and overpoweringly sexist jape, more like a television sitcom than like anything else Cyril had ever written. On these fragments it took a long time for inspiration to strike—more than ten years.

When I finally figured out what to do with "The Meeting," though, it seemed to me to be worth the wait—not least because it won a Hugo as Best Short Story at the World Science Fiction Convention in Toronto in 1973. It was the first writing Hugo I had ever received (I'd won three as Best Editor), and, what was more important, the only one ever accorded to Cyril. (He had, after all, had the bad judgment to do much of his writing before such awards existed.)

At about the same time, at another convention, I found myself on a panel with Ben Bova and Katherine MacLean, talking about what we might have done if we had been born into an age when science-fiction writing could not exist because the conditions that made it possible were absent. That took care of fourteenth-century England; I went right home and wrote "Mute Inglorious Tam."

The third story, whatever I did, kept turning itself into a science-fiction version of *I Love Lucy*, with all its arrant pat-on-the-head disparagement of The Little Woman. I saw no way of changing that. Finally I took a deep breath, screwed up my courage and let it have its way as "The Gift of Garigolli."

But that is the end of it. Unless some long-lost fragment or completed story turns up (there are a few unaccounted for, but they are no doubt permanently vanished by now), there won't be any more collaborations between Cyril Kornbluth and myself.

I regret this a lot. Working with Cyril Kornbluth was one of the happiest and best parts of my writing career. By the time he died we both had established ourselves as independent writers and undoubtedly further collaborations would have been at best occasional. But they would have been fun. . . .

# Mute Inglorious Tam

On a late Saturday afternoon in summer, just before
the ringing of Angelus, Tam of the Wealdway straightened from the furrows in his plowed strip of Oldfield
and stretched his cracking joints.

He was a small and dark man, of almost pure
Saxon blood. Properly speaking, his name was only
Tam. There was no need for further identification.
He would never go a mile from a neighbor who had
known him from birth. But sometimes he called
himself by a surname—it was one of many small
conceits that complicated his proper and straightforward life—and he would be soundly whipped for it if
his Norman masters ever caught him at it.

He had been breaking clods in the field for fifteen
hours, interrupted only by the ringing of the canoni-
cal hours from the squat, tiny church, and a mouth-
ful of bread and soft cheese at noon. It was not easy
for him to stand straight. It was also not particularly
wise. A man could lose his strip for poor tilth, and
Tam had come close enough, often enough. But there
were times when the thoughts that chased themselves around his head made him forget the steady

221

chop of the wooden hoe, and he would stand entranced, staring toward Lymeford Castle, or the river, or toward nothing at all, while he invented fanciful encounters and impossible prosperings. It was another of Tam's conceits, and a most dangerous one, if it were known. The least it might get him was a cuff from a man-at-arms. The most was a particularly unpleasing death.

Since Salisbury, in Sussex, was flat ground, its great houses were not perched dramatically on crags, like the keeps of robber barons along the Rhine or the grim fortresses of the Scottish lairds. They were the least they could be to do the job they had to do, in an age which had not yet imagined the palace or the cathedral.

In the year 1303 Lymeford Castle was a dingy pile of stone. It housed Sir and Lady Robert Bowen (sometimes they spelled it Bohun, or Beauhun, or Beauhaunt) and their household servants and men-at-arms in very great discomfort. It did not seem so to them particularly. They had before them the housing of their Saxon subjects to show what misery could be. The castle was intended to guard a bridge across the Lyme River: a key point on the high road from Portsmouth to London. It did this most effectively. William of Normandy, who had taken England by storm a couple of centuries earlier, did not mean for himself or his descendants to be taken in the same way on another day. So Lymeford Castle had been awarded to Sir Robert's great-great-great-grandfather on the condition that he defend it, and thereby defend London as well against invasion on that particular route from the sea.

That first Bowen had owned more than stones. A castle must be fed. The castellan and his lady, their household servants and their armed men could not be expected to till the field and milk the cows. The founder of Sir Robert's line had solved the problem of feeding the castle by rounding up a hundred of the defeated Saxon soldiers, clamping iron rings around their necks and setting them to work at the great task of clearing the untidy woods which surrounded the castle. After cleaning and plowing from sunup to sunset the slaves were free to gather twigs and mud, with which they made themselves kennels to sleep in. And in that first year, to celebrate the harvest and to insure a continuing supply of slaves, the castellan led his men-at-arms on a raid into Salisbury town itself. They drove back to Lymeford, with whips, about a hundred Saxon girls and women. After taking their pick, they gave the rest to the slaves, and the chaplain read a single perfunctory marriage service over the filthy, ring-necked slaves and the weeping Salisbury women. Since the male slaves happened to be from Northumbria, while the women were Sussex bred, they could not understand each other's dialects. It did not matter. The huts were enlarged, and next midsummer there was another crop, this time of babies.

The passage of two centuries had changed things remarkably little. A Bowen (or Beauhaunt) still guarded the Portsmouth-London high road. He still took pride in his Norman blood. Saxons still tilled the soil for him and if they no longer had the iron collar, or the name of slaves, they still would dangle from the gallows in the castle courtyard for any of a very large number of possible offenses against his authority. At Runnymede, many years before, King John had signed the Great Charter conferring some sort of rule of law to protect his barons against arbitrary acts, but no one had thought of extending those rights to the serfs.

They could die for almost anything or for nothing at all: for trying to quit their master's soil for greener fields; for failing to deliver to the castle their bushels of grain, as well as their choicest lambs, calves and girl-children; for daring in any way to flout the divine law that made one kind of man ruler and another kind ruled. It was this offense to which Tam was prone, and one day, as his father had told him the day before he died, it would cost him the price that no man can afford to pay, though all do.

Though Tam had never even heard of the Magna Carta, he sometimes thought that a world might sometime come to be in which a man like himself might own the things he owned as a matter of right and not because a man with a sword had not decided to take them from him. Take Alys his wife. He did not mind in any real sense that the men-at-arms had bedded her before he had. She was none the worse for it in any way that Tam could measure; but he had slept badly that night, pondering why it was that no one needed to consult him about the woman the priest had sworn to him that day, and whether it might not be more—more—he grappled for a word ("fair" did not occur to him) and caught at "right"— more right that he should say whose pleasures his property served.

Mostly he thought of sweeter and more fanciful things. When the falconers were by, he sometimes stole a look at the hawk stooping on a pigeon and thought that a man might fly if only he had the wings and the wit to move them. Pressed into driving the castellan's crops into the granary, he swore at the dumb oxen and imagined a cart that could turn its wheels by itself. If the Lyme in flood could carry a tree bigger than a house faster than a man could run, why could that power not pull a plow? Why did a man have to plant five kernels of corn to see one come up? Why could not all five come up and make him five times as fat?

He even looked at the village that was his home, and wondered why it had to be so poor, so filthy and so small; and that thought had hardly occurred even to Sir Robert himself.

In the year 1303 Lymeford looked like this:

The Lyme River, crossed by the new stone structure that was the fourth Lymeford Bridge, ran south to the English Channel. Its west bank was overgrown with the old English oak forest. Its right bank was the edge of the great clearing. Lymeford Castle, hard by the bridge, covered the road and curved northeast to London. For the length of the clearing, the road was not only the king's highway, it was also the Lymeford village street. At a discreet distance from the castle it began to be edged with huts, larger or smaller as their tenants were rich or fecund. The road widened a bit halfway to the edge of the clearing, and there on its right side sat the village church.

The church was made of stone, but that was about all you could say for it. All the wealth it owned it had to draw from the village, and there was not much wealth there to draw. Still, silver pennies had to be sent regularly to the bishop, who in turn would send them on to Rome. The parish priest of Lymeford was an Italian who had never seen the bishop, to whom it had never occurred to try to speak the language and who had been awarded the living of Lymeford by a cardinal who was likewise Italian and likewise could not have described its location within fifty miles. There was nothing unusual in that, and the Italian collected the silver pennies while his largely Norman, but Saxon speaking, locum tenens scraped along on donations of beer, dried fish and the odd occasional calf. He was a dour man who would have been a dreadful one if he had had a field of action that was larger than Lymeford.

Across the street from the church was The Green, a cheerless trampled field where the compulsory archery practice and pike drill were undergone by every physically able male of Lymeford, each four weeks, except in the worst of winter and when plowing or harvest was larger in Sir Robert's mind than the defense of his castle. His serfs would fight when he told them to, and he would squander their lives with the joy a man feels in exercising the one extravagance he permits himself on occasion. But that was only at need, and the fields and crops were forever. He saw to the crops with some considerable skill. A three-field system prevailed in Lymeford. There was Oldfield, east of the road, and the first land brought under cultivation by the slaves two hundred years ago. There was Newfield, straddling the road and marked off from Oldfield by a path into the woods called the Wealdway, running southeast from The Green into the oak forest at the edge of the clearing. There was Fallowfield, last to be cleared and planted, which for the most part lay south of the road and the castle. From the left side of the road to the river, The Mead spread its green acres. The Mead was held in common by all the villagers. Any man might turn his cows or sheep to graze on it anywhere. The farmed fields, however, were divided into long, narrow strips, each held by a villager who would defend it with his fists or his sickle against the encroachment of a single inch. In the year 1303 Oldfield and Newfield were under cultivation, and Fallowfield was being rested. Next year it would be Newfield and Fallowfield farmed, and Oldfield would rest.

While Angelus clanged on the cracked church bell, Tam stood with his head downcast. He was supposed to be praying. In a way he was, the impenetrable rote-learned Latin slipping through his brain like the reiteration of a mantra, but he was also pleasantly occupied in speculating how plump his daughter might become if they could farm all three fields each year without destroying the soil, and at the same time thinking of the pot of fennel-spiced beer that should be waiting in his hut.

As the Angelus ceased to ring, his neighbor's hail dispelled both dreams.

Irritated, Tam shouldered his wooden-bladed hoe and trudged along the Wealdway, worn deep by two hundred years of bare peasant feet.

His neighbor, Hud, fell in with him. In the bastard Midland-Sussex hybrid that was the Lymeford dialect, Hud said, "Man, that was a long day."

"All the days are long in the summer."

"You were dreaming again, man. Saw you."

Tam did not reply. He was careful of Hud. Hud was as small and dark as himself, but thin and nervous rather than blocky. Tam knew he got that from his father Robin, who had got it from his mother Joan—who had got it from some man-at-arms on her wedding night spent in the castle. Hud was always asking, always talking, always seeking new things. But when Tam, years younger, had dared to try to open his untamable thoughts to him, Hud had run straight to the priest.

"Won't the players be coming by this time of year, man?" he pestered.

"They might."

"Ah, wouldn't it be a great thing if they came by tomorrow? And then after Mass they'd make their pitch in The Green, and out would come the King of

England and Captain Slasher and the Turkish Champion in their clothes colored like the sunset, and St. George in his silver armor!"

Tam grunted. " 'Tisn't silver. Couldn't be. If it was silver the robbers in the Weald would never let them get this far."

The nervous little man said, "I didn't mean it *was* silver. I meant it *looked* like silver."

Tam could feel anger welling up in him, drowning the good aftertaste of his reverie and the foretaste of his fennel beer. He said angrily, "You talk like a fool."

"Like a fool, is it? And who is always dreaming the sun away, man?"

"God's guts, leave off!" shouted Tam, and clamped his teeth on his words too late. He seldom swore. He could have bitten his tongue out after he uttered the words. Now there would be confession of blasphemy to make, and Father Bloughram, who had been looking lean and starved of late, would demand a penance in grain instead of any beggarly saying of prayers. Hud cowered back, staring. Tam snarled something at him, he could not himself have said what, and turned off the deep-trodden path into his own hut.

The hut was cramped and murky with wood smoke from its open hearth. There was a smoke hole in the roof that let some of it out. Tam leaned his hoe against the wattled wall, flopped down onto the bundle of rags in the corner that was the bed for all three of the members of his family and growled at Alys his wife: "Beer." His mind was full of Hud and anger, but slowly the rage cooled and the good thoughts crept back in: Why not a softer bed, a larger hut? Why not a fire that did not smoke, as his returning grandfather, who wore a scar from the Holy Land to his grave, had told him the Saracens had? And with the thought of a different kind of life came the thought of beer; he could taste the stuff now, sluicing the dust from his throat; the bitterness of the roasted barley; the sweetness of the fennel. "Beer," he called again, and became aware that his wife had been tiptoeing about the hut.

"Tam," she said apprehensively, "Joanie Brewer's got the flux."

His brows drew together like thunderclouds. "No beer?" he asked.

"She's got the flux, and not for all the barley in Oldfield could she brew beer. I tried to borrow from Hud's wife, and she had only enough for him, she showed me—"

Tam got up and knocked her spinning into a corner with one backhanded blow. "Was there no beer yesterday?" he shouted. "God forgive you for being the useless slut you are! May the Horned Man and all his brood fly away with a miserable wretch that won't brew beer for the husband that sweats his guts out from sunup to sunset!"

She got up cringing, and he knocked her into the corner again.

The next moment there was a solid crack across his back, and he crashed to the dirt floor. Another blow took him on the legs as he rolled over, and he looked up and saw the raging face of his daughter Kate and the wooden-bladed hoe upraised in her hands.

She did not strike him a third time, but stood there menacingly. "Will you leave her alone?" she demanded.

"Yes, you devil's get!" Tam shouted from the floor, and then, "You'd like me to say no, wouldn't you? And then you'd beat in the brains of the old fool that gave you a name and a home."

Weeping, Alys protested, "Don't say that, husband. She's your child, I'm a good woman, I have nothing black on my soul."

Tam got to his feet and brushed dirt from his leather breeches and shirt. "We'll say no more about it," he said. "But it's hard when a man can't have his beer."

"You wild boar," said Kate, not lowering the hoe. "If I hadn't come back from The Mead with the cow, you might have killed her."

"No, child," Tam said uneasily. He knew his temper. "Let's talk of other things." Contemptuously she put down the hoe, while Alys got up, sniffling, and began to stir the peaseporridge on the hearth. Suddenly the smoke and heat inside the hut was more than Tam could bear, and muttering something, he stumbled outside and breathed in the cool air of the night.

It was full dark now and, for a wonder, stars were out. Tam's Crusader grandfather had told him of the great bright nights in the mountains beyond Acre, with such stars that a man could spy friend's face from foe's at a bowshot. England had nothing like that, but Tam could make out the Plow, fading toward the sunset, and Cassiopeia pursuing it from the east. His grandfather had tried to teach him the Arabic names for some of the brighter stars, but the man had died when Tam was ten and the memories were gone. What were those two, now, so bright and so close together? Something about twin peacocks? Twins at least, thought Tam, staring at Gemini, but a thought of peacocks lingered. He wished he had paid closer attention to the old man, who had been a Saracen's slave for nine years until a lucky raid had captured his caravan and set him free.

A distant sound of yelping caught his ear. Tam read the sound easily enough; a vixen and her half-grown young, by the shrillness. The birds came into the plowed fields at night to steal the seed, and the foxes came to catch the birds, and this night they had found something big enough to try to catch them— wolf, perhaps, Tam thought, though it was not like them to come so near to men's huts in good weather. There were a plenty of them in Sir Robert's forest, with fat deer and birds and fish beyond counting in the streams; but it was what a man's life was worth to take them. He stood there, musing on the curious chance that put venison on Sir Robert's table and peaseporridge on his, and on the lights in the sky, until he realized Alys had progressed from abject to angry and must by now be eating without him.

After the evening meal Alys scurried over to Hud's wife with her tale of beastly husbands, and Kate sat on a billet of wood, picking knots out of her hair.

Tam squatted on the rags and studied her. At fifteen years, or whatever she was, she was a wild one. How had it happened that the babe who cooed and grasped at the grass whistle her father made her had turned into this stranger? She was not biddable. Edwy's strip adjoined Tam's in Fallowfield, and Edwy had a marriageable son. What was more reasonable than that Kate should marry him? But she had talked about his looks. True, the boy was no beauty. What did that matter? When, as a father should, he had brushed that aside, she had threatened plainly to run away, bringing ruin and the rope on all of them. Nor would she let herself be beaten into good sense, but instead kicked—with painful accuracy—and bit and scratched like a fiend from hell's pit.

He felt a pang at that thought. Oh, Alys was an

honest woman. But there were other ways the child
of another could be fobbed off on you. A moment of
carelessness when you didn't watch the cradle—it
was too awful to think of, but sometimes you had to
think of it. Everybody knew that Old People liked
nothing better than to steal somebody's baby and slip
one of their own into the cradle. He and Alys had
duly left bowls of milk out during the child's infancy,
and on feast days bowls of beer. They had always
kept a bit of iron by Kate, because the Old People
hated iron. But still. . . .

Tam lighted a rushlight soaked in mutton fat at
what was left of the fire. Alys would have something
to say about his extravagance, but a mood for talking
was on him, and he wanted to see Kate's face. "Child,"
he said, "one Sunday now the players will come by
and pitch on The Green. And we'll all go after Mass
and see them play. Why, St. George looks as if he
wears armor all of silver!"

She tugged at her hair and would not speak or look
at him.

He squirmed uncomfortably on the ragged bed.
"I'll tell you a story, child," he offered.

Contemptuously, "Tell your drunken friend. I've
heard the two of you, Hud and yourself, lying away
at each other with the beer working in you."

"Not that sort of story, Kate. A story no one has
ever told."

No answer, but at least her face was turned toward
him. Emboldened, he began:

" 'Tis a story of a man who owned a great strong
wain that could move without oxen, and in it he—"

"What pulled it, then? Goats?"

"Nothing pulled it, child. It moved by itself. It—"
he fumbled, and found inspiration—"it was a gift
from the Old People, and the man put on it meal and

dried fish and casks of water, and he rode in it to one of those bright stars you see just over church. Many days he traveled, child. When he got there—"

"What road goes to a star, man?"

"No road, Kate. This wain rode in the air, like a cloud. And then—"

"Clouds can't carry casks of water," she announced. "You talk like Edwy's mad son that thinks he saw the Devil in a turnip."

"Listen now, Kate!" he snapped. "It is only a story. When the man came to—"

"Story! It's a great silly lie."

"Neither lie nor truth," he roared. "It is a story I am telling you."

"Stories should be sense," she said positively. "Leave off your dreaming, father. All Lymeford talks of it, man. Even in the castle they speak of mad Tam the dreamer."

"Mad, I am?" he shouted, reaching for the hoe. But she was too quick for him. She had it in her hands; he tried to take it from her, and they wrestled, rock against flame, until he heard his wife's caterwauling from the entrance, where she'd come running, called by the noise; and when he looked around, Kate had the hoe from him and space to use it and this time she got him firmly atop the skull—and he knew no more that night.

In the morning he was well enough, and Kate was wisely nowhere in sight. By the time the long day was through he had lost the anger.

Alys made sure there was beer that night, and the nights that followed. The dreams that came from the brew were not the same as the dreams he had tried so hard to put into words. For the rest of his life, sometimes he dreamed those dreams again, immense dreams, dreams that—had he had the words, and the skill, and above all the audience—a hundred generations might have remembered. But he didn't have any of those things. Only the beer.

# The Gift of Garigolli

Garigolli to Home Base

Greeting, Chief,

I'm glad you're pleased with the demographics and cognitics studies. You don't mention the orbital mapping, but I suppose that's all complete and satisfactory.

Now will you please tell me how we're going to get off this lousy planet?

Keep firmly in mind, Chief, that we're not complainers. You don't have a better crew anywhere in the Galaxy and you know it. We've complied with the Triple Directive, every time, on every planet we've explored. Remember Arcturus XII? But this time we're having trouble. After all, look at the disproportion in mass. And take a look at the reports we've sent in. These are pretty miserable sentients, Chief.

So will you let us know, please, if there has ever been an authorized exception to Directive Two? I don't mean we aren't going to bust a link to comply—if we can—but frankly, at this moment, I don't see how.

And we need to get out of here fast.
*Garigolli*

Although it was a pretty morning in June, with the blossoms dropping off the catalpa trees and the algae blooming in the twelve-foot plastic pool, I was not enjoying either my breakfast or the morning mail.

The letter from the lawyer started, the way letters from lawyers do, with

## RE: GUDSELL VS. DUPOIR

and went on to advise Dupoir (that's me, plus my wife and our two-year-old son Butchie) that unless a certified check arrived in Undersigned's office before close of business June 11th (that was tomorrow) in the amount of $14,752.03, Undersigned would be compelled to institute Proceedings at once.

I showed it to my wife, Shirl, for lack of anything better to do.

She read it and nodded intelligently. "He's really been very patient with us, considering," she said. "I suppose this is just some more lawyer-talk?"

It had occurred to me, for a wild moment, that maybe she had $14,752.03 in the old sugar bowl as a surprise for me, but I could see she didn't. I shook my head. "This means they take the house," I said. "I'm not mad any more. But you won't sign anything for your brother after this, will you?"

"Certainly not," she said, shocked. "Shall I put that letter in the paper-recycling bin?"

"Not just yet," I said, taking off my glasses and hearing aid. Shirl knows perfectly well that I can't hear her when my glasses are off, but she kept on talking anyway as she wiped the apricot puree off Butchie's chin, rescued the milk glass, rinsed the plastic infant-food jar and propped it in the "plastics" carton, rinsed the lid and put it in the "metals" box and poured my coffee. We are a very ecological household. It astonishes me how good Shirl is at things like that, considering.

I waved fruit flies away from the general direction of my orange juice and put my glasses back on in time to catch her asking, wonderingly, "What would they do with our house? I mean, I'm not a demon decorator like Ginevra Freedman. I just like it comfortable and neat."

"They don't exactly want the house," I explained. "They just want the money they'll get after they sell it to somebody else." Her expression cleared at once. Shirl always likes to understand things.

I sipped my coffee, fending off Butchie's attempt to grab the cup, and folded the letter and laid it across my knees like an unsheathed scimitar, ready to taste the blood of the *giaour*, which it kind of was. Butchie indicated that he would like to eat it, but I didn't see that that would solve the problem. Although I didn't have any better way of solving it, at that.

I finished the orange juice, patted Butchie's head and, against my better judgment, gave Shirl the routine kiss on the nose.

"Well," she said, "I'm glad that's settled. Isn't it nice the way the mail comes first thing in the morning now?"

I said it was very nice and left for the bus but, really, I could have been just as happy if Undersigned's letter had come any old time. The fruit flies were pursuing me all the way down the street. They seemed to think they could get nourishment out of me, which suggested that fruit flies were about equal in intelligence to brothers-in-law. It was not a surprising thought. I had thought it before.

> Garigolli to Home Base
> Chief,
> The mobility of this Host is a constant pain in the spermatophore. Now he's gone off on the day-cycle early, and half the crew are still stuck in his domicile. Ultimate Matrix knows how they'll handle it if we don't get back before they run out of group empathy.
> You've got no reason to take that tone, Chief. We're doing a good job and you know it. "Directive One: To remain undetected by sentients on planet being explored." A hundred and forty-four p.g., right? They don't have a clue we're here, although I concede that that part is fairly easy, since they are so much bigger than we are. "Directive Three: Subject to Directives One and Two, to make a complete study of geographic, demographic, ecological and cognitic factors and to transmit same to Home Base." You actually complimented us on those! It's only Directive Two that's giving us trouble.
> We're still trying, but did it ever occur to you that maybe these people don't *deserve* Directive Two?
>
> *Garigolli*

I loped along the jungle trail to the bus stop, calculating with my razor-sharp mind that the distance from the house was almost exactly 14,752.03 centimeters. As centimeters it didn't sound bad at all. As money, $14,752.03 was the kind of sum I hadn't written down since Commercial Arithmetic in P.S. 98.

I fell in with Barney Freedman, insurance underwriter and husband of Ginevra, the Demon Decorator. "Whatever became of Commerical Arithmetic?" I asked him. "Like ninety-day notes for fourteen thousand seven hundred and fifty-two dollars and three cents at six percent simple interest? Although why anybody would be dumb enough to lend anybody money for ninety days beats me. If he doesn't have it now, he won't have it in ninety days."

"You're in some kind of trouble."

"Shrewd guess."

"So what did Shirl do now?"

"She co-signed a note for her brother," I said. "When he went into the drying-out sanitarium for the gold treatment. They wouldn't take him on his own credit, for some reason. They must have gold-plated him. He said the note was just a formality, so Shirl didn't bother me with it."

We turned the corner. Barney said, "Ginevra didn't bother me once when the telephone company—"

"So when Shirl's brother got undrunk," I said, "he told her not to worry about it and went to California. He thought he might catch on with the movies."

"Did he?"

"He didn't even catch cold with the movies. Then they sent us the bill. Fourteen thou—well, they had it all itemized. Three nurses. Medication. Suite. Occupational Therapy. Professional services. Hydrotherapy. Group counseling. One-to-one counseling. Limousine. Chauffeur for limousine. Chauffeur's helper for limousine. Chauffeur's helper's hard-boiled eggs for lunch. Salt for chauffeur's helper's hard-boiled—"

"You're getting hysterical," Barney said. "You mean he just skipped?" We were at the bus stop, with a gaggle of other prosperous young suburbanites.

I said, "Like a flat rock on a pond. So we wrote

him, and of course the letters came back. They didn't
fool around, the Institute for Psychosomatic Adjustment didn't."

"That's a pretty name."

"I telephoned a man up there to explain, when we
got the first letter. He didn't sound pretty. Just tired.
He said my wife shouldn't sign things without reading them. And he said if his house was—something
about joint tenancy in fee simple, he would break his
wife's arm if she was the type that signed things
without reading them, and keep on rebreaking it
until she stopped. Meanwhile they had laid out a lot
of goods and services in good faith, and what was I
going to do about it?"

The bus appeared on the horizon, emitting jet
trails of Diesel smog. We knotted up by the sign. "So
I told him I didn't know," I said, "but I know now.
I'll get sued, that's what I'll do. The Dupoirs always
have an answer to every problem."

Conversation was suspended for fifteen seconds of
scrimmage while we entered the bus. Barney and I
were lucky. We wound up with our heads jammed
affectionately together, not too far from a window
that sucked in Diesel fumes and fanned them at us. I
could see the fruit flies gamely trying to get back to
my ear, but they were losing the battle.

Barney said, "Hey. Couldn't you sell your house to
somebody you trusted for a dollar, and then they
couldn't—"

"Yes, they could. And then we'd both go to jail. I
asked a guy in our legal department."

"Huh." The bus roared on, past knots of other
prosperous young suburbanites who waved their fists
at us as we passed. "How about this. I hope you
won't take this the wrong way. But couldn't there be

some angle about Shirl being, uh, not exactly *competent* to sign any kind of—"

"I asked about that too, Barney. No hope. Shirl's never been hospitalized, she's never been to a shrink, she runs a house and a husband and a small boy just fine. Maybe she's a little impulsive. But a lot of people are impulsive, the man said."

Garigolli to Home Base

Chief,

I think we've got it. These people use a medium of exchange, remember? And the Host doesn't have enough of it! What could be simpler?

With a little modification there are a couple of local organisms that should be able to concentrate the stuff out of the ambient environment, and then—

And then we're off the impaling spike!

*Garigolli*

The bus jerked to a stop at the railroad station and we boiled out in successive rollers of humanity which beached us at separate parts of the platform.

The 8:07 slid in at 8:19 sharp and I swung aboard, my mighty thews rippling like those of the giant anthropoids among whom I had been raised. With stealthy tread and every jungle-trained sense alert I stalked a vacant seat halfway down the aisle on the left, my fangs and molars bared, my liana-bound, flint-tipped *Times* poised for the thrust of death. It wasn't my morning. Ug-Fwa the Hyena, scavenger of the mighty Limpopo, bounded from the far vestibule giving voice to his mad cackle and slipped into the vacant seat. I and the rest of the giant anthropoids glared, unfolded our newspapers and pretended to read.

The headlines were very interesting that morning. PRES ASKS $14,752.03 FOR MISSILE DEFENSE. "SLICK" DUPOIR SOUGHT IN DEFAULT CASE. RUMOR RED PURGE OF BROTHER-IN-LAW. QUAKE DEATH TOLL SET AT 14,752.03. BODY OF SKID ROW CHARACTER IDENTIFIED AS FORMER PROSPEROUS YOUNG SUBURBANITE; BROTHER-IN-LAWS FLIES FROM COAST, WEEPS "WHY DIDN'T HE ASK ME FOR HELP?" FOSTER PARENTS OF "BUTCHIE" DUPOIR OPEN LE-GAL FIGHT AGAINST DESTITUTE MA AND PA, SAY "IF THEY LOVE HIM WHY DON'T THEY SUPPORT HIM?" GLIDER SOARS 14,752.03 MILES. DUPOIR OFF 147.52—no, that was a fly speck, not a decimal point—OFF 14,752.03 FOR NEW LOW, RAILS AND BROTHERS AND LAW MIXED IN ACTIVE TRADING. I always feel you're more efficient if you start the day with the gist of the news straight in your mind.

I arrived at the office punctually at 9:07, late enough to show that I was an executive, but not so late that Mr. Horgan would notice it. The frowning brow of my cave opened under the grim rock front that bore the legend "International Plastics Co." and I walked in, nodding good morning to several persons from the Fourteenth Floor, but being nodded to myself only by Hermie, who ran the cigar stand. Hermie culti-vated my company because I was good for a dollar on the numbers two or three times a week. Little did he know that it would be many a long day before he saw a dollar of mine, perhaps as many as 14,752.03 of them.

Garigolli to Home Base
Further to my last communication, Chief,
We ran into a kind of a setback. We found a suitable organic substrate and implanted a col-ony of modified organisms which extracted gold from environmental sources, and they were per-

forming beautifully, depositing a film of pure
metal on the substrate, which the Host was
carrying with him.

Then he folded it up and threw it in a waste
receptacle.

We're still working on it, but I don't know,
Chief, I don't know.

*Garigolli*

I find it a little difficult to explain to people what I
do for a living. It has something to do with making
the country plastics-conscious. I make the country
plastics-conscious by writing newspaper stories about
plastics which only seem to get printed in neighbor-
hood shopping guides in Sioux Falls, Idaho. And by
scripting talk features about plastics which get run
from 11:55 P.M. to 12:00 midnight on radio stations
the rest of whose programs time is devoted to
public-service items like late jockey changes at Wheel-
ing Downs. And by scripting television features which
do not seem ever to be run on any station. And by
handling the annual Miss Plastics contest, at least up
to the point where actual contestants appear, when it
is taken over by the people from the Fourteenth
Floor. And by writing the monthly page of Plastics
Briefs which goes out, already matted, to 2,000 papers in North America. Plastics Briefs is our best bet
because each Brief is illustrated by a line drawing of
a girl doing something with, to or about plastics, and
her costume is always brief. As I said, all this is not
easy to explain, so when people ask me what I do I
usually say, "Whatever Mr. Horgan tells me to."

This morning Mr. Horgan called me away from a
conference with Jack Denny, our Briefs artist, and
said: "Dupoir, that Century of Plastics Anniversary
Dinner idea of yours is out. The Fourteenth Floor

says it lacks thematic juice. Think of something else for a winter promotion, and think big!" He banged a plastic block on his desk with a little plastic hammer.

I said, "Mr. Horgan, how about this? Are we getting the break in the high-school chemistry textbooks we should? Are we getting the message of polythene to every boy, girl, brother-in-law—"

He shook his head. "That's small," he said, and went on to explain: "By which I mean it isn't big. Also there is the flak we are getting from the nature nuts, which the Fourteenth Floor does not think you are dealing with in a creative way."

"I've ordered five thousand pop-up recycling bins for the test, Mr. Horgan. They're not only plastic, they're *recycled* plastic. We use them in my own home, and I am confident—"

"Confidence," he said, "is when you've got your eyes so firmly fixed on the goal that you trip on a dog-doodie and fall in the crap."

I regrouped. "I think we can convert the present opposition from the ecology movement to—"

"The ecology movement," he said, "is people who love buzzards better than babies and catfish better than cars."

I fell back on my last line of defense. "Yes, Mr. Horgan," I said.

"Personally," Mr. Horgan said, "I *like* seeing plastic bottles bobbing in the surf. It makes me feel, I don't know, like part of something that is going to last forever. I want you to communicate that feeling, Dupoir. Now go get your Briefs out."

I thought of asking for a salary advance of $14,752.03, but hesitated.

"Is there something else?"

"No, Mr. Horgan. Thank you." I left quietly.

Jack Denny was still waiting in my office, doodling

still-life studies of cornucopias with fruits and nuts spilling out of them. "Look," he said, "how about this for a change? Something symbolic of the season, like 'the rich harvest of Plastics to make life more gracious,' like?"

I said kindly, "You don't understand copy, Jack. Do you remember what we did for last September?"

He scowled. "A girl in halter and shorts, very brief and tight, putting up plastic storm windows."

"That's right. Well, I've got an idea for something kind of novel this year. A little two-act drama. Act One: She's wearing halter and shorts and she's taking down the plastic screens. Act Two: She's wearing a dress and putting up the plastic storm windows. And this is important. In Act Two there's wind, and autumn leaves blowing, and the dress is kind of windblown tight against her. Do you know what I mean, Jack?"

He said evenly, "I was the youngest child and only boy in a family of eight. If I didn't know what you meant by now I would deserve to be put away. Sometimes I think I *will* be put away. Do you know what seven older sisters can do to the psychology of a sensitive young boy?" He began to shake.

"Draw, Jack," I told him hastily. To give him a chance to recover himself I picked up his cornucopias. "Very nice," I said, turning them over. "Beautiful modeling. I guess you spilled some paint on this one?"

He snatched it out of my hand. "Where? That? That's gilt. I don't have any gilt."

"No offense, Jack. I just thought it looked kind of nice." It didn't, particularly, it was just a shiny yellow smear in a corner of the drawing.

"Nice! Sure, if you'd let me use metallic inks. If

you'd go to high-gloss paper. If you'd *spend* a few bucks—"

"Maybe, Jack," I said, "it'd be better, at that, if you took these back to your office. You can concentrate better there, maybe."

He went out, shaking.

I stayed in and thought about my house and brother-in-law and the Gudsell Medical Credit Bureau and after a while I began to shake too. Shaking, I phoned a Mr. Klaw, whom I had come to think of as my "account executive" at Gudsell.

Mr. Klaw was glad to hear from me. "You got our lawyer's note? Good, good. And exactly what arrangements are you suggesting, Mr. Dupoir?"

"I don't know," I said openly. "It catches me at a bad time. If we could have an extension—"

"Extensions we haven't got," he said regretfully. "We had one month of extensions, and we gave you the month, and now we're fresh out. I'm really sorry, Dupoir."

"With some time I could get a second mortgage, Mr. Klaw."

"You could at that, but not for $14,752.03."

"Do you want to put me and my family on the street?"

"Goodness, no, Mr. Dupoir! What we want is the sanitarium's money, including our commission. And maybe we want a *little* bit to make people think before they sign things, and maybe that people who should go to the county hospital *go* to the county hospital instead of a frankly de luxe rest home."

"I'll call you later," I said.

"Please do," said Mr. Klaw sincerely.

Tendons slack as the limp lianas, I leafed listlessly through the *dhowani*-bark jujus on my desk, studying Jack Denny's draftsmanship with cornucopias. The yellow stain, I noted, seemed to be spreading, even as a brother-in-law's blood might spread on the sands of the doom-pit when the cobras hissed the hour of judgment.

Mr. Horgan rapped perfunctorily on the doorframe and came in. "I had the impression, Dupoir, that you had something further to ask me at our conference this morning. I've learned to back those judgments, Dupoir."

"Well, sir—" I began.

"Had that feeling about poor old Globus," he went on. "You remember Miss Globus? Crying in the file room one day. Seems she'd signed up for some kind of charm school. Couldn't pay, didn't like it, tried to back out. They wanted their money. Attached her wages. Well. Naturally, we couldn't have that sort of financial irresponsibility. I understand she's a PFC in the WAC now. What was it you wanted, Dupoir?"

"Me, Mr. Horgan? Wanted? No. Nothing at all."

"Glad we cleared that up," he grunted. "Can't do your best work for the firm if your mind's taken up with personal problems. Remember, Dupoir. We want the country plastics conscious, and forget about those ecology freaks."

"Yes, Mr. Horgan."

"And big. Not small."

"Big it is, Mr. Horgan," I said. I rolled up Jack Denny's sketches into a thick wad and threw them at him in the door, but not before he had closed it behind him.

Garigolli to Home Base
Listen Chief,

I appreciate your trying to work out a solution for us, but you're not doing as well as we're doing, even. Not that that's much.

We tried again to meet that constant aura of medium-of-exchange need for the Host, but he destroyed the whole lash-up again. Maybe we're misunderstanding him?

Artifacts are out. He's too big to see anything we make. Energy sources don't look promising. Oh, sure, we could elaborate lesser breeds that would selectively concentrate, for instance, plutonium or one of the uraniums. I don't think this particular Host would know the difference unless the scale was very large, and then, blooie, critical mass.

Meanwhile morale is becoming troublesome. We're holding together, but I wouldn't describe the condition as *good*. Vellitot has been wooing Dinnoliss in spite of the secondary directives against breeding while on exploration missions. I've cautioned them both, but they don't seem to stop. The funny thing is they're both in the male phase.

*Garigolli*

Between Jack Denny and myself we got about half of the month's Plastics Briefs done before quitting time. Maybe they weren't big, but they were real windblown. All factors considered, I don't think it is very much to my discredit that two hours later I was moodily drinking my seventh beer in a dark place near the railroad station.

The bartender respected my mood, the TV was off, the juke box had nothing but blues on it and there was only one fly in my lugubrious ointment, a little man who kept trying to be friendly.

From time to time I gave him a scowl I had copied from Mr. Horgan. Then he would edge down the bar for a few minutes before edging back. Eventually he

got up courage enough to talk, and I got too gloomy
to crush him with my mighty thews, corded like the
jungle-vines that looped from the towering *nganga*-
palms.

He was some kind of hotelkeeper, it appeared.
"My young friend, you may think you have problems, but there's no business like my business. Mortgage, insurance, state supervision, building and
grounds maintenance, kitchen personnel and pur-
chasing, linen, uniforms, the station wagon and the
driver, carpet repairs—oh, God, carpet repairs! No
matter how many ash trays you put around, you
know what they do? They steal the ashtrays. Then
they stamp out cigarettes on the carpets." He began
to weep.

I told the bartender to give him another. How
could I lose? If he passed out I'd be rid of him. If he
recovered I would have his undying, doglike affec-
tion for several minutes, and what kind of shape was
I in to sneer at that?

Besides, I had worked out some pretty interesting
figures. "Did you know," I told him, "that if you
spend $1.46 a day on cigarettes, you can save
$14,752.03 by giving up smoking for 10,104 and a
quarter days?"

He wasn't listening, but he wasn't weeping any
more either. He was just looking lovingly at his
vodka libre, or whatever it was. I tried a different
tack. "When you see discarded plastic bottles bobbing in the surf," I asked, "does it make you feel like
part of something grand and timeless that will go on
forever?"

He glanced at me with distaste, then went back to
adoring his drink. "Or do you like buzzards better
than babies?" I asked.

"They're all babies," he said. "Nasty, smelly, upchucking babies."

"Who are?" I asked, having lost the thread. He shook his head mysteriously, patted his drink and tossed it down.

"Root of most evil," he said, swallowing. Then, affectionately, "Don't know where I'd be with it, don't know where I'd be without it."

He appeared to be talking about booze. "On your way home, without it?" I suggested.

He said obscurely, "Digging ditches, without it." Then he giggled. "Greatest business in the world! But oh! the worries! The competition! And when you come down to it it's just aversion, right?"

"I can see you have a great aversion to liquor," I said politely.

"No, stupid! The *guests*."

Stiffly I signaled for Number Eight, but the bartender misunderstood and brought another for my friend, too. I said, "You have an aversion to the guests?"

He took firm hold on the bar and attempted to look squarely into my eyes, but wound up with his left eye four inches in front of my left eye and both our right eyes staring at respective ears. "The *guests* must be made to feel an aversion to *alcohol*," he said. "Secret of the whole thing. Works. Sometimes. But oh! it costs."

Like the striking fangs of Nag, the cobra, faster than the eye can follow, my trained reflexes swept the beer up to my lips. I drank furiously, scowling at him. "You mean to say you run a drunk farm?" I shouted.

He was shocked. "My boy! No need to be vulgar. An 'institute,' eh? Let's leave the aversion to the drunks."

"I have to tell you, sir," I declared, "that I have a personal reason for despising all proprietors of such institutions!"

He began to weep again. "You, too! Oh, the general scorn."

"In my case, there is nothing general—"

"—the hatred! The unthinking contempt. And for what?"

I snarled. "For your blood-sucking ways."

"Blood, old boy?" he said, surprised. "No, nothing like that. We don't use blood. We use gold, yes, but the gold cure's old hat. Need new gimmick. Can't use silver, too cheap. Really doesn't matter what you say you use. All aversion—drying them out, keeping them comfy and aversion. But no blood."

He wiggled his fingers for Number Nine. Moodily I drank, glaring at him over my glass.

"In the wrong end of it, I sometimes think," he went on meditatively, staring with suspicious envy at the bartender. "*He* doesn't have to worry. Pour it out, pick up the money. No concern about expensive rooms standing idle, staff loafing around picking their noses, overhead going on, going on—you wouldn't be*lieve* how it goes on, whether the guests are there to pay for it or not—"

"Hah," I muttered.

"You've simply no idea what I go through," he sobbed. "And then they won't pay. No, really. Fellow beat me out of $14,752.03 just lately. I'm taking it out of the co-signer's hide, of course, but after you pay the collection agency, what's the profit?"

I choked on the beer, but he was too deep in sorrow to notice.

Strangling, I gasped, "Did you say fourteen thousand—?"

He nodded. "Seven hundred and fifty-two dollars,

yes. And three cents. Astonishes you, doesn't it, the deadbeats in this world?"

I couldn't speak.

"You wouldn't think it," he mourned. "All those salaries. All those rooms. The hydrotherapy tubs. The *water* bill."

I shook my head.

"Probably you think my life's a bowl of roses, hey?"

I managed to pry my larynx open enough to wheeze, "Up to this minute, I did. You've opened my eyes."

"Drink to that," he said promptly. "Hey, barman!"

But before the bartender got there with Number Ten the little man hiccoughed and slid melting to the floor, like a glacier calving into icebergs.

The bartender peered over at him. "Every *damn* night," he grumbled. "And who's going to get him home this time?"

My mind working as fast as *Ngo*, the dancing spider, spinning her web, I succeeded in saying, "Me. Glad to oblige. Never fear."

Garigolli to Home Base
Chief,

All right, I admit we haven't been exactly 144 p.g. on this project, but there's no reason for you to get loose. Reciting the penalties for violating the Triple Directive is uncalled-for.

Let me point out that there has been no question at any time of compliance with One or Three. And even Directive Two, well, we've done what we could. "To repay sentients in medium suitable to them for information gained." These sentients are tricky, Chief. They don't seem to empathize, really. See our reports. They often take without giving in return among themselves, and it seems to me that under the circumstances a certain modification of Directive Two would have been quite proper.

But I am not protesting the ruling. Especially since you've pointed out it won't do any good. When I get old and skinny enough to retire to a sling in Home Base I guess I'll get that home-base mentality too, but way out here on the surface of the exploration volume it looks different, believe me.

And what is happening with the rest of our crew back at Host's domicile I can't even guess. They must be nearly frantic by now.

                                                    *Garigolli*


There was some discussion with a policeman he wanted to hit (apparently under the impression that the cop was his night watchman playing hookey), but I finally got the little man to the Institute for Psychosomatic Adjustment.

The mausoleum that had graduated my brother-in-law turned out to be three stories high, with a sun porch and a slate roof and bars on the ground-floor bay windows. It was not all that far from my house. Shirl had been pleased about that, I remembered. She said we could visit her brother a lot there, and in fact she had gone over once or twice on Sundays, but me, I'd never set eyes on the place before.

Dagger-sharp fangs flecking white spume, none dared dispute me as I strode through the great green corridors of the rain forest. Corded thews rippling like pythons under my skin, it was child's play to carry the craven jackal to his lair. The cabbie helped me up the steps with him.

The little man, now revealed as that creature who in anticipation had seemed so much larger and hairier, revived slightly as we entered the reception hall. "Ooooh," he groaned. "Watch the bouncing, old boy. That door. My office. Leather couch. Much obliged."

I dumped him on the couch, lit a green-shaded lamp on his desk, closed the door and considered.

Mine enemy had delivered himself into my power. All I had to do was seize him by the forelock. I seemed to see the faces of my family—Shirl's smiling sweetly, Butchie's cocoa-overlaid-with-oatmeal— spurring me on.

There had to be a way.

I pondered. Life had not equipped me for this occasion. Raffles or Professor Moriarity would have known what to do at once, but, ponder as I would, I couldn't think of anything to do except to go through the drawers of his desk.

Well, it was a start. But it yielded very little. Miscellaneous paper clips and sheaves of letterheads, a carton of cigarettes of a brand apparently flavored with rice wine and extract of vanilla, part of a fifth of Old Rathole and five switchblade knives, presumably taken from the inmates. There was also $6.15 in unused postage stamps, but I quickly computed that, even if I went to the trouble of cashing them in, that would leave me $14,745.88 short.

Of Papers to Burn there were none.

All in all, the venture was a bust. I wiped out a water glass with one of the letterheads (difficult, because they were of so high quality that they seemed likelier to shatter than to wad up), and forced down a couple of ounces of the whiskey (difficult, because it was of so low).

Obviously anything of value, like for instance co-signed agreements with brothers-in-law, would be in a safe, which itself would probably be in the offices of the Gudsell Medical Credit Bureau. Blackmail?

But there seemed very little to work with, barring one or two curious photographs tucked in among the envelopes. Conceivably I could cause him some slight embarrassment, but nowhere near $14,752.03 worth. I had not noticed any evidence of Red espionage that might put the little man (whose name, I learned from his letterhead, was Bermingham) away for 10,104 and a quarter days, while I saved up the price of reclaiming our liberty.

There seemed to be only one possible thing to do.

Eyes glowing like red coals behind slitted lids, I walked lightly on velvet-soft pads to the *kraal* of the witch-man. He was snoring with his mouth open. Totally vulnerable to his doom.

Only, how to inflict it?

It is not as easy as one might think to murder a person. Especially if one doesn't come prepared for it. Mr. Horgan doesn't like us to carry guns at the office, and heaven knows what Shirl would do with one if I left it around home. Anyway, I didn't have one.

Poison was a possibility. The Old Rathole suggested itself. But we'd already tried that, hadn't we?

I considered the switchblade knives. There was a technical problem. Would *you* know where the heart is? Granted, it had to be inside his chest somewhere, and sooner or later I could find it. But what would I say to Mr. Bermingham after the first three or four exploratory stabs woke him up?

The only reasonably efficient method I could think of to insure Mr. Bermingham's decease was to burn the place down with him in it. Which, I quickly perceived, meant with whatever cargo of drying-out drunks the Institute now possessed in it too, behind those barred windows.

At this point I came face to face with myself.

I wasn't going to kill anybody. I wasn't going to steal any papers.

What I was going to do was, I was going to let Mr. Klaw's lawyers go ahead and take our house, because I just didn't know how to do anything else. I hefted the switchblades in my hand, threw them against the wall and poured myself another slug of Mr. Bermingham's lousy whiskey, wishing it would kill me right there and be a lesson to him.

Garigolli to Home Base
Now, don't get excited, Chief,
But we have another problem.

Before I get into it, I would like to remind you of a couple of things. First, I was against exploring this planet in the first place, remember? I said it was going to be very difficult, on the grounds of the difference in mass between its dominant species and us. I mean, really. Here we are fighting member to member against dangerous beasts all the time, and the beasts, to the Host and his race, are only microorganisms that live unnoticed in their circulatory systems, their tissues, their food and their environment. Anybody could tell that this was going to be a tough assignment, if not an impossible one.

Then there's the fact that this Host moves around so. I told you some of our crew got left in his domicile. Well, we've timed this before, and almost always he returns within 144 or 216 time-units—at most, half of one of his planet's days. It's pretty close to critical, but our crew is tough and they can survive empathy-deprival that long. Only this time he has been away, so far, nearly 432 time-units. It's bad enough for those of us who have been with him. The ones who were cut off back at his domicile must have been through the tortures of the damned.

Two of them homed in on us to report just a few time-units ago, and I'm afraid you're not going to like what's happened. They must have been pretty panicky. They decided to try meeting the Second Directive themselves. They modified some microorganisms to provide some organic chemicals they thought the Host might like.

Unfortunately the organisms turned out to have an appetite for some of the Host's household artifacts, and they're pretty well demolished. So we not only haven't *given* him anything to comply with Directive Two, we've *taken* something from him. And in the process maybe we've called attention to ourselves.

I'm giving it to you arced, Chief, because I know that's how you'd like it. I accept full responsibility.

Because I don't have any choice, do I?
                                        *Garigolli*


"What the Hell," said the voice of Mr. Bermingham, from somewhere up there, "are you doing in my office?"

I opened my eyes, and he was quite right. I was in Mr. Bermingham's office. The sun was streaming through Mr. Bermingham's Venetian blinds, and Mr. Bermingham was standing over me with a selection of the switchblade knives in his hands.

I don't know how Everyman reacts to this sort of situation. I guess I ran about average. I pushed myself up on one elbow and blinked at him.

"Spastic," he muttered to himself. "Well?"

I cleared my throat. "I, uh, I think I can explain this."

He was hung over and shaking. "Go ahead! Who the devil are you?"

"Well, my name is Dupoir."

"I don't mean what's your name, I mean— Wait a minute. Dupoir?"

"Dupoir."

"As in $14,752.03?"

"That's right, Mr. Bermingham."

"You!" he gasped. "Say, you've got some nerve coming here this way. I ought to teach you a lesson."

I scrambled to my feet. Mighty thews rippling, I tossed back my head and bellowed the death challenge of the giant anthropoids with whom I had been raised.

Bermingham misunderstood. It probably didn't sound like a death challenge to him. He said anxiously, "If you're going to be sick, go out there and do it. Then we're going to straighten this thing out."

I followed his pointing finger. There on one side of the foyer was the door marked *Staff Washroom,* and on the other the door to the street through which I had carried him. It was only the work of a second to decide which to take. I was out the door, down the steps, around the corner and hailing a fortuitous cab before he could react.

By the time I got to the house that Mr. Klaw wanted so badly to take away from us it was 7:40 on my watch. There was no chance at all that Shirl would still be asleep. There was not any very big chance that she had got to sleep at all that night, not with her faithful husband for the first time in the four years of our marriage staying out all night without warning, but no chance at all that she would be still in bed. So there would be explaining to do. Nevertheless I insinuated my key into the lock of the back door, eased it open, slipped ghost-like through and gently closed it behind me.

I smelled like a distillery, I noticed, but my keen, jungle-trained senses brought me no other message. No one was in sight or sound. Not even Butchie was either chattering or weeping to disturb the silence.

I slid silently through the mud-room into the half-bath where I kept a spare razor. I spent five minutes trying to convert myself into the image of a prosperous young executive getting ready to be half an hour late at work, but it was no easy job. There was nothing but soap to shave with, and Butchie had knocked it into the sink. What was left was a blob of jelly, sculpted into a crescent where the dripping tap had eroded it away. Still I got clean, more or less, and shaved, less.

I entered the kitchen, and then realized that my jungle-trained senses had failed to note the presence of a pot of fresh coffee perking on the stove. I could hear it plainly enough. Smelling it was more difficult; its scent was drowned by the aroma of cheap booze that hung in the air all around me.

So I turned around and yes, there was Shirl on the stairway, holding Butchie by one hand like Maureen O'Sullivan walking Cheeta. She wore an expression of unrelieved tragedy.

It was clearly necessary to give her an explanation at once, whether I had one or not. "Honey," I said, "I'm *sorry*. I met this fellow I hadn't seen in a long time, and we got to talking. I know we should have called. But by the time I realized the time it was so late I was afraid I'd wake you up."

"You can't wear that shirt to the office," she said woefully. "I ironed your blue and gray one with the white cuffs. It's in the closet."

I paused to analyze the situation. It appeared she wasn't angry at all, only upset—which, as any husband of our years knows, is 14,752.03 times worse. In spite of the fact that the reek of booze was making me giddy and fruit flies were buzzing around Shirl's normally immaculate kitchen, I knew what I had to do. "Shirl," I said, falling to one knee, "I apologize."

That seemed to divert her. "Apologize? For what?"

"For staying out all night."

"But you explained all that. You met this fellow you hadn't seen in a long time, and you got to talking. By the time you realized the time it was so late you were afraid you'd wake me up."

"Oh, Shirl," I cried, leaping to my feet and crushing her in my mighty thews. I would have kissed her, but the reek of stale liquor seemed even stronger. I was afraid of what close contact might do, not to mention its effect on Butchie, staring up at me with a thumb and two fingers in his mouth. We Dupoirs never do anything by halves.

But there was a tear in her eye. She said, "I watched Butchie, honestly I did. I always do. When he broke the studio lamp I was watching every minute, remember? He was just too fast for me."

I didn't have any idea what she was talking about. That is not an unfamiliar situation in our house, and I have developed a technique for dealing with it. "What?" I asked.

"He was too fast for me," Shirl said woefully. "When he dumped his vitamins into his raisins and oatmeal I was right there. I went to get some paper napkins, and that was when he did it. But how could I know it would ruin the plastics bin?"

I went into Phase Two. "What plastics bin?"

"*Our* plastics bin." She pointed. "Where Butchie threw the stuff."

At once I saw what she meant. There was a row of four plastic popup recycling bins in our kitchen, one for paper, one for plastics, one for glass and one for metals. They were a credit to us, and to Mr. Horgan and to the Fourteenth Floor. However, the one marked "plastics" was not a credit to anyone any more. It had sprung a leak. A colorless fluid was oozing out of the bottom of it and, whatever it was, it was deeply pitting the floor tiles.

I bent closer and realized where the reek of stale booze was coming from: out of the juices that were seeping from our plastics bin.

"What the devil?" I asked.

Shirl said thoughtfully, "If vitamins can do that to plastic, what do you suppose they do to Butchie's insides?"

"It isn't the vitamins. I know that much." I reached in and hooked the handle of what had been a milk jug, gallon size. It was high-density polythene and about 400 percent more indestructible than Mount Rushmore. It was exactly the kind of plastic jug that people who loved buzzards better than babies have been complaining about finding bobbing around the surf of their favorite bathing beaches, all the world over.

Indestructible or not, it was about 90 percent destroyed. What I pulled out was a handle and part of a neck. The rest drizzled off into a substance very like the stuff I had shaved with. Only that was soap, which one expects to dissolve from time to time. High-density polythene one does not.

The fruit flies were buzzing around me, and everything was very confusing. I was hardly aware that the front doorbell had rung until I noticed that Shirl had gone to answer it.

What made me fully aware of this was Mr. Bermingham's triumphant roar: "Thought I'd find you here, Dupoir! And who are these people—your confederates?"

Bermingham had no terrors for me. I was past that point. I said, "Hello, Mr. Bermingham. This confederate is my wife, the littler one here is my son. Shirl, Butchie—Mr. Bermingham. Mr. Bermingham's the one who is going to take away our house."

Shirl said politely, "You must be tired, Mr. Bermingham. I'll get you a cup of coffee."

Garigolli to Home Base
Chief,

I admit it, we've excreted this one out beyond redemption. Don't bother to reply to this. Just write us off.

I could say that it wasn't entirely the fault of the crew members who stayed behind in the Host's domicile. They thought they had figured out a way to meet Directive Two. They modified some organisms—didn't even use bacteria, just an enzyme that hydrated polythene into what they had every reason to believe was a standard food substance, since the Host had been observed to ingest it with some frequency. There is no wrong-doing there, Chief. Alcohols are standard foods for many organic beings, as you know. And a gift of food has been held to satisfy the second Directive. And add to that they were half out of their plexuses with empathy deprivation.

Nevertheless I admit the gift failed in a fairly basic way, since it seems to have damaged artifacts the Hosts hold valuable.

So I accept the responsibility, Chief. Wipe this expedition off the records. We've failed, and we'll never see our home breeding-slings again.

Please notify our descendants and former co-parents and, if you can, try to let them think we died heroically, won't you?

*Garigolli*

Shirl has defeated the wrath of far more complex creatures than Mr. Bermingham by offering them coffee—me, for instance. While she got him the clean cup and the spoon and the milk out of the pitcher in the refrigerator, I had time to think.

Mr. Horgan would be interested in what had happened to our plastics Eco-Bin. Not only Mr. Horgan. The Fourteenth Floor would be interested. The ecology freaks themselves would be interested, and maybe would forget about liking buzzards better than babies long enough to say a good word for International Plastics Co.

I mean, this was *significant*. It was big, by which I mean it wasn't little. It was a sort of whole new horizon for plastics. The thing about plastics, as everyone knows, is that once you convert them into trash they *stay* trash. Bury a maple syrup jug in your back yard and five thousand years from now some descendant operating a radar-controlled peony-planter from his back porch will grub it up as shiny as new. But the gunk in our Eco-Bin was making these plastics, or at least the polythene parts of them, biodegradable.

What was the gunk? I had no idea. Some random chemical combination between Butchie's oatmeal and his vitamins? I didn't care. It was there, and it worked. If we could isolate the stuff, I had no doubt that the world-famous scientists who gave us the plastic storm window and the popup Eco-Bin could duplicate it. And if we could duplicate it we could sell it to hard-pressed garbagemen all over the world. The Fourteenth Floor would be very pleased.

With me to think was ever to act. I rinsed out one of Butchie's baby-food jars in the sink, scraped some of the stickiest parts of the melting plastic into it and capped it tightly. I couldn't wait to get it to the office.

Mr. Bermingham was staring at me with his mouth open. "Good Lord," he muttered, "playing with filth at his age. What psychic damage we wreak with bad early toilet training."

I had lost interest in Mr. Bermingham. I stood up and told him, "I've got to go to work. I'd be happy to walk you as far as the bus."

"You aren't going anywhere, Dupoir! Came here to talk to you. Going to do it, too. Behavior was absolutely inexcusable, and I demand— Say, Dupoir, you don't have a drink anywhere about the house, do you?"

"More coffee, Mr. Bermingham?" Shirl said politely. "I'm afraid we don't have anything stronger to offer you. We don't keep alcoholic beverages here, or at least not very long. Mr. Dupoir drinks them."

"Thought so," snarled Bermingham. "Recognize a drunk when I see one: shifty eyes, irrational behavior, duplicity—oh, the duplicity! Got all the signs."

"Oh, he's not like my brother, really," Shirl said thoughtfully. "My husband doesn't go out breaking into liquor stores when he runs out, you know. But I don't drink, and Butchie doesn't drink, and so about all we ever have in the house is some cans of beer, and there aren't any of those now."

Bermingham looked at her with angry disbelief. "You too! I *smell* it," he said. "You going to tell me I don't know what good old ethyl alcohol smells like?"

"That's the bin, Mr. Bermingham. It's a terrible mess, I know."

"Funny place to keep the creature," he muttered to himself, dropping to his knees. He dipped a finger into the drippings, smelled it, tasted it and nodded. "Alcohol, all right. Add a few congeners, couple drops of food coloring, and you've got the finest Chivas Regal a bellboy ever sold you out of a bottle with the tax stamp broken." He stood up and glared at me. "What's the matter with you, Dupoir? You not only don't pay your honest debts, you don't want to pay the bartenders either?"

I said, "It's more or less an accident."

"Accident?"

Then illumination struck. "Accident you should find us like this," I corrected. "You see, it's a secret new process. We're not ready to announce it yet. Making alcohol out of old plastic scraps."

He questioned Shirl with his eyes. Getting her consent, he poured some of Butchie's baby-food orange juice into a glass, scooped in some of the drippings from the bin, closed his eyes and tasted. "Mmm," he said judiciously. "Sell it for vodka just the way it stands."

"Glad to have an expert opinion," I said. "We think there's millions in it."

He took another taste. "Plastic scraps, you say? Listen, Dupoir. Think we can clear all this up in no time. That fool Klaw, I've told him over and over, ask politely, don't make trouble for people. But no, he's got that crazy lawyer's drive for revenge. Apologize for him, old boy, I really do apologize for him. Now look," he said, putting down the glass to rub his hands. "You'll need help in putting this process on the market. Business acumen, you know? Wise counsel from man of experience. Like me. And capital. Can help you there. I'm loaded."

Shirl put in, "Then what do you want our house for?"

"House? My dear Mrs. Dupoir," cried Mr. Bermingham, laughing heartily, "I'm not going to take your house! Your husband and I will work out the details in no time. Let me have a little more of that delightful orange juice and we can talk some business."

Garigolli to Home Base
Joy, joy
Chief!
Cancel all I said. We've met Directive Two, the Host is happy, and we're on our way Home!
Warm up the breeding slings, there's going to be a hot time in the old hammocks tonight.
*Garigolli*

Straight as the flight of Ung-Glitch, the soaring vulture, that is the code of the jungle. I was straight with Mr. Bermingham. I didn't cheat him. I made a handshake deal with him over the ruins of our Econ-Bin, and honored it when we got to his lawyers. I traded him 40 percent of the beverage rights to the stuff that came out of our bin, and he wrote off that little matter of $14,752.03.

Of course, the beverage rights turned out not to be worth all that much, because the stuff in the bin was organic and alive and capable of reproduction, and it did indeed reproduce itself enthusiastically. Six months later you could buy a starter drop of it for a quarter on any street corner, and what that has done to the vintners of the world you know as well as I do. But Bermingham came out ahead. He divided his 40 percent interest into forty parts and sold them

for $500 each to the alumni of his drunk tank. And
Mr. Horgan—

Ah, Mr. Horgan.

Mr. Horgan was perched on my doorframe like
Ung-Glitch awaiting a delivery of cadavers for dinner
when I arrived that morning, bearing my little glass
jar before me like the waiting line in an obstetrician's
office. "You're late, Dupoir," he pointed out. "Troubles me, that does. Do you remember Metcalf? Tall,
blonde girl that used to work in Accounts Receiv-
able? Never could get in on time, and—"

"Mr. Horgan," I said, "look." And I unscrewed my
baby-food jar and dumped the contents on an unpopped
pop-up Econ-Bin. It took him a while to see what was
happening, but once he saw he was so impressed he
forgot to roar.

And, yes, the Fourteenth Floor was very pleased.

There wasn't any big money in it. We couldn't sell
the stuff, because it was so happy to give itself away
to everyone in the world. But it meant a promotion
and a raise. Not big. But not really little, either.
And, as Mr. Horgan said, "I *like* the idea of helping
to eliminate all the litter that devastates the land-
scape. It makes me feel, I don't know, like part of
something clean and natural."

And so we got along happily as anything—happily,
anyway, until the time Shirl bought the merry-go-
round.

# The Meeting

Harry Vladek was too large a man for his Volkswagen, but he was too poor a man to trade it in, and as things were going he was going to stay that way a long time. He applied the brakes carefully ("Master cylinder's leaking like a sieve, Mr. Vladek; what's the use of just fixing up the linings?"—but the estimate was a hundred and twenty-eight dollars, and where was it going to come from?) and parked in the neatly graveled lot. He squeezed out of the door, the upsetting telephone call from Dr. Nicholson on his mind, locked the car up and went into the school building.

The Parent-Teachers Association of the Bingham County School for Exceptional Children was holding its first meeting of the term. Of the twenty people already there, Vladek knew only Mrs. Adler, the principal, or headmistress, or owner of the school. She was the one he needed to talk to most, he thought. Would there be any chance to see her privately? Right now she sat across the room at her scuffed golden oak desk in a posture chair, talking in low, rapid tones with a gray-haired woman in a tan suit. A teacher? She seemed too old to be a parent, although his wife had told him some of the kids seemed to be twenty or more.

It was 8:30 and the parents were still driving up to the school, a converted building that had once been a big country house—almost a mansion. The living room was full of elegant reminders of that. *Two* chandeliers. Intricate vine-leaf molding on the plaster above the dropped ceiling. The pink-veined white marble fireplace, unfortunately prominent because of the unsuitable andirons, too cheap and too small, that now stood in it. Golden oak sliding double doors to the hall. And visible through them a grim, fireproof staircase of concrete and steel. They must, Vladek thought, have had to rip out a beautiful wooden thing to install the fireproof stairs for compliance with the state school laws.

People kept coming in, single men, single women, and occasionally a couple. He wondered how the couples managed their baby-sitting problem. The subtitle on the school's letterhead was "an institution for emotionally disturbed and cerebrally damaged children capable of education." Harry's nine-year-old Thomas was one of the emotionally disturbed ones. With a taste of envy he wondered if cerebrally damaged children could be baby-sat by any reasonably competent grownup. Thomas could not. The Vladeks had not had an evening out together since he was two, so that tonight Margaret was holding the fort at home, no doubt worrying herself sick about the call from Dr. Nicholson, while Harry was representing the family at the PTA.

As the room filled up, chairs were getting scarce. A young couple was standing at the end of the row near him, looking around for a pair of empty seats. "Here," he said to them. "I'll move over." The woman smiled politely and the man said thanks. Emboldened by an ashtray on the empty seat in front of him, Harry pulled out his pack of cigarettes and offered it to them, but it turned out they were nonsmokers. Harry lit up anyway, listening to what was going on around him.

Everybody was talking. One woman asked another, "How's the gall bladder? Are they going to take it out after all?" A heavy, balding man said to a short man with bushy sideburns, "Well, my accountant says the tuition's medically deductible if the school is for pyscho*somatic*, not just for psycho. That we've got to clear up." The short man told him positively, "Right, but all you need is a doctor's letter; he recommends the school, refers the child to the school." And a very young woman said intensely, "Dr. Shields was very optimistic, Mrs. Clerman. He says without a doubt the thyroid will make Georgie accessible. And then—" A light-coffee-colored black man in an aloha shirt told a plump woman, "He really pulled a wing-ding over the weekend, two stitches in his face, busted my fishing pole in three places." And the woman said. "They get so bored. My little girl has this thing about crayons, so that rules out coloring books altogether. You wonder what you can do."

Harry finally said to the young man next to him, "My name's Vladek. I'm Tommy's father; he's in the beginners group."

"That's where ours is," said the young man. "He's Vern. Six years old. Blond like me. Maybe you've seen him."

Harry did not try very hard to remember. The two or three times he had picked Tommy up after class he had not been able to tell one child from another in the great bustle of departure. Coats, handkerchiefs, hats, one little girl who always hid in the supply closet and a little boy who never wanted to go home and hung onto the teacher. "Oh, yes," he said politely.

The young man introduced himself and his wife; they were named Murray and Celia Logan. Harry leaned over the man to shake the wife's hand, and she said, "Aren't you new here?"

"Yes. Tommy's been in the school a month. We moved in from Elmira to be near it." He hesitated, then added, "Tommy's nine, but the reason he's in the beginners group is that Mrs. Adler thought it would make the adjustment easier."

Logan pointed to a suntanned man in the first row. "See that fellow with the glasses? He moved here from *Texas*. Of course, he's got money."

"It must be a good place," Harry said questioningly.

Logan grinned, his expression a little nervous.

"How's your son?" Harry asked.

"That little rascal," said Logan. "Last week I got him another copy of the *My Fair Lady* album, I guess he's used up four or five of them, and he goes around singing 'luv-er-ly, luv-er-ly.' But *look* at you? No."

"Mine doesn't talk," said Harry.

Mrs. Logan said judiciously, "Ours talks. Not *to* anybody, though. It's like a wall."

"I know," said Harry, and pressed. "Has, ah, has Vern shown much improvement with the school?"

Murray Logan pursed his lips. "I would say, yes. The bedwetting's not too good, but life's a great deal smoother in some ways. You know, you don't hope for a dramatic breakthrough. But in little things, day by day, it goes smoother. Mostly smoother. Of course there are setbacks."

Harry nodded, thinking of seven years of setbacks, and two years of growing worry and puzzlement before that. He said, "Mrs. Adler told me that, for instance, a special outbreak of destructiveness might mean something like a plateau in speech therapy. So the child fights it and breaks out in some other direction."

"That too," said Logan, "but what I meant was, you know, the ones you don't expect." He brooded silently a moment, then said with relief, "Oh, they're starting."

Vladek nodded, stubbing out his cigarette and absent-mindedly lighting another. His stomach was knotting up again. He wondered at these other parents, who seemed so safe and, well, untouched. Wasn't it the same with them as with Margaret and himself? And it had been a long time since either of them had felt the world comfortable around them, even without Dr. Nicholson pressing for a decision. He forced himself to lean back and look as tranquil as the others.

Mrs. Adler was tapping her desk with a ruler. "I think everybody who is coming is here," she said. She leaned against the desk and waited for the room to quiet down. She was short, dark, plump and surprisingly pretty. She did not look at all like a competent professional. She looked so unlike her role that, in fact, Harry's heart had sunk three months ago when their correspondence about admitting Tommy had been climaxed by the long trip from Elmira for the interview. He had expected a steel-gray lady with rimless glasses . . . a Valkyrie in a white smock like the nurse who had held wriggling, screaming Tommy while waiting for the suppository to quiet him down for his first EEG . . . a disheveled old fraud . . . he didn't know what. Anything except this pretty young woman. Another blind alley, he had thought in despair. Another, after a hundred too many already. First, "Wait for him to outgrow it." He doesn't.

Then, "We must reconcile ourselves to God's will." But you don't want to. Then give him the prescription three times a day for three months. And it doesn't work. Then chase around for six months with the Child Guidance Clinic to find out it's only letterheads and one circuit-riding doctor who doesn't have time for anything. Then, after four dreary, weepy weeks of soul-searching, the State Training School, and find out it has an eight-year waiting list. Then the private custodial school, and find they're fifty-five hundred dollars a year—without medical treatment! —and where do you get fifty-five hundred dollars a year? And all the time everybody warns you, as if you didn't know it: "Hurry! Do something! Catch it early! This is the critical stage! Delay is fatal!" And then this soft-looking little woman; how could she do anything?

She had rapidly shown him how. She had questioned Margaret and Harry incisively, turned to Tommy, rampaging through that same room like a rogue bull, and turned his rampage into a game. In three minutes he was happily experimenting with an indestructible old windup cabinet Victrola, and Mrs. Adler was saying to the Vladeks, "Don't count on a miracle cure. There isn't any. But improvements, yes, and I think we can help Tommy."

Perhaps she had, thought Vladek bleakly. Perhaps she was helping as much as anyone ever could.

Meanwhile Mrs. Alder had quickly and pleasantly welcomed the parents, suggested they remain for coffee and get to know each other, and introduced the PTA president, a Mrs. Rose, tall, prematurely gray and very executive. "This being the first meeting of the term," she said, "there are no minutes to be read; so we'll get to the committee work reports. What about the transportation problem, Mr. Baer?"

The man who got up was old. More than sixty; Harry wondered what it was like to have your life crowned with a late retarded child. He wore all the trappings of success—a four-hundred-dollar suit, an electronic wrist watch, a large gold fraternal ring. In a slight German accent he said, "I was to the district school board and they are not cooperating. My lawyer looked it up and the trouble is all one word. What the law says, the school board may, that is the word, may reimburse parents of handicapped children for transportation to private schools. Not shall, you understand, but may. They were very frank with me. They said they just didn't want to spend the money. They had the impression we're all rich people here."

Slight sour laughter around the room.

"So my lawyer made an appointment, and we appeared before the full board and presented the case—we don't care, reimbursement, a school bus, anything so we can relieve the transportation burden a little. The answer was no." He shrugged and remained standing, looking at Mrs. Rose, who said:

"Thank you, Mr. Baer. Does anybody have any suggestions?"

A woman said angrily, "Put some heat on them. We're all voters!"

A man said, "Publicity, that's right. The principle is perfectly clear in the law, one taxpayer's child is supposed to get the same service as another taxpayer's child. We should write letters to the papers."

Mr. Baer said, "Wait a minute. Letters I don't think mean anything, but I've got a public relations firm; I'll tell them to take a little time off my food specialties and use it for the school. They can use their own know-how, how to do it; they're the experts."

This was moved, seconded and passed, while Murray Logan whispered to Vladek, "He's Marijane Garlic Mayonnaise. He had a twelve-year-old girl in very bad shape that Mrs. Adler helped in her old private class. He bought this building for her, along with a couple of other parents."

Harry Vladek was musing over how it felt to be a parent who could buy a building for a school that would help your child, while the committee reports continued. Some time later, to Harry's dismay, the business turned to financing, and there was a vote to hold a fund-raising theater party for which each couple with a child in the school would have to sell "at least" five pairs of orchestra seats at sixty dollars a pair. Let's get this straightened out now, he thought, and put up his hand.

"My name is Harry Vladek," he said when he was recognized, "and I'm brand-new here. In the school and in the county. I work for a big insurance company, and I was lucky enough to get a transfer here so my boy can go to the school. But I just don't know anybody yet that I can sell tickets to for sixty dollars. That's an awful lot of money for my kind of people."

Mrs. Rose said, "It's an awful lot of money for most of us. You can get rid of your tickets, though. We've got to. It doesn't matter if you try a hundred people and ninety-five say no just as long as the others say yes."

He sat down, already calculating. Well, Mr. Crine at the office. He was a bachelor and he did go to the theater. Maybe work up an office raffle for another pair. Or two pairs. Then there was, let's see, the real estate dealer who had sold them the house, the lawyer they'd used for the closing—

Well. It had been explained to him that the tuition, while decidedly not nominal, eighteen hundred dollars a year in fact, did not cover the cost per child. Somebody had to pay for the speech therapist, the dance therapist, the full-time psychologist and the part-time psychiatrist, and all the others and it might as well be Mr. Crine at the office. And the lawyer.

And half an hour later Mrs. Rose looked at the agenda, checked off an item and said, "That seems to be all for tonight. Mr. and Mrs. Perry brought us some very nice cookies, and we all know that Mrs. Howe's coffee is out of this world. They're in the beginners' room, and we hope you'll all stay to get acquainted. The meeting is adjourned."

Harry and the Logans joined the polite surge to the beginners room, where Tommy spent his mornings. "There's Miss Hackett," said Celia Logan. That was the beginners' teacher. She saw them and came over, smiling. Harry had seen her only in a tentlike smock, her armor against chocolate milk, finger paints and sudden jets from the "water play" corner of the room. Without it she was handsomely middle-aged in a green pants suit.

"I'm glad you parents have met," she said. "I wanted to tell you that your little boys are getting along nicely. They're forming a sort of conspiracy against the others in the class. Vern swipes their toys and gives them to Tommy."

"He *does?*" cried Logan.

"Yes, indeed. I think he's beginning to relate. And, Mr. Vladek, Tommy's taken his thumb out of his mouth for minutes at a time. At least half a dozen times this morning, without my saying a word."

Harry said excitedly, "You know, I thought I noticed he was tapering off. I couldn't be sure. You're positive about that?"

"Absolutely," she said. "And I bluffed him into

drawing a face. He gave me that glare of his when the others were drawing; so I started to take the paper away. He grabbed it back and scribbled a kind of Picasso-ish face in one second flat. I wanted to save it for Mrs. Vladek and you, but Tommy got it and shredded it in that methodical way he has."

"I wish I could have seen it," said Vladek.

"There'll be others. I can see the prospect of real improvement in your boys," she said, including the Logans in her smile. "I have a private case afternoons that's really tricky. A nine-year-old boy, like Tommy. He's not bad except for one thing. He thinks Donald Duck is out to get him. His parents somehow managed to convince themselves for two years that he was kidding them, in spite of three broken TV picture tubes. Then they went to a psychiatrist and learned the score. Excuse me, I want to talk to Mrs. Adler."

Logan shook his head and said, "I guess we could be worse off, Vladek. Vern giving something to another boy! How do you like that?"

"I like it," his wife said radiantly.

"And did you hear about that other boy? Poor kid. When I hear about something like that— And then there was the Baer girl. I always think it's worse when it's a little girl because, you know, you worry with little girls that somebody will take advantage; but our boys'll make out, Vladek. You heard what Miss Hackett said."

Harry was suddenly impatient to get home to his wife. "I don't think I'll stay for coffee, or do they expect you to?"

"No, no, leave when you like."

"I have a half-hour drive," he said apologetically and went through the golden oak doors, past the ugly but fireproof staircase, out onto the graveled parking lot. His real reason was that he wanted very much to get home before Margaret fell asleep so he could tell her about the thumb-sucking. Things were happening, definite things, after only a month. And Tommy drew a face. And Miss Hackett said—

He stopped in the middle of the lot. He had remembered about Dr. Nicholson, and besides what was it, exactly, that Miss Hackett had said? Anything about a normal life? Not anything about a cure? "Real improvement," she said, but improvement how far?

He lit a cigarette, turned and plowed his way back through the parents to Mrs. Adler. "Mrs. Adler," he said, "may I see you just for a moment?"

She came with him immediately out of earshot of the others. "Did you enjoy the meeting, Mr. Vladek?"

"Oh, sure. What I wanted to see you about is that I have to make a decision. I don't know what to do. I don't know who to go to. It would help a lot if you could tell me, well, what are Tommy's chances?"

She waited a moment before she responded. "Are you considering committing him, Mr. Vladek?" she demanded.

"No, it's not exactly that. It's—well, what can you tell me, Mrs. Adler? I know a month isn't much. But is he ever going to be like everybody else?"

He could see from her face that she had done this before and had hated it. She said patiently, " 'Everybody else,' Mr. Vladek, includes some terrible people who just don't happen, technically, to be handicapped. Our objective isn't to make Tommy like 'everybody else.' It's just to help him to become the best and most rewarding Tommy Vladek he can."

"Yes, but what's going to happen later on? I mean, if Margaret and I—if anything happens to us?"

She was suffering. "There is simply no way to

know, Mr. Vladek," she said gently. "I wouldn't give up hope. But I can't tell you to expect miracles."

Margaret wasn't asleep; she was waiting up for him, in the small living room of the small new house. "How was he?" Vladek asked, as each of them had asked the other on returning home for seven years.

She looked as though she had been crying, but she was calm enough. "Not too bad. I had to lie down with him to get him to go to bed. He took his gland-gunk well, though. He licked the spoon."

"That's good," he said and told her about the drawing of the face, about the conspiracy with little Vern Logan, about the thumb-sucking. He could see how pleased she was, but she only said: "Dr. Nicholson called again."

"I told him not to bother you!"

"He didn't bother me, Harry. He was very nice. I promised him you'd call him back."

"It's eleven o'clock, Margaret. I'll call him in the morning."

"No, I said tonight, no matter what time. He's waiting, and he said to be sure and reverse the charges."

"I wish I'd never answered the son of a bitch's letter," he burst out and then, apologetically: "Is there any coffee? I didn't stay for it at the school."

She had put the water on to boil when she heard the car whine into the driveway, and the instant coffee was already in the cup. She poured it and said, "You have to talk to him, Harry. He has to know tonight."

"Know tonight! Know tonight," he mimicked savagely. He scalded his lips on the coffee cup and said, "What do you want me to do, Margaret? How do I make a decision like this? Today I picked up the phone and called the company psychologist, and when his secretary answered, I said I had the wrong number. I didn't know what to say to him."

"I'm not trying to pressure you, Harry. But he has to know."

Vladek put down the cup and lit his fiftieth cigarette of the day. The little dining room—it wasn't that, it was a half breakfast alcove off the tiny kitchen, but they called it a dining room to each other—was full of Tommy. The new paint on the wall where Tommy had peeled off the cups-and-spoons wallpaper. The Tommy-proof latch on the stove. The one odd aqua seat that didn't match the others on the kitchen chairs, where Tommy had methodically gouged it with the handle of his spoon. He said, "I know what my mother would tell me, talk to the priest. Maybe I should. But we've never even been to Mass here."

Margaret sat down and helped herself to one of his cigarettes. She was still a good-looking woman. She hadn't gained a pound since Tommy was born, although she usually looked tired. She said, carefully and straightforwardly, "We agreed, Harry. You said you would talk to Mrs. Adler, and you've done that. We said if she didn't think Tommy would ever straighten out we'd talk to Dr. Nicholson. I know it's hard on you, and I know I'm not much help. But I don't know what to do, and I have to let you decide."

Harry looked at his wife, lovingly and hopelessly, and at that moment the phone rang. It was, of course, Dr. Nicholson.

"I haven't made a decision," said Harry Vladek at once. "You're rushing me, Dr. Nicholson."

The distant voice was calm and assured. "No, Mr. Vladek, it's not me that's rushing you. The other little boy's heart gave out an hour ago. That's what's rushing you."

"You mean he's dead?" cried Vladek.

"He's on the heart-lung machine, Mr. Vladek. We can hold him for at least eighteen hours, maybe twenty-four. The brain is all right. We're getting very good waves on the oscilloscope. The tissue match with your boy is satisfactory. Better than satisfactory. There's a flight out of JFK at six fifteen in the morning, and I've reserved space for yourself, your wife and Tommy. You'll be met at the airport. You can be here by noon; so we have time. Only just time, Mr. Vladek. It's up to you now."

Vladek said furiously, "I can't decide that! Don't you understand? I don't know how."

"I do understand, Mr. Vladek," said the distant voice and, strangely, Vladek thought, it seemed he did. "I have a suggestion. Would you like to come down anyhow? I think it might help you to see the other boy, and you can talk to his parents. They feel they owe you something even for going this far, and they want to thank you."

"Oh, no!" cried Vladek.

The doctor went on: "All they want is for their boy to have a life. They don't expect anything but that. They'll give you custody of that child—your child, yours and theirs. He's a very fine little boy, Mr. Vladek. Eight years old. Reads beautifully. Makes model airplanes. They let him ride his bike because he was so sensible and reliable, and the accident wasn't his fault. The truck came right up on the sidewalk and hit him."

Harry was trembling. "That's like giving me a bribe," he said harshly. "That's telling me I can trade Tommy in for somebody smarter and nicer."

"I didn't mean it that way, Mr. Vladek. I only wanted you to know the kind of boy you can save."

"You don't even know the operation's going to work!"

"No," agreed the doctor. "Not positively. I can tell you that we've transplanted animals, including primates, and human cadavers, and one pair of terminal cases; but you're right, we've never had a transplant into a well body. I've shown you all the records, Mr. Vladek. We went over them with your own doctor when we first talked about this possibility, five months ago. This is the first case since then when the match was close and there was a real hope for success, but you're right, it's still unproved. Unless you help us prove it. For what it's worth, I think it will work. But no one can be sure."

Margaret had left the kitchen, but Vladek knew where she was from the scratchy click in the earpiece: in the bedroom, listening on the extension phone. He said at last, "I can't say now, Dr. Nicholson. I'll call you back—in half an hour. I can't do any more than that right now."

"That's a great deal, Mr. Vladek. I'll be waiting right here for your call."

Harry sat down and drank the rest of his coffee. You had to be an expert in a lot of things to get along, he was thinking. What did he know about brain transplants? In one way, a lot. He knew that the surgery part was supposed to be straightforward, but the tissue rejection was the problem, but Dr. Nicholson thought he had that licked. He knew that every doctor he had talked to, and he had now talked to seven of them, had agreed that medically it was probably sound enough, and that every one of them had carefully clammed up when he got the conversation around to whether it was right. It was his decision, not theirs, they all said, sometimes just by their silence. But who was he to decide?

Margaret appeared in the doorway. "Harry. Let's go upstairs and look at Tommy."

He said harshly, "Is that supposed to make it easier for me to murder my son?"

She said, "We talked that out, Harry, and we agreed it isn't murder. Whatever it is. I only think that Tommy ought to be with us when we decide, even if he doesn't know what we're deciding."

The two of them stood next to the outsize crib that held their son, looking in the night light at the long fair lashes against the chubby cheeks and the pouted lips around the thumb. Reading. Model airplanes. Riding a bike. Against a quick sketch of a face and the occasional, cherished, tempestuous, bruising flurry of kisses.

Vladek stayed there the full half hour and then, as he had promised, went back to the kitchen, picked up the phone and began to dial.

# *Afterword*

**B**ecause Cyril Kornbluth was foolish enough to die just as he was hitting his stride—and because fame is not only fickle but often painfully brief—there are many readers of science fiction who have hardly heard his name now. That's a pity. Apart from his collaboration work (that with me, a great many short pieces with other old Futurians and two novels with Judith Merril), Cyril wrote on his own a quantity of short stories and eight or nine novels, ranging in quality from good to wonderful.

Most of the novels were not science fiction, and they are nowhere to be found in the normal channels of commerce any more. The three sf novels—*Takeoff*, *Not This August* and *The Syndic*—have been reissued fairly recently and diligent search may turn them up. The short stories have all been collected and a selection of them called *The Best of C. M. Kornbluth* is still in print. (I happen to think it's a very good selection, but then I edited the volume.) Now and then you will even see one of Cyril's best short stories, "The Little Black Bag," turning up in reruns of the adaptation by Rod Serling on late-night television.

They are all worth searching out, because there's a lot of pleasure to be found in all of them . . . along with the pain of knowing that there isn't any more. Cyril started out good, and kept on getting better as long as he lived. I don't know what he would have written if he had lived to do it. I just know that it would have been *fine*.

ROBERT A. HEINLEIN

"Heinlein knows more about blending provocative scientific thinking with strong human stories than any dozen other contemporary science fiction writers."
—*Chicago Sun-Times*

"Robert A. Heinlein wears imagination as though it were his private suit of clothes. What makes his work so rich is that he combines his lively, creative sense with an approach that is at once literate, informed, and exciting."
—*New York Times*

Seven of Robert A. Heinlein's best-loved titles are now available in superbly packaged new Baen editions, with embossed series-look covers by artist John Melo. Collect them all by sending in the order form below: